Peaceful Plots

Beth M James

Dusken Publishing

Written by Beth M James
Copyright © 2019 Beth M James
ISBN 978-0-9889428-5-1

Cover Photography: Mike/Beth James

This book is dedicated to my dad:
Stanley E Hopkins
(he buried people)

Acknowledgments
Deb Waite for Maggie (a real cemetery ghost)
Stuart Hanzlik, an ex-police officer who helped with the "what if"
scenarios
And as always, thank you to Ellis and Mike for your hardcore reviews
and edits

Other Books by Beth M James

The Calling's Return
(Book 3, Dream or Reality Series)

The Promise of Return
(Book 2, Dream or Reality Series)

The Calling
(Book 1, Dream or Reality Series)

Gitana – Life Plan

Five Common Elements

A lightning storm

Lost keys

A haunted house (or rumored to be)

A stack of thick books

A person named Max

The Common Elements Romance Project

Chapter 1

Max Riley rose from his office chair to match the height of the man standing on the other side of his desk. He made himself clear. "You're not getting one more penny from me. This time you're out of luck."

"I'm not done yet." The man opposite him leaned in as well. His voice turned hard. "You've loaned me money before and it's paid off for you. Big time. This deal is even better. We could both win on this one."

"Half a million dollars isn't small change for a loan." Max shook his head. "I don't have the money."

"How about half?"

"Half won't do you any good," Max said with a leery eye.

The man in the gray suit paced Max's office, stopping at the mantel above the gas fireplace. He selected one of the pictures of Max's daughters to focus on and stared at it for a moment.

"Max." The man called him by his name, almost pleading. "I know you can come up with the money. I've already committed and they're waiting." He returned to his spot in the front of the desk. "What if you sold this place? Last year ...

that company wanted to buy your land ..." He snapped his fingers as he tried remembering the name.

"Satchel Casing?"

"That's it. I bet you could approach them again."

Max growled. "The business is just a front to buy up land for profit."

His blood pressure rose at the thought of a company ripping apart his land and changing the countryside. He tapped his finger on the desk. "This place is not for sale. Get that through your head right now."

"You should." He gestured his head toward the picture he had admired. "Your daughters don't want it."

"Leave my daughters out of this." Max stiffened.

The man placed his hands on his hips and smiled as if knowing he got to him. "I have three months to come up with the money. I want you in."

"I won't change my mind."

"You'll lose out, Max. You'll lose out." He turned to leave. At the door, he stopped. A cold smile played on his lips. "Think long and hard about the consequences and what could happen. I can't wait any longer. This deal has to go through."

"Not with me." Max's patience was at an end with the man's threat. "It's best you leave."

Max watched the man disappear and then listened as he slammed the front door shut. How in the hell did he get in there in the first place? If he met with anyone, his business took place in town. Never at his house.

He glanced at the drink waiting for him on his desk—

Jamison on the rocks. Max downed the whiskey before he headed upstairs to make sure the man had left.

Dusk covered the Wisconsin sky, offering a soft warm hue. He grabbed his coat to take a walk outside and clear his mind.

He headed to the cemetery, next to his land, and went straight for the grave next to the family plot. Max spotted the shot glass resting on the base of the headstone. He peered into the glass. Damn squirrels got to the whiskey again. He was hoping for another shot to ease his nerves.

Max looked around. All was peaceful in Hope River Cemetery. He smiled, thinking how Riley, his youngest daughter, had her own name for the place—the gated community. He wished she'd come home. Phoenix was too far away.

Leaving the cemetery, he strolled across the yard toward the orchard on the other side of the house. The door to the red shed was open. Max frowned. He always closed and locked the small building. As he moved closer, he heard what he thought was the shuffling of gas cans being moved and then a clang as one hit the other.

Max charged toward the shed.

Chapter 2

Riley Walsh tightened her grip around the steering wheel of the rented Camry as she reached the bridge crossing into Wisconsin. She paid attention to the striped lines marking the lanes as the snow unleashed from the sky.

"Really? Now?" she said with disbelief. This was the end of September. Fall was about sunshine, crisp air, and trees showcasing their brilliant colors of orange, reds, and yellows. As she glanced along both sides of the freeway, she saw only one tree that had turned red. Snow shouldn't be in the forecast.

She didn't see the pothole in time. The front end of the car bounced violently as the wheel hit, and she cringed, hoping no damage occurred. The lid on the pink urn in the passenger seat rattled, threatening to open.

"Hang on, Mom. Almost home." Riley reached over to adjust the container and the seatbelt that held it upright. "Soon you'll be with Dad again."

Riley had been awake for almost twenty-four hours. Her world had turned upside down after Shannon, her older sister, called to say the police had found Dad in the backyard shed with a rope around his neck. Riley tried justifying why he'd ended his life so abruptly.

Suicide. The word hung on her like an iron weight.

In her head, she replayed her last conversation with Dad. He'd been fine. He laughed. He said he had some business issues but nothing to be concerned about. The conversation had focused more on her and about the chance for her promotion at Sikerte Investment Firm where she worked.

His death just didn't make sense.

A tear rolled to Riley's chin, and she wiped it away. As she reached the exit and headed south, her throat constricted and she swallowed hard, not wanting to cry again.

Her phone buzzed from the cup holder where she set it. The screen lighted to show the call was from Gary Snefner, her co-worker and friend. What could he possibly want now? She answered three of his calls between the time her flight landed and when she'd picked up the rental car. With her leaving work on short notice to head home, he offered to help her with a client, getting their paperwork in order, after one of the newer investors at the firm messed it up.

She growled, more at herself than the caller. The snow began to stick to the road. She couldn't take his call and risk an accident.

As the phone continued to buzz, her anxiety rose. She always picked up the phone when Gary called. They worked well together, protecting each other's backs. He promised to keep her posted, letting her know what was going on, especially with the chance of her getting promoted to office manager.

What a bad time to take off work.

Riley wiggled her fingers, one hand and then the other, as she realized how tightly she'd been hanging on to the steering wheel. Two more miles of country roads. She couldn't wait to get out of the car. She was exhausted.

She slowed after passing the cemetery with its tall cedar and oak trees. She turned into the narrow dirt driveway that curved through the grove of pine, oak, and maple trees. The trees along the property line kept the house hidden from view, but now she was there.

Riley's stomach fluttered as she gazed at the 1920s Arts and Crafts-style home that looked more like a fairy-tale cottage, with its low gabled roof, than a house.

"We're home, Mom."

She sat for a minute with the car turned off, unsure if she was ready to go inside. Once she did, it meant that Dad's death was real. Thinking about it made her shudder.

Movement near the cemetery gate caught her attention. A man wearing a dark green coat stood next to the Walsh family plot. His hair fell to his shoulders and curled at the ends. A short, trimmed mustache and beard dressed his face. He was handsome even from a distance. Riley sensed he had been watching her, but when she spotted him, he turned and disappeared. A local? She had to remember that other people visited the cemetery as well. Growing up, they always thought it was part of their yard.

Turning toward the passenger seat, Riley held the top of the seat belt to avoid hitting or breaking the urn when she unbuckled it. She left the rest of her bags in the car as she hugged Mom's ashes to her chest and headed for the porch.

The large open room held a swing on one side where she'd sit and read in the mornings when home. On the other side sat two white rockers with a wooden table where they enjoyed glasses of wine in the evening. Near the front door, a new mat stated "Welcome." Riley stomped her feet on the coarse material to remove the dirt and snow from her shoes. She reached for the handle to open the door, but it jerked out of her hand. Delana, child number one, jumped toward her. Riley braced herself and held the urn tighter.

"Auntie!" Her niece hopped up and down while trying to hug her.

"Delana." Riley smiled. The ten-year-old blocked the door in her excitement, keeping Auntie from entering as she shivered in the cold.

Delana gasped when she saw the pink urn. Her eyes grew. "Is that a present?"

Riley gazed down at Mom in her arms. "Nope. It's Grandma."

The child wrinkled her nose and made a sour face, not knowing what to think.

"Is that you, Riley?" Shannon popped into the hallway. "Delana, let your aunt in. Close the door."

Riley stepped inside, relieved to feel heat. She couldn't believe how grown-up Delana was getting. At ten years old, her niece had the figure of a ballerina with long legs and a graceful posture, just like her mom.

"I know," Shannon agreed as if reading her mind. They

watched the child run off to the den. "Wait until you see the other two."

Riley placed Mom on the table next to the wall, wanting to give her sister a hug. They clung to each other, in greeting and in sorrow. Neither one could hold back the tears.

Shannon was the first to pull away. She grabbed them both tissues from the table in the hall. They blew their noses at the same time, making them laugh.

"How are you holding up?" Riley asked as she dabbed at her nose. She noticed her sister had lost weight since the last time they met. Thin lines of stress appeared on her face and neck as well.

"Probably the same as you," Shannon said and reached out to pull a strand of hair from her sister's cheek. "But we'll get through this. Together."

Like Mom, Shannon was always the caring one and kept the peace, especially when Riley was in trouble. Riley was like her dad, the stubborn Irish redhead.

"So, what's going on with you?" Shannon changed the subject. "Any boyfriends?"

"No," Riley said, wishing her sister didn't ask every time they talked on the phone or in person.

She had trouble finding men, being picky like their father. Maxwell Walsh didn't find a woman until he turned thirty-two years old, the same age as Shannon now. Mom was eight years younger than Dad. Who would think Mom would go first? Fifty-four was way too young to die from a weak heart.

A loud crash made them jump. The noise sounded like it came from the kitchen down the hall.

"Must be Conner," Shannon guessed. "He's putting away the groceries. Come say hi to him."

Riley took off her boots. The luggage could wait a little longer. She followed her sister to the kitchen, at the end of the hallway. Dad had built a couple of new wings on the house and this was one of them. While most of the house had dark wood, the kitchen bounced light from every corner. Whites, blues, and stainless steel. The style didn't fit the rest of the house, but Dad didn't care as long as Mom smiled. She had wanted a bright, airy room to cook and hang out in, so he fulfilled her wish.

"Riley." Conner smiled in greeting.

Shannon's husband wore his body well. In his mid-forties, he loved to run and kept his figure lean and muscled. He was handsome, in a business kind of way, with gray-speckled hair styled so that it always looked windblown. Knowing Conner, Riley bet he used a lot of product to get his "casual" look.

He walked toward her with a carton of milk in his hands. Riley met him around the edge of the island. She gave him a hug and a kiss to the cheek.

He retreated to the refrigerator. "Hey, I'm sorry about your dad killing himself. How you doing?"

Riley winced at his words. Killing himself. She didn't like the sound of it. Knowing he meant no harm, she shrugged and turned her head to stare at the gray tiled floor. "It's hard to take. I'm still in shock."

Conner opened the refrigerator door and tossed in the

milk. "What a trip. Max killing himself."

Riley swallowed hard and forced herself to stay in control. If only Conner would be a little more sympathetic. He was always a precise talker, more businesslike than personal. But he could show more sympathy.

She glanced over at Shannon, noting that his words affected her too. Riley couldn't ignore it. "That's a little harsh to say."

"What?" He pulled a box of oatmeal from one of the bags and set it on the counter. "Killing? I call it like it is. Your dad knew what he was doing. I get it. He didn't want to go through the treatment or deal with the pain."

Riley frowned. What he said didn't make sense. Treatment? What did he know that she didn't? "What are you talking about?"

Conner looked to Shannon with a silent are-you-kidding-me expression. He turned back to her. "His cancer."

A truck slammed into her. No one told her. Riley's arms began to shake. A lump grew in her throat. She swallowed hard in order to talk. "Can-cancer? What kind of cancer did he have?"

"Lung." Her sister's voice softened. "Stage four."

"He didn't smoke." Everything turned numb on her. Her legs gave out and she slid on to the stool at the center island. Why hadn't Dad mentioned anything to her when they talked on the phone? He must have known at that time. She could have helped him.

"You're right. He didn't smoke."

14

"Did he go to the Mayo Clinic?" The place was in Rochester, Minnesota. An easy drive.

"I don't know." Shannon shrugged, clueless.

Riley rolled out questions Shannon and Conner couldn't answer. Her brother-in-law's nostrils flared as if angry—at her. She had a right to know. She fumed. "We need to call his doctor. Find out what happened."

"Why?" Conner growled as if her idea had been ridiculous. "Talking to him isn't going to do any good now."

"He can provide us with some answers. Tell us what happened. Why." She held the edge of the counter to steady herself. "What if the cancer is hereditary?"

Conner raised his hands. "Okay. Okay. Just settle down. I will find out. I know his doctor. We've done business before in Milwaukee. I'll call him."

"That would be great," Shannon chimed in to break the tension. She came over to hug Riley. "I didn't know how bad he was either. I could see him not wanting us to know. Why he ended his life like he did."

Riley let out a sob but controlled the rest, keeping the tears from falling.

Shannon left to grab a bottle of wine and a corkscrew from the pantry. "I think it's about time for some wine." She returned and set them on the counter for Riley to help, while she found three wine glasses.

Riley looked to her sister. "When did you find out, Shannon?"

"The day he died. Conner learned Dad's cancer spread to more than just his lung. The doctor wanted him to go through some pretty aggressive chemo therapy and radiation. They didn't know if that would cure him or not."

Red wine. The label had a castle-like design. Stone Legend Hall. Merlot. Worked for her.

"Think of how much harder it would've been on you girls," Conner said as if to justify their dad's actions. "He was dying. I bet only a few more months and he'd have been dead anyway."

Riley's mouth dropped. Shannon glared at her husband.

"How do you know that?" Riley choked on the words.

"He let me in on his secret. He knew for a while."

She sat on the stool, stunned. This didn't sound like Dad. He always told them how he was healthy as an ox. Again, she thought back to their conversation. They had never discussed any illness or cancer. He was fine.

Shannon passed the first glass to her, and Riley accepted without hesitation. She took a large gulp. And then another. The wine was dry but robust with a hint of … cinnamon? She took another drink but couldn't place the taste.

"Did they ever find a note?"

"I don't believe so." Her sister looked at Conner. "Did the police say anything to you?"

He fumbled for words. "I … No, I never asked. Wait, once I asked. I don't think he left anything."

"Most people leave some type of note when they commit suicide," Shannon said, more to herself than to them. She then turned to Riley. "Conner has been handling the details with the police. Calling his death a suicide—it isn't official yet. Not until after the autopsy. They need to rule out other possibilities."

Riley's head jerked back. It couldn't have been an accident, not with a rope around his neck. "You mean like foul play? Murder?"

"Ridiculous," Conner stated. "Let the man rest in peace."

She agreed. Who would hurt her dad? She shuddered, unable to think about the medical examiner doing an autopsy on him. Her stomach churned. Maybe she should have eaten something before the wine.

A block of cheese was sitting on the counter. She leaned over and stretched to pull it toward her.

"Wait." Riley realized what this meant. "We can't bury him until they release him from the medical examiner's office."

"I believe you're right." Shannon nodded. "Plans may need to change a bit."

Damn. Riley took seven days off from work. Was that going to be enough? She had to get back before her tasks piled up.

She opened the block of sharp cheddar. Shannon already had the knife and cutting board out on the counter. Conner rummaged through one of the grocery bags and pulled out a box of fancy crackers.

In silence, they made themselves a snack of cheese, crackers, and salami. As she ate, Riley reviewed her work email from her phone. She answered three from two of the financial advisors. She also sent a text to Gary telling him that she'd call later.

"What? Are you working?" Shannon's lips tightened like a mother about ready to scold her child.

"I still have my job. It doesn't end."

"Family time, girl. Family time."

"Where are the kids?" Riley asked, changing the subject on purpose.

Shannon lifted her head to point her chin upward. "Upstairs." She wiped her hands on a towel. "They need to come down for a snack."

Riley took another gulp of wine. "I'll capture the beasts."

She set her glass down and then headed up the stairs. She stopped midway and ran her fingers down the wallpaper—a simple vintage floral design with soft tones of beige, green, and pink flowers. The paper had torn along the edges from their picking at it through the years.

Riley straightened a few of the family pictures hanging on the walls above the wainscoting. All the photographs were black and white with ornate silver frames—their great grandparents, Dad with his brothers and one sister, Mom on the farm where she grew up. A little depressing in a way. Everything was so old. Dated. Everyone in the pictures was dead.

She reached the narrow loft area where she used to watch TV, do her homework, and work on the computer. Her bedroom was on the left while Shannon's was to the right. In between their rooms, Dad built a Jack and Jill bathroom when they reached their teen years. He had reduced the size of their bedrooms to obtain a decent-sized bathroom. Their bedrooms were still spacious so neither one of them minded. Dad selected the white tile and black fixtures. He let them be creative with the rest. They opted for a Paris theme with white, black, and pink decor.

She heard the kids in her old room, as expected. Mom and Dad kept plenty of toys for the grandkids to play with when they came to visit. Taking in the sight, Riley found that they had plenty to keep them occupied. Flynn, now eight years old, made a ruckus as he hauled the trucks and games out of the closet. He found a doll and tossed it to Delana. She picked up the doll, fixed her dress, and then handed it to her little sister. "Here, Elise. Here's a doll for you to play with."

Riley's youngest niece sat on the floor. While the two older children had dark blond hair like their dad, the little one had short, red hair. She looked like a porcelain doll with her curly locks, round blue eyes, and full ruby lips.

"Hi, Elise." Riley bent down to play with one of her curls. "You're getting so big."

"Her birthday's coming up," Delana said while dressing one of the Barbies in a gown. "She'll be four."

Riley rounded her mouth as if surprised. Elise stared at her aunt while clutching her doll. She looked to her sister and then back to her aunt again. Riley was heartbroken. She didn't think Elise remembered her.

"Auntie," Flynn called out. "Look it. Look what I found."

He pulled out a yellow tractor from the bin. She smiled. Last time they saw each other, the two of them had used the tractor and a dump truck for moving dirt around Grandpa's garden. He wasn't too happy, but they had fun for hours.

Riley stood and made her way over to Flynn, careful to avoid stepping on the toys. She leaned down and gave him a hug.

"How are you doing, Flynn?" She tousled his hair. He swept his head away from her as if annoyed at the attention. He wanted to play.

She loved kids but never thought about having one of her own. A co-worker had two teenage boys who fought all the time. She always came to work looking haggard and ready to pull out her hair. Another co-worker, one of the financial advisors, kept busy every night taking his kids to baseball, soccer, and gymnastics. Riley didn't know how they did it. She would be frazzled as a parent. Shannon was the only one she knew who breezed through parenting with gold stars. The perfect mom raising three lovely kids.

"Who wants a snack?" Conner called from the bottom of the stairs.

"I do!" The oldest two yelled in unison and sprang up from the floor.

Damn. She forgot. Another reason why she'd be a bad parent.

Flynn dropped the tractor and ran past her. He disappeared out the door. Delana put her doll to bed and kissed her goodnight before standing up. She stepped over the toys and grabbed her sister's hand. Her voice turned soft when she said, "Come on, Elise. Let's go downstairs. See Mommy."

Shannon used to do the same with her. She'd always make sure that her little sister wasn't left behind … until they turned into teens. Riley became the rebel then, telling her sister to stop pretending to be her mom. She wondered how long before Elise would say the same thing to Delana.

As the kids sat at the small table near the bay window in the kitchen to eat their snacks, Riley went to collect her luggage from the car. She hauled her belongings to the solarium, now her bedroom after Shannon needed the upstairs for her family.

Riley loved the room with all the high windows, billowy white curtains, and crystal chandelier hanging from the ceiling. The antique furniture included a cozy chair, dark ornate tables, and a black iron daybed. There was no closet, but Mom had found an armoire at one of the local antique stores that matched the tables and fit perfectly against the wall.

Before turning on the light, she dropped her luggage on the daybed. She went to the far window and pulled back the curtain to see outside. The window faced the cemetery. She searched for the statue of the angel between the trees.

The angel stood tall with her head slightly tilted and her eyes down. The artist had done a beautiful job showing peace and serenity in the angel's expression. He also captured her strength in the way her shoulders were pulled back to hold the half-spread wings. She was ready to protect and defend the graves if needed. With all the strange things that occurred in this house over the years—floors creaking, lights flickering, and unexplained banging—Riley believed the angel was there to protect her from evil as well.

But she hadn't protected Dad.

What the hell were they going to do with the house? Sell? She lived in Arizona. She had a job. Shannon lived in

Milwaukee. Conner's job was there.

Her cell phone rang. She picked it up and read Gary's name on the screen before swiping to answer the call.

"Riley. How's it going?"

"I'm here. At the house."

Papers shuffled on his desk. He was at work. "Hey, I need your help."

"Client?"

"Stocks dropped. People are calling and wanting to know what to do. No one's here to calm them down."

She winced. "Sorry."

"I'm not going to tell you twice that you're missed around here. We need you back. And don't forget about your up-coming interview. You're scheduled for next Monday."

"Monday?" What the hell was he talking about? Her flight came in that morning. Her heart beat faster. What if she couldn't make it to the office in time? If her flight was delayed? "Who set that up?"

"Joe Abernet."

Her boss. Riley rubbed her head and paced the small room. "What if I need to stay longer? I'm not sure if a week will be enough time."

"You need to come back for the interview," Gary said in a low voice as if others were around to hear him. "Rita's climbing up Joe's ass. She's putting on the charm."

Riley stopped and stared at her carry-on bag without seeing it. "How much ass-kissing? Wait—I don't want to know."

Rita had no right to the job. Riley knew what the investors needed and how to handle the customers. She took the brunt of the angry clients who roared their complaints when they lost thousands of dollars. She didn't like it either but that's how the market worked.

"What time is the interview?"

"Two o'clock."

"Gary, I don't know if I can make it into the office by two."

"You said your flight comes in at noon, right?"

"Yes."

"I'll pick you up and we'll head straight to the office."

She bit her lip and tossed around other possible solutions to what she could do. Interview by phone? Fly in on Sunday, the day before?

"All right. All right. We'll make it work." She'd talk to Shannon. Tomorrow they planned to start making the funeral arrangements. Maybe her sister already had. Wouldn't that be awesome? Riley cursed when she remembered the roadblock. "Shit, I don't know when the medical examiner will release Dad's body."

A long pause came from the other end. "What?

She hadn't told him about Dad committing suicide. If news circled through the office, Riley wasn't sure how her co-workers would react. She'd rather be there, in person, to tell them what happened instead of having them gossip without knowing the facts. She had to think fast and give him something. "They're not sure what caused his death yet. I just found out he had lung cancer."

"Oh wow. Did he smoke?"

"No, he didn't."

"The damn environment," Gary said. He went on a rant about the pollution and how the corporate world wasn't doing enough to prevent global warming.

Riley didn't want to participate, having other things to do. Hot, she went over to the window and unlatched the French-door styled panes. The cold air gusted into the room. She lifted her face to the breeze until her cheeks turned cold. She then closed the window again.

A shadow of a man moved in the cemetery. He seemed to be pacing. What was he doing there in the dark? Was it the guy she had seen earlier? This one seemed taller, lankier. He had on a long coat and Fedora hat.

"Anyway," Gary's voice changed, bringing her back to their conversation. "I gotta go. No one cared to stick around tonight and help out."

"I'll get back with you in a few days," she told him. "I am checking my emails."

"Yeah," he said with a heavy sigh on his end.

"I'm sorry, Gary. I'd be there to help if I could."

"Yeah, yeah. It's all right. I know."

He didn't know. It wasn't all right. She had to keep her insides from crumbling. Too many things were going on at once.

Riley looked out the window after hanging up. The man from the cemetery had disappeared. The night sky took over, and the angel was no longer in view. She went back to her unpacking. Once finished, she was ready for more wine.

The smoke from the fireplace in the den managed to filter down the hall. Riley closed her bedroom door to keep it out. Whoever tended the fire wasn't doing a great job. When she entered the room, Conner crouched next to the fire and tried cramming a log into the already-full space. He wasn't a Boy Scout.

"Let me help," she said and motioned for him to give her the chunk of wood.

"Have at it." He handed her the log, glad to pass on the duty.

First thing she did was check the damper and found that it was only half open. She hit the handle with her fist to open it all the way. She then arranged the burning wood without adding the log in her hand. She set it back into the bin next to the wall.

"That should do it." She rubbed her hands together, proud of the smokeless glow that now radiated from the large stone fireplace. She turned around, hoping that Conner would have watched and been impressed. He had left the room. Oh well.

She moseyed around the den while she waited for Shannon to join her. The room had an old English charm, making it cozy and the perfect place to hang out. The oversized blue-striped couch in the center of the room, facing the fireplace, held enough pillows and blankets for three people to snuggle in. On each side was a wide red chair with leopard-print toss pillows. The chairs didn't match the couch, but somehow Mom managed to make it work. She loved to decorate and would have made a great home interior designer.

A pang of sadness filled her heart. She heard Dad's cheery

greeting when he walked into the room. She and Shannon would attach themselves to him like leeches.

She turned and spotted Dad's table in the back corner of the room. If he wanted to be with the family but had to work, he sat at the makeshift desk. The table, made of burled oak, had two flush drawers supported by fancy curved brackets. Going over to the table, she opened one of the drawers and found it stuffed with papers and receipts. The other held writing tablets, pens, and pencils ready for use. He didn't use the space often, spending most of his time in the office downstairs.

A few clunking noises sounded from upstairs. She assumed Shannon and Conner were putting the kids to bed. She heard some protests but the noise settled quickly.

Riley remembered the wine. She went to retrieve it from the kitchen and then came back with the bottle in hand and her glass from before. She plopped down on the couch. Beat.

She finished the first glass and started pouring round two when Shannon and Conner trudged down the stairs. They went into the kitchen and were talking privately. She couldn't hear what they were gabbing about and that was fine. Soon they left the kitchen and joined her. Both carried their glasses, another bottle of wine, and a replenished plate of crackers and sliced cheese like they had earlier.

"What a day." Shannon joined her on the couch. She set the snacks down on the coffee table.

"I hear you," Riley said in agreement. "I'm still in shock."

Shannon rubbed the back of her scalp as if to erase everything going on in her brain.

"Where do we even start?" Riley asked. "Funeral?"

"The will," Conner suggested before he popped a cracker into his mouth. He chewed, drank some of his wine, and then asked, "Did anyone contact Max's lawyer?"

Riley and her sister glanced at each other and then at him. By Shannon's dumbfounded look, neither one of them had thought about contacting the lawyer. Of course, it made sense.

"And the police," Riley said.

Conner sat straighter in the red chair. "Why the police?"

"Aren't they the ones who found him? Don't they need to investigate or something?"

"Why?" He poured himself more wine, filling it almost to the top. "He killed himself. End of story."

The words ground her insides. "But what if he didn't?"

She still couldn't comprehend the fact that her dad killed himself. This just wasn't like him.

Conner held up his hands. "I'll take care of it. I'll handle the police and the lawyer." As an afterthought, he said, "If you want."

"Fine with me," Riley said and her sister agreed. The funeral arrangements would be hard enough. Conner's help would spare them some time.

"So, how's life going for you in Arizona?" he asked while relaxing in his chair to enjoy the wine and a handful of snacks.

"It's been busy." She reached over and grabbed a piece of cheese.

"You still handling the money?"

27

"I don't handle any money," she said, as he seemed to always ask and forget.

"Are you making money for yourself? You should have a good stash set aside by now."

Riley didn't respond. She struggled with investing money when she lived paycheck to paycheck.

"Any rich boyfriends tucked away? Dating anyone from your work?"

Conner was a nice guy, great husband, and responsible father. But he acted like the guys at Sikerte's Investment Firm. They were only interested in making their first million by the age of forty. They were also cheap dates and too cocky for her taste. Conner had the same attitude—overly confident and sure of himself. The one difference between the men at work and Conner was that he had a great wife. The men at Sikerte's were on their second and third wives. What she couldn't understand was why Conner would think she'd want to hook up with a guy from work.

"I don't have time for a boyfriend."

Shannon gave her the "sister" eye. "If you'd stop looking at your emails you might find time."

"What?" She slid her phone into her back pocket.

"Do you know how many times you've checked your emails since you've been here?"

Riley stiffened and looked toward the door, ready for an escape. She didn't need the scolding. She had to help with the Lensten account. Shannon didn't get it. This was her life. Work. 24-7.

Her sister sensed her mood. She changed the subject. "When do you need to be back to work?"

"Next Monday. Day of my interview."

"What if we can't have the funeral by then?" Shannon frowned.

"If needed, I'll come back." Riley sighed. "In the meantime, I still have to work."

"This is your dad," Shannon said in a sharp tone. "They're not a company to work for if they don't let you take off for your own dad's funeral."

"I'm here. They approved my time." Riley defended her work. She decided to take the heat off herself. "How about you?"

Shannon swirled the wine in her glass. "The kids are in school, so they'll need to return home." She glanced at Conner. "We'll have to figure out our plan as well, once we know more about the funeral."

Conner cleared his voice. "I'll call the lawyer tomorrow. See if there's anything needed. How we can get the ball rolling."

"And the police," Riley reminded him.

"And them too," he said without much interest. He looked to Shannon. "We'll head out Sunday."

"What? You're leaving?" Riley's heart stopped, not wanting to be left alone in the house.

"No, no." Shannon patted her leg. "Conner has to return to work. He's taking the kids home so they can go to school on Monday. Helen and Phil, his parents, are going to take care of them while I'm here. I'm not leaving."

Riley let out her breath. She slouched back into the couch. There was no way she could do this alone.

"We have too much to do for me to leave," Shannon said, mirroring her thoughts.

"Here, here," Riley agreed and raised her glass to her sister's. "Let the fun begin."

Chapter 3

The morning sun streamed into the solarium and woke Riley. Last night, she forgot to close the curtains and now the sun shone across the bed. She liked the bright light more than the creepy darkness during the night when she felt someone was in her room. She shivered, recalling how the air had changed with her unexpected guest.

Riley stayed in bed for another fifteen minutes to enjoy the early morning. She melted into the warmth of the down comforter and the silky sheets. She couldn't afford the luxury of spending time in bed at the apartment. Work kept her busy, and she was up by five a.m. Besides, the cheap mattress she bought six months ago now sagged in the middle. Most of the time, she woke with a backache.

Resting on her side, she checked her emails—a mistake since it meant another twenty minutes of being lazy. Shannon was probably ready to go.

Getting out of bed, Riley shuffled over to the window. No threat of snow or clouds in sight. The angel, with her hands out and head down, continued to watch over the family plot.

Soon she'd be watching over Dad and Mom as well.

She glanced over at the urn sitting on top of the dresser. The bright pink urn clashed with the darker decorations of the bedroom, making its own statement. The urn suited Mom, who'd bought it ten years ago when a male friend had bought one for his wife who died of cancer. Mom, being particular about what she wore, thought it equally fitting to make sure she picked out her final resting place. After the funeral, no one would see what Mom had bought.

Riley walked away from the window and grabbed a small throw from the chair nestled in the corner. She wrapped it around her shoulders. For the time being, she wanted to stay in her pajamas. The soft, thick cotton blanket would keep her warm as she left her bedroom to see what was going on.

Conner's voice was clear and strong when she headed down the hall to the kitchen. He was on his cell phone. When he saw her enter the kitchen, he tipped his head in greeting and then left for some privacy. She could've left, she supposed, but coffee called to her.

Dad's electric stainless-steel percolator made the best java—much better than the automatic drip coffee makers. On hangover mornings, she'd watch the water percolate up to the glass top until the liquid turned dark. She'd then pour some out, even if the green light hadn't come on to say that the coffee was ready.

She lifted the pot and guessed it was about half full. Riley grabbed a large mug from the cupboard and filled it with the brew. The steam warmed her face as she inhaled the Columbian blend. The hot liquid would burn her lips. She blew on the dark liquid to cool it before taking the first sip.

Yes. The best coffee ever.

"Good morning." Shannon breezed into the kitchen. She wore a dark blue tunic, leggings, and black fashion boots. She was halfway through putting on her makeup. Her hair was still wet. She'd come down to refill her cup.

"Good morning," Riley responded and sat at the island with the small blanket keeping her warm and cozy.

"Our appointment with the funeral home is at nine."

Riley checked her watch. 7:36. She had some time. Not much though. She sipped her coffee and watched Shannon fill a pot with water, add eggs, and then place it on the stove while turning on the burner. She was in mom-mode, getting breakfast ready for the kids.

"Did they say where Dad is?" Riley asked as her brain started working for the day. "Will we see him there?"

The sudden vision of seeing marks on his neck made her shudder. She didn't want to remember Dad that way. Thankfully he hadn't used a gun.

"I believe he's still at the medical examiner's office." Shannon opened the bread and popped two slices into the toaster, then glanced toward her. "Can you drive today? Conner's taking the children shopping for boots before they leave."

"Sure." Riley was hoping to drop off her rental car today to save money. She planned to drive Dad's Buick while she stayed at the house. The car was parked in the garage and the keys still hung on the hook near the back door. Another idea popped into her head. "Do you think Conner could pick us up at the rental car place? I'd like to drop the car off."

Shannon hesitated. She made a face.

"Or could you drive Dad's car so I can drop off my rental? Then we won't need to worry about time."

By her expression, Shannon liked that plan better.

Filling her cup again, Riley kicked her butt in gear to get ready in time. She used the downstairs bathroom to take her shower. She decided on the natural look, wearing only mascara to save time. Dressing in black pants and a black button-down shirt with a light-blue, lacey tank underneath, she hoped the outfit would be warm enough. She'd planned to wear jeans but after seeing Shannon dress up, Riley decided she better too. She wasn't sure of the protocol on what to wear for planning a funeral.

Back in the kitchen, the kids were finishing their breakfast. The flat screen TV hanging from the wall blared the news. Riley caught the last part of the weather. The day would be sunny and the temperature would continue to warm up. No snow for the next week.

Yes.

Still, she needed a coat. She went to the closet near the back porch, where all their heavier coats were stored. Mom was the one to find her a coat when she came back for a visit. Now she had to dig for one. The closet was too dark to see inside. She found the string hanging near the side wall and tugged until the light clicked on. Over twenty coats filled the tiny space. The shelf above stored bins filled with mittens and hats. On the floor were different boots piled together.

"Really, Mom? You didn't toss any of our stuff?" Riley couldn't believe it.

"What's that?" Shannon called out.

"Nothing," Riley yelled back. "I'm talking to myself."

She filed through the coats and found an old navy double-breasted peacoat that she wore in high school. Simple, wearable, and not too dated. The silk lining was ripped on the inside but no one would see it. Good enough. A bonus was that it actually fit.

The kids were pretty loud in the kitchen. Elise cried when she spilled food on her shirt. Flynn ran around with his arms out, pretending to be an airplane. Delana tried vying for her mom's attention. Shannon went about her business as if the world were calm. This was her life. Riley wondered if she could handle all the chaos that early in the morning—every day.

Glancing out the back-door window, she decided to wait outside for Shannon since she had a few minutes. Riley opened the door and slipped out to the porch for some quiet. As she crossed the lawn, her shoes became wet from the soggy ground. Damn, she should have thought about that sooner. Instead of heading back, she sprinted across the rest of the yard and ducked around the trees into the cemetery.

The grass was cut shorter in the gated community, making it easier to walk. A slight breeze blew up as she made her way to the angel. Riley lifted the collar on the coat to keep her neck warm. She glanced about to see what was new since the last time she'd been there.

The cemetery was L-shaped, with the lower, older section near Dad's house. The area closest to them was hilly with mature trees. The statues were taller and more ornate on their side. She found her favorite log-style headstone—still in place. Next, she searched for the section with the little lambs. In the middle, a larger statue of an angel holding a blanket and a book stood over the children who died too young. Most of those children were from the 1800s.

A stone building with a green oxidized roof separated the old part of the cemetery from the new part. The vines climbing the walls had thinned out, leaving the branches showing. The place was used for funeral services, and she guessed that Dad's service would be held there.

The new section, at the top of the L and near the road, was less hilly with neat rows of plant stands decorating the lawn. The headstones were flat in the ground, making it easier for the caretaker to mow, which she didn't like. Half the stones were hidden because the grass crept over their names and dates. The new section also housed two granite buildings—columbarium niches for those cremated. One of her friends from high school had been laid to rest in the smaller one. She died in a car accident after driving through a red light.

Riley shuddered, not wanting to think of her friend's death. She had another one to deal with now. One more heart-wrenching for her.

She went to join the angel in front of the family plot.

On each side of her was an angled, gothic-style bench with a tall back—her favorite spot. The benches didn't match the rest of the cemetery, looking more like stone church pews, but Dad wanted them. And like the different styles in the house, he made it work.

She liked sitting on the bench to the right of the angel, giving her a wide view of the cemetery. She enjoyed the peacefulness the landscape carried. This was her place to think. The lawn was quiet today, aside from a few leaves that tumbled across the lawn.

The family plot was surrounded by a two-foot stone wall. Her paternal grandparents were to the right, in front. Mom and Dad's shared grave was to the left. Their headstone, an upright gray marble slab in the shape of a tree trunk, was already in place and had been there for a decade. Behind them rested her two single aunts, an uncle who died in the war, a cousin, and her great-grandparents.

"Hello."

Riley jumped.

"Jesus!" she said and placed her hand on the bench's armrest.

"Sorry, I didn't mean to frighten you."

"Good place for it." She let out a nervous laugh while regaining her composure.

He was the man with the light curled hair and dark green jacket she'd seen yesterday. His coat hung open and he wore a tan Henley underneath. She noticed his necklace—a silver medal star. And his hard chest. He worked out.

"I'm Geo."

"Riley," she said.

"Max's youngest daughter."

He looked more like a Colorado free-spirit than a Midwest hunter, even though he kept a bright orange hat tucked into one of his coat pockets.

"You knew my father?" She shoved her hands underneath her armpits to keep them warm. She forgot gloves, but then she hadn't planned to stay long.

He nodded. "I knew him very well. I rent the place out back."

Riley wrinkled her nose, taking a moment to think. She didn't remember any houses near her dad's property. Except for the one on his land, an abandoned shack. Shannon and her friends had avoided the place as kids, thinking it was haunted. Even as teenagers, the place creeped them out when going there to drink or to smoke a joint. They never stayed too long. And never at night.

"You're not talking about the old hunting shack, are you?"

"That's it."

"Really? Are you sure? It should've been torn down years ago."

"The shack is actually a nice place to live. I did some repairs to it."

"I sure hope so. How long have you lived there?"

Why didn't she know about it? Dad never mentioned him or renting out the shack.

"About six months."

"What?" Her voice went an octave higher. She'd been

back to visit. Wouldn't she have seen or heard work being done?

He raised his hand to calm her down. He explained, "I rented out land from your dad and started growing grapes. My grandfather worked as the caretaker here." He motioned around them. "I lived with him until he died. Since the hunting shack is next to the vineyard, I negotiated a deal with your dad, about a year ago, to include it in the rent of the property. It's taken some time to make it livable."

"Oh yeah," she said, remembering her dad talking about the man who grew grapes and made damn good wine. "You're the winemaker."

"That's me."

Riley nodded. "We drank a … red blend. Yes, a red, the last time I came home. I liked it."

"Thanks."

She frowned. "But you don't own a winery, correct?"

"Correct. I sell the grapes. The wine that I make is for myself." He smiled. "And for your dad."

Both turned quiet, reflecting on her dad.

Geo hesitated. "For what it's worth, your dad was great. My prayers go out to you and your family."

She pressed her lips together. The lump in her throat returned. How many times was she going to hear those words in the next week or so? Shannon was the social one and would keep her calm. Not Riley. She feared turning into a blubbering idiot.

"Definitely a tragedy," he said. He kicked a small pile of leaves away with his booted foot.

Riley leaned against the back of the bench and looked out at the road, beyond the cemetery, as a car passed. She said, "I guess he saved himself from all the pain he would have gone through."

A breeze blew across her face, colder than expected. She turned her head down and stared at the ground.

Geo shifted. He stuffed his hands in his jacket pockets. "I know this must be hard on you. I'm having a hard time believing it myself." He shuffled his feet. "If you don't mind me asking …," he hesitated and then said, "Do you think your father took his own life?"

His question threw her off guard. Harsher than expected, she asked, "Why would you think differently?"

Geo bowed slightly. "My apologies. I meant no offense. I heard rumors. That's all. He just didn't seem the type to die at his own hands."

Okay, what was he saying? Did he know something they didn't? She eyed him with some skepticism.

As if sensing he upset her, Geo backed up. "If there's anything I can do to help, please let me know."

The back door to Dad's house opened. Shannon stepped out and called her name. Her sister carried both their purses.

Riley waved. "Be right there."

Time to go.

When she turned back to Geo, he was gone.

Her head started to hurt.

What a way to start the day.

Chapter 4

Riley sat next to her sister in the small, dark office as they made the arrangements at the funeral home. The chairs were small and hard to sit in. Sally, the rail-thin funeral director with short, shaggy gray hair sat behind a desk stacked with paperwork in thick folders. The assistant left them with a pot of coffee and Styrofoam cups. She had set them on the side table when they arrived.

They paid close attention as Sally explained the different types of funerals they could have, mentioning that the funeral home would be a lovely place to hold the wake. After conferring with her sister, Riley told her that both wake and funeral would be at the stone building inside the cemetery.

Next, Sally explained what Dad had pre-arranged. She showed them the copper-colored casket and burial vault he purchased. The vault would have a dove emblem on the cover. The rest they had to decide.

Riley frowned at her sister. They had been there for an hour. Silently she asked, "How long is this going to take?"

Reading her expression, Shannon shrugged.

The morning soon turned into the afternoon as Sally placed a thick folder in front of them.

"Let's first pick out the memorial cards." She swiped her thumb across her tongue and thumbed through the pages to where the cards started. Finding the place, she pushed the book closer to them, allowing them time to go through the samples.

Riley took over, glancing at each card and flipping the pages. Way too many styles to choose from. She glanced at her sister, hoping for help. Instead, Shannon rose from her chair to get them more coffee.

With a sigh, Riley continued the search. Did they want a picture of Dad? An eagle? A mountain scene? Wait. She spotted one with an angel. "How about this one, Shannon?"

"Looks good to me," she said while opening a creamer cup for her coffee.

"How lovely." Sally smiled in a perfect saleswoman way. "One of my favorites."

Riley wondered if she said that to all her customers, wanting them to feel good about their choice.

Sally wrote the style number down on the form. She then leaned forward and turned the pages to the next section. "Now let's pick out the verse to print on the inside of the cards."

Ten pages of verses—all in small print.

You've got to be kidding me.

Riley tilted her head back to stretch her neck. She would not read through all the verses listed. She looked to

Shannon.

Her sister scooted forward with cup of coffee in hand. "Which ones are your more popular verses?"

"Well, let me see...*The Lord's Prayer, They Say There is a Reason, A Letter from Heaven*..." She pointed to each one. "Or there's—"

"Oh," Shannon exclaimed, spotting one. She pointed with her finger. "Here. *Now I Lay Me Down to Sleep*."

"Yeah, I like that," Riley agreed. "Dad used to say the prayer to us before we fell asleep for the night."

Sally wrote it down. Verse done. Next came the Thank You cards.

Riley groaned. They had to do the same thing again for the thank you cards? She took a sip of her coffee to keep from swearing in front of the nice lady.

"I think we can pass on Thank You cards," Shannon said.

The funeral director raised her eyebrows. "Are you sure? We can order the thank you cards to match the angel on the memorial cards."

Shannon kept her smile polite. "No, we can manage those on our own."

Riley knew her sister. They could get a box of cards for a helluva lot cheaper at the store, saving them money and fulfilling the same purpose.

Next came the obituary notice for the newspaper. They had homework to do for the notice. What did they want to say about him? Sally reminded them that everyone in the community knew and respected Maxwell Walsh. She suggested they look at a few examples, read through the online obituaries, write it up, and then send it to her. Riley liked the idea. She had a headache. Her stomach growled.

The assistant popped her head into the office and announced that a phone call waited for Sally on Line 2. The funeral director excused herself and left the room.

"I'm hungry." Riley leaned over to Shannon.

"So am I," her sister said and placed a hand on her stomach when it growled.

As they waited for Sally to return, Riley checked her emails. Four more from work. Gary had persuaded the boss to delay her interview by an hour. She wished it were rescheduled for Tuesday, but she couldn't complain. The extra hour would help.

What was she going to wear to her interview? She didn't bring any business clothes with her. Would her funeral outfit work? She could shop for a suit before she left. They'd have time. Shannon would help pick the perfect outfit.

"Okay," Sally said as she entered the room again.

Riley jumped, surprised she came back so soon.

The funeral director sat behind the desk again and gave her a subtle yet sympathetic smile. "There's one more item on our list to do and that is choosing the flower arrangements. We should be done here in the next half hour, so you can meet with the pastor. He has time to meet you in ..." she glanced at her watch, "forty minutes. We'll make sure you have time to get there without being late."

She had a crumb on her lip. The woman had eaten something—a cookie or a muffin—and didn't offer any to them.

Riley's stomach growled again.

Getting lunch was out of the question as they rushed from the funeral home to the church. As Sally stated, the slightly bald pastor was waiting for them.

He asked questions at the pace of a turtle. Did they want to have one or more readings? A eulogy? Songs? Riley let Shannon make most of the decisions. Pastor Rupert walked them through their next set of questions about the service. The frail man had been at the church forever. The other pastor Dad liked had retired eons ago. This one had to be getting close to that time as well.

"Will it be an open or closed casket?" he asked from behind his desk.

Riley's attention returned to the present. Her throat constricted. Did they have an option?

"Dad wanted an open casket," Shannon said with her eyes unfocused, lost in thought.

"But what if he has marks?"

The pastor cleared his throat. "Makeup will take care of that sort of thing."

"Everyone looks like wax in all that makeup," Riley said, not keen on the idea. "They look dead and nothing like themselves when they were alive. What's the point?"

"I really don't want to see any of his marks." Shannon's eyes glazed over as if playing it out in her head.

"Good point, sis. I'm afraid people will be looking for the marks on his neck as they're paying their respects." Riley shuddered. This isn't how she wanted anyone to remember

Dad.

"Closed," they said in unison.

Riley held her stomach as they sat in the two plain chairs in front of the wood desk piled with papers and bulletins. She was queasy, beyond the hunger stage. She released her stomach and rubbed her hands across her face. She needed to get out of there. Talk about something else. Food.

Sally, the funeral director, and Pastor Rupert were godsends, helping them in every way possible; however, all the questions and choices became too much. Her cup runneth over. What she wouldn't do for a cheeseburger and fries.

Pastor Rupert leaned forward. "Ms. Walsh, are you all right?"

Riley jerked when she realized he was talking to her. Guilt must have shrouded her face.

"We're starved," Shannon said, answering for them both, "and overwhelmed."

"Understood." He smiled with empathy. "The planning of a loved one's funeral is hard, especially when the passing is unexpected. Do we need to take a break?"

Yes, Riley thought but knew it meant being confined inside the tiny office even longer. She said in her best I-am-paying-attention voice, "Let's continue. Please."

The rest of the meeting went well. In less than twenty minutes, they left the pastor's office and church. Riley welcomed the fresh air to stabilize herself. The sun shined, making the day seem warmer than the predicted temperature—in the forties.

"I need a drink." Shannon let out a huge breath of air as she walked straight to Dad's car.

"I need food," Riley said as she followed close behind.

They went to eat at the Irish pub on the outskirts of Hudson. Dad's favorite bar. Riley ordered a hamburger, and Shannon chose a salad. Both remained silent as they shoveled in the first few bites.

"So, what's with all the phone checking today?" Shannon asked between bites.

"What do you mean?" Riley glanced up as she tossed a French fry into her mouth.

"Your nose was buried in your phone ten times at the funeral home. Five times at the church. Not even Conner is that bad."

Riley shrugged. "I need to keep up with my messages. If not, they get out of control."

Shannon raised her eyebrow. "And you don't think checking your phone eight hundred times a day is out of control?"

"What?" Riley's defenses went up. She drank some beer from her mug. "I'm not that bad."

Her sister's lips pursed together to keep from spouting off again.

They finished eating and then headed back to the house. Riley, having a headache, was in a bad mood. Pulling into the driveway, she noticed that Conner and the kids were back from their shopping. The police were there for a visit as well.

"What's going on?" Shannon asked her husband when they

entered the house.

"Fucking police," Conner said and paced the front hall. "Getting into everybody's business."

The police weren't around.

Riley frowned. "Where are they?"

"Out back." Conner wiped his nose and sniffed.

Her back went rigid. She avoided that area of the yard, near the back field where Dad was found inside the old shed. Crime scene tape surrounded the place to keep people out. She didn't want to even look that way. But why the visit again? She then remembered Geo's suspicion.

"Did they find something?"

"Procedure," Conner said and raised his hands, using air quotes.

She hesitated, unsure if she should walk over and help the police or stay in the house. Would they know if she drank a beer before driving home? She wasn't drunk. The hamburger—all that meat—had to absorb most of the alcohol.

"How long are they going to be here?"

"Fuck if I can tell you." Conner paced. "You girls stay inside. I'll handle this."

Shannon turned somber as she went to the kitchen. "Can't they leave it alone?"

Riley could tell her sister reached her fill of "death" for the day.

"Where's Delana?" Shannon asked Flynn, who sat at the table playing his electronic game.

"Outside." He sniffled and then wiped his nose on his

sleeve.

"Ugh." Shannon groaned at her son. "Go get a tissue." She then peered out the window toward the cemetery. "Delana needs to come in. Do her homework before night and bedtime."

"Homework?" Riley was surprised.

"School is harder this year. She has homework in almost every class. Missing days doesn't help."

"I suppose." Riley could relate. One week was a long time for her to miss work. Which reminded her, she needed to call Gary again and find out what was going on. She started for her phone and then stopped. Shannon yelled at her once today for checking her emails. She wanted to avoid another scolding for being on her phone too much.

"Math is the worst class." Her sister continued on while scanning the contents of the refrigerator. "Delana doesn't get it, and the way they teach them now is different from how we learned."

"I'll help."

Shannon glanced over at her. Her eyes lightened. "Really?"

"Yeah, why not." It'd keep her from checking emails and calling Gary. "I'll get her and bring her in."

Once outside, Riley's boots crunched against the hard grass. Glancing to the other side of the yard—the forbidden side—she saw two police officers standing near the yellow tape. They were in a heavy discussion as one pointed to the ground. She couldn't see the small red shed hidden behind the trees. Trying to think back, she didn't remember much being in the shed—an old gas can and a couple of folding lawn chairs.

49

It was pretty small and the dirt floor was uneven and always damp. She debated about going over to check on them.

Riley couldn't do it. She wasn't ready to get that close to where Dad's life ended.

She tripped over a tree root, making her pay attention to where she was walking.

The cemetery.

She weaved her way between the trees.

Delana was giggling and seemed to be talking to someone as she danced around a headstone like it was a prop in a recital. Her blond hair bounced as she moved from one grave to the next while her hips swayed back and forth. A smile curved on Riley's lips. That girl was going to have all the boys after her. Poor Shannon. She would have her hands full with her oldest daughter, especially when she reached her teen years.

"Auntie!"

"Hi, Delana. What are you doing?"

"Playing. You wanna join me?"

"If we had time I would, but your mom wants you inside. Pronto."

Her mouth turned down in disappointment.

"I hear you need to do your homework."

This time she groaned. Whatever amused her beforehand ended. Riley had broken into her playtime. She felt bad. Aunties were supposed to be fun.

She coaxed her. "You don't want to get so far behind that your friends become smarter than you, do you?"

"They all are. I get terrible grades all the time." Her

shoulders slumped as she stomped her way toward her aunt.

Riley held out her hand for her niece to take. "Let me help. I can teach you some things they don't know."

Her eyes lit up. "Like boys?"

"Boys?" Riley laughed. "You're too young for boys."

Her niece frowned.

"Okay, maybe one trick."

Her eyes lit up again, and she looked like her mom with the way her smile spread across her face.

Delana took her hand and stumbled when she glanced behind her. She yelled out, "Bye, Maggie."

Riley glanced across the cemetery but saw no one. She searched the trees to see if the person hid behind one of them to avoid being seen. She asked, "Who's Maggie?"

"My friend. I met her the last time we were here."

"Oh." Riley came up short on what to say. Was Maggie her imaginary friend? "Do you play here a lot with her?"

"No," Delana said. "Only when she wants to come out and play. She doesn't like other people too much. Kind of scared of them."

"I see."

Delana skipped as they crossed the lawn. She still held her aunt's hand.

With the sun going down, the air was a bit chilly. Riley wished she had a warmer coat and gloves. She shivered. "Brrrr."

"You're cold?" Her niece squinted up at her with teeth showing.

"I am." She was turning into a wimp by living in Arizona.

51

"I'm hot."

"And you were running around," Riley said.

"Did you know this was Grandpa's happy home?" she asked while making Riley's arm swing with hers. "He super loved it here."

Riley looked at the house with the dark wood, additions, and coziness with a cottage feel. She had reservations about it being a happy home. When they were growing up, all the creaks and groans at night made it sound like someone was walking around. But for Dad, Delana was probably right. He loved the house, but he should. He put his heart and a lot of labor into the place.

"It makes him mad when people see him for his money."

Delana's statement—more for an adult to say than a ten-year-old—made Riley stop. "What do you mean by that? Who told you? Grandpa?"

"Maggie."

Her imaginary friend?

The girl was making her tired, and they hadn't started her homework yet. They continued to walk toward the back door of the house.

"Maggie said Grandpa was hurt."

"True," Riley said, taking a moment to think about what to say to a ten-year-old. "He was sick. He had cancer."

Delana dropped her hand yet continued to walk next to her with head down. Her bottom lip trembled as if she was going to cry.

"It's okay, Delana. We're all sad." Riley leaned over and hugged her niece.

She sniffled. "Grandpa would never ever kill himself."

Riley's muscles pulled tight like a bowstring. Her niece wasn't supposed to know how Dad had died. Shannon made her promise she wouldn't talk about the suicide in front of the kids. So how did she find out?

"Who told you that?"

"Maggie."

Of course. Riley rolled her eyes. "Did you overhear someone say it?"

"No," she said in an annoyed voice because Auntie didn't listen to her. "Maggie told me."

"How would she know?"

"He told her. A man didn't like Grandpa. He's the one who hurt him."

She sucked in her breath and stared at Delana as she bounced up the stairs to the door.

How in the hell was she going to tell Shannon that her daughter just told her what happened? She'd immediately blame Riley for telling her daughter.

"Ohh, this isn't good," she mumbled, entering the house behind Delana. This was going to blow up in her face.

"What do you two want for dinner?" Shannon called out from the kitchen.

"Pancakes!" Delana yelled as she scrambled out of her boots and coat. She shuffled into the kitchen while pulling up her pants.

"No pancakes," Shannon said. "That's for breakfast. How

about eggs?"

Riley raised her eyebrows at her sister. "Really?"

Shannon shrugged her shoulders.

Delana left the kitchen to get her school backpack. Riley sat on the bar stool at the counter and waited. She eyed the bottle of wine on the side table. No, not yet.

Wine did sound good.

They drank a lot of wine when she came home to visit. Dad kept his inventory well stocked. He stored at least five cases in the cellar. The wine always continued to flow. Was the drinking to help Riley relax? Be festive during the holidays? Or did they drink to forget life in general with all the chaos and drama from working so hard. No matter, this place was her safe haven.

No more.

Riley let out a heavy breath.

"What's up? You seem pensive."

"Huh?" She glanced up at her sister.

"Why so glum?"

Riley pulled her hair back, away from her face. "Oh, just thinking about Mom and Dad."

Shannon set three small plates out on the breakfast table in the kitchen. She nodded and said, "I know what you mean. All these things we used to do. What we had with them." She looked around. "The house seems so empty."

Conner trudged into the room with his fists tight and his mouth in a snarl. He saw Shannon and then found Riley. "The cops want to talk to you."

"Me?"

He stared at her as if she had done something wrong.

"No, the both of you."

Chapter 5

Riley's heart skipped a beat when Conner said the cops wanted to talk to Shannon and her.

"Where are they?"

"In the living room, waiting."

The most formal place in the house. She slid off the stool. Shannon brushed off her hands on her pants and straightened her shirt.

Conner pointed his finger, waving it toward the both of them. "Don't you give them too much information. If they question too much, tell them you want a lawyer present."

Shannon nodded obediently. Riley wondered why he'd turned so anal. She needed to find out what happened to Dad. What if they found more information? What if it wasn't a suicide? Her mind refused to go further.

First sight, walking into the living room, Riley's mouth fell open. Wow. She stared at the one cop—a knock-out, like the private investigators on a TV series. His short black hair shined in the light. His sharp blue eyes and sexy five o'clock shadow got her attention. He opted to wear a gray, fitted suit that stated French model as opposed to blue-collar worker.

When he looked up at her sister, he did a double take. Riley had witnessed the reaction many times before—an instant attraction to her sister. From that moment on, Riley was lost to them as if she were part of the furniture and walls.

"Are you Ms. Riley Walsh?" He held out his hand to her sister.

"No, I'm Mrs. Doyle. Shannon." She shook his hand.

The disappointment grayed his eyes. She was the married one and not the single daughter.

"I'm Detective Torrence." He hesitated with letting go of her hand when he shook it. Not a noticeable difference but one that Riley recognized when someone wanted to keep the connection.

Shannon let go of his hand and motioned toward her. "This is my sister Riley."

"Hello," he said and shook her hand—professional all the way. He stepped back. "My apologies for bothering the two of you in this time of grief. I am sorry for your loss."

They both nodded.

"What can we do for you, detective?" Shannon brought his attention back to her. She motioned for him to sit on the blue velvet chair. She sat on the stiff white couch. Riley decided to stand. The other police officer stayed quietly in the background.

"My understanding is that your father hired a lawyer … a Mr. Hathaway."

Shannon looked to her to respond.

"Yes, that's correct. He's handled the family estate since the beginning. Do you know him?"

Detective Torrence glanced at her for a second before turning his attention to Shannon. "I'm sorry to inform you that he has passed away as well."

"What?" Riley's response came too hard and fast. She crossed her arms over her stomach. Both Shannon and the detective looked at her in an odd way. Riley couldn't believe another one. Dead. Was it a coincidence? She gulped and fumbled for words. "I met him a few times. He's the one who handled our dad's finances."

"Yes, he did."

Her head spun. Geo's caution and Delana's comment now made her think. Was there a bad guy lurking about? No, there couldn't be. This wasn't a crime show. "How did he die?"

"Heart attack." Detective Torrence kept his gaze on her as if wanting to observe her reaction.

Riley chose her words carefully. "I can't believe it. How awful."

"What does this mean for us?" Shannon gave her some relief from the detective and his burning eyes.

"You'll need to contact their office. They are assigning another lawyer to help."

"How do you know?" Riley asked.

"Part of the investigation."

"Why? Is there something else going on?" She shot him a questioning look, hoping for a little more information.

"Normal procedure." He wouldn't give any details. This was his time to question them, not her time to ask. He glanced down at his notes. "Ms. Walsh, you live in Arizona?"

"Yes, I do."

"Can you give me your address?"

Riley provided him with her address and responded to his other "routine" questions. Where was she on the day he died? When did she last speak to him? What was their conversation about? Was there anything unusual going on in her life, her father's life? Once the detective finished, satisfied with her answers, he turned to Shannon and asked the same questions.

"Can either one of you tell us about Maxwell Walsh's finances?"

Detective Torrence turned to Riley. She wanted to roll her eyes. He obviously had the information already. "I handle his investments. Dad has an account—a portfolio—with Sikerte, an investment firm in Arizona. Yes, I work there. No, I don't manage his money. I'm not licensed."

Her palms turned sweaty. She wanted him to stop looking at her like she was a suspect. She wasn't guilty of anything here. Now she understood why Conner warned them. In a minute, she was ready to tell him she wanted her lawyer.

Wait ... he was now dead.

The detective turned slightly in his chair to focus on her. "How about his current finances? Anything unusual?"

"Not that I'm aware. Can you tell me what I should be looking for? Was our dad in trouble or something?"

"No, no." He held out his hand to assure them. "We're

doing routine work here." He wrote on his notepad and then raised his head. "But if you do find anything unusual, please give us a call."

He reached into his coat pocket and pulled out two cards.

Riley's eyes narrowed. He wasn't telling them everything. "Why are you here, looking around?"

"Routine procedures. Today we searched the shed again where your father was found, including the surrounding area."

"What are you looking for?" Shannon rounded her eyes, wanting to help in any way.

Riley smiled inwardly. Her sister had the hots for him as well.

He hesitated before answering. "Any evidence that we can find to help with the case." His dark eyes focused on Shannon. "Your help is appreciated."

Of course, he's more interested in Shannon. Riley snorted through her nose.

Detective Torrence glanced toward her when she made the noise but chose to ignore her. He stood and stretched to show his tall, lean frame. He eyed Shannon as if checking her reaction. The slight smile she offered encouraged him to strut even more. He adjusted the button on his suitcoat. The detective tugged on his pants, adjusting the waist after sitting. Oh yeah, he was aware of his male potion.

"Again, I'm sorry for your loss. He contributed to our fund for getting a K-9 unit. Your dad was a generous man to this community."

"I'm glad he was a help to you." Shannon's face saddened. She placed her hands on her thighs for a moment and then stood.

Detective Torrence almost stepped forward as if to give her a hug but stopped himself. Instead, he held out his hand. As he shook her hand, his eyes deepened with sympathy. "If you need any help, we're here." He turned to shake Riley's hand. "If you find anything unusual, please don't hesitate to call."

Riley left, letting Shannon show him and the other officer out.

Wait. She turned around and found them in the hall. She asked, "When do we get Dad back?"

The detective held the front door and faced them before going out. "That is up to the coroner. I'll see if I can find out for you."

"Thanks." She guessed the detective would return again—specifically for Shannon.

She's married, buddy.

Chapter 6

At the table, Conner leaped out of his chair when Riley entered the kitchen. He was practically on top of her. "What did he want from you?"

She figured he'd been listening to the conversation with ears fully open. She shrugged. "Not much. He told us that Dad's lawyer died of a heart attack."

He grunted. She sensed he already knew. Conner grabbed a beer from the refrigerator. "That's what he came here for? To tell you about the lawyer?" He twisted the top off and took a swig. "Why were the police here? Why are they interested in Max's finances?"

He was listening in to their conversation, she confirmed. Riley studied her brother-in-law. Why was he so agitated? She answered, "He wanted to inform us that the firm is retaining a new lawyer to replace Mr. Hathaway."

"I have a lawyer. We'll use him."

Riley shook her head. "Our lawyer's office has all Dad's information."

"I see that as an issue."

She frowned at his odd statement. She wanted to ask why, but instead thought it through. With Dad and the lawyer dying, the firm would have to get someone else up to speed on Dad's finances and the trust. Would it be better if someone else looked into his finances? Make sure everything was in order?

The subject dropped when the kids trampled into the room looking for food. Delana carried her books and backpack. She placed them on the floor until after dinner. Ham and eggs worked—nice and easy to make. Once they ate, she spent the next few hours helping her niece struggle through most of her homework. Shannon was right. Math had changed since they'd been in school.

Eight o'clock.

"Up to bed," Riley said, having enough of homework. Her ass was tired from sitting on the hard chair.

"I can't play?" Delana eyed the books and papers spread out across the table. Her lip turned outward with disappointment.

"Only for a bit." After all the school work, Delana deserved playtime before going to bed.

A chill ran through Riley. The room turned colder.

Delana giggled. She hurried to put her homework back into the folders and then into her backpack. She grabbed her books.

"Come on, let's go upstairs," her niece whispered.

Riley stood and stretched. "You go on up and play. I need a break."

Delana gave her an odd look and then shrugged.

"Come on, Maggie," she said and trotted out of the room

with her "friend."

Left alone, Riley listened for the others. Shannon and Conner were in the den. She knew not to disturb them based on the heavy conversation they were having. Not so much an argument but close. A little voice told her to get some fresh air—take a walk in the cemetery. Taking a bottle of wine and a glass, she threw on her coat and headed outside. Remembering that she had nothing to open the bottle with, she darted back inside to grab a corkscrew.

Outside, the crisp, fresh air helped. In fact, she was glad to take a few deep breaths to clear her head. The wind from earlier in the day had died down and made the temperature bearable. As she made her way to the cemetery, an owl hooted from above. She stopped to search for it—she hadn't seen an owl in ages. He called out a few more times, fluttered, and then flew off. She caught his form before he disappeared in the night sky. By the bird's size, she guessed a barn owl.

Riley entered the cemetery and again stopped. She wasn't the only one visiting the graves. Geo stood with his head down, looking toward the grave off to the side of the family's plot. Curious about what he was doing, she tiptoed closer and tried to be quiet so not to disturb him.

He bent down and picked up a shot glass resting on the base of the headstone. She'd seen the glass there on many occasions but most times, like now, it was empty. Next, he opened a bottle of whiskey and poured the liquor into the glass. Riley recognized the label on the bottle.

Jamison. Perfect choice. He downed the whiskey and poured another shot. This time he placed the glass next to the headstone. Mystery solved.

A leaf crunched under her foot.

Geo turned with hands up, ready to protect himself.

Riley jumped back. He relaxed. She blushed, guilty of spying on him. To relieve the awkward moment, she asked, "You're going to waste good whiskey?"

He chuckled. "Not in the least." He raised the bottle. "My grandfather's favorite drink since spending time with Maxwell Walsh."

It was her turn to laugh. "Yes, my dad had a way of influencing people. I remember being in the bar here in town, and they didn't have Irish Car Bombs on their drink menu. The next day, they sold them as a specialty drink for happy hour in honor of my dad."

"I drank a few of those at the bar." Geo took a swig from the bottle he held.

"Do you leave the whiskey in the glass?" She pointed toward the full shot.

"I do."

"Ummm, I've never seen it full."

Geo's smile grew. "I expect that either your dad, in his early morning walk, poured it into his coffee, or there's a squirrel out there who's becoming an alcoholic."

She chuckled and then realized she was imposing on his private time. She backed away. "I'm sorry to interrupt your … your ritual. I'll leave."

"No, stay," he said and motioned for her to join him. He

did a double-take when she stepped closer. He lifted the bottle again. "It looks like you could use a shot as well."

Riley took offense. "Do I look that bad?"

"Oh no," he said as she smoothed down her hair. He cleared his throat as if knowing he better correct himself. "I just … you look tired."

He was right. She was tired. He didn't need to point it out though.

"Would you like a hit?"

She fumbled with her coat, reaching inside the front and found the wine. She pulled it out. "I brought my own libation. Care to join me?"

Geo twisted to check the label. "Ah, one of my wines. Nice."

She tucked the bottle underneath her arm before reaching into her coat again. "I only have one glass, but I'm willing to share."

"I'm fine with that," he said, eying her with approval.

Riley blushed again. Did he just flirt with her?

The guys she dated back home weren't into flirting. Their dates were set up like business meetings—matter-of-fact with crisp politeness. No one relaxed until a few drinks were in them. And then they'd talk about themselves and their achievements.

"Shall we sit?" He held his hand out for her to go first.

She walked over to the closest Goth bench and settled in. She looked up at the angel, who smiled at her with motherly love. An odd sensation overcame her, as if someone had wanted her to meet Geo tonight … or for him

66

to meet her.

Riley placed the bottle of wine in between her legs and the glass in the middle, giving him room to sit on the other side. She pulled out the corkscrew. "I'm not sure if I've had this one of yours before. I don't recognize the picture on the label."

Geo leaned over to check out the fall scene. "This cab has a hint of spice and smokiness. I made this blend last year. I gave your dad two bottles, and he liked it so much that he bought another six a week later to have on hand."

"He drank that much wine?" Riley joked but it didn't surprise her.

"Your dad liked wine." Geo chuckled. "I think that's why he let me rent out his land for growing grapes."

"He does keep your wine separate, in a different rack from the other wines—like his special stash." She struggled with the corkscrew and he offered to help. She let him take over.

He glanced over at her as he continued the task of opening the bottle. "Your dad treated me well. He was instrumental in my success." He pulled out the cork. "I think he tended to my grapes more than I did."

"I can picture him doing that." Dad liked to be hands-on in all his business investments to ensure success.

"I can say this is one of the best batches I made. It goes well on a cold fall night."

She chuckled. "And sitting in a cemetery."

Riley held up the wine glass, and he poured the dark red liquid from the bottle, careful not to spill. She swirled the wine with care since he filled it higher than restaurant style. Now wasn't the time to be fancy with examining the clarity or watching the legs the wine left on the glass. She sipped the first taste, let it sit in her mouth to enjoy the flavor, and nodded with approval. "Yes, very good." She took another drink before changing the subject. "You like coming here?"

"I do." He leaned closer to her. "The place is peaceful. I can look out at the graves and realize that life isn't so bad."

Riley laughed. "I guess I never looked at it that way. For me, I like the comfort of knowing that people are settled in. I get a sense of calm, like everything will be okay. Or I used to."

"What do you mean?"

She took a larger sip of wine before handing the glass to him. "I'm not sure. Something isn't quite right. I've noticed since I've been back."

"Unsettled ghosts?" he teased.

She looked into the darkness. The lights on the street illuminated part of the graves. "The vibe is different from what I remember. It's more like a chill versus a warm fuzzy."

Geo crossed his lower legs and settled in, leaning back against the bench. He followed her gaze. "It does seem colder with winter closing in."

He handed her the glass back. She liked his blue eyes and how his lips curved into a soft smile.

She took another drink. "What made you decide to become a wine maker?"

"I needed a new occupation. I learned how to make

wine from my uncle years ago. He made his with a few makeshift jugs and balloons." He paused as if recollecting the memory. He smiled. "Dandelion wine."

Riley wrinkled her nose. "You turned weeds into wine?"

"Yeah," Geo said with a laugh. "That shit could knock your socks off. Think of it like the moonshine of wines. I started there. After a year, I spent time overseas and learned how the Europeans made wine."

"And you've lived here for three years now?" She tried to remember what he had said the first time they met.

"I've lived here three years, in Wisconsin, with my grandpa. I'd say six months at the shack."

"What made you come here?"

"My grandfather was the caretaker here at the cemetery."

"I remember you saying that. But why did *you* come here?"

"Good question." He stalled for time as he took a sip of wine.

"Were you in some kind of trouble?" Riley dared to ask. The wine began to affect her, making her bolder.

"Trouble?" Geo coughed as the word came out. "Why do you say that?"

He rubbed his chin and seemed amused by her curiosity.

"I can spot someone who is as ..." she tried to find the right words, "as edgy as I am."

"I'm not edgy," he said in defense.

"On the outside you're not. But on the inside, you are." She leaned toward him. "Or maybe you have a secret that you're not telling me."

Geo let out a breath of air, as if surprised that he was more transparent than he realized. He said, "I've had my share of hard times and bad situations."

"Oh, like what?"

"In a previous life, I served in the military, as a cop, and then a detective." He gulped down more of the wine.

She left it alone, seeing his jaw tighten. On another day he might be willing to tell her more. They were silent for a while as they enjoyed the wine. Riley glanced toward the house. A light upstairs turned off. Shannon had put the kids to bed. The air grew colder as the moon rose in the sky.

"Did you talk to the detective today?"

"How did you know he was here?" She tilted her head at an angle. Was he snooping?

"One police car and one unmarked car were in your driveway. I saw them doing more investigative work around the shed as I checked on my vines."

"Yes, I talked to them, but they didn't offer much info. Do you think they were looking for a note? I think it's strange that my dad didn't leave one."

"I would think, for you girls, he would have."

He spoke some truth. Dad would justify his actions, not wanting them to be upset or feel guilty. She poured more wine into the glass and then gave him the bottle.

Geo moved closer to the center of the bench.

She didn't mind. She liked his company and how good she felt around him.

Her phone buzzed inside the back pocket of her jeans. She had turned the switch to vibrate when they were at the funeral home. Now she ignored it.

Riley leaned forward, resting her lower arms on her thighs. She dangled her wine glass between her knees.

"Do you remember what you said to me before, about my dad?" She lowered her head. "I'm now wondering the same. I believe Detective Torrence was searching for evidence, like he knew it was more than suicide. He asked questions about Dad's finances. He wondered if I'd found anything unusual when I was going through his accounts."

"Have you started going through them?"

She shook her head.

"It's not a bad idea for you to start, see if there's anything odd."

"Like what?"

He shrugged. "Large amounts of money going out. Money being transferred. Bills that don't look right."

"Have you talked to him?"

Geo shot her a look. "Who?"

"The detective."

He hesitated and was careful with his words. "Yes. General questioning."

"What did he want to know?"

"If I had noticed anything unusual. If Max had said anything to me."

"And?"

"I knew your dad was preoccupied last month. He stayed home more often than usual. He didn't go to his two favorite spots—the local bar or the coffee shop."

She thought about that. If Dad wasn't doing his normal

routine, something must have bothered him. Maybe she could find something in his office, giving them a clue as to why he wasn't himself.

The night darkened. All the lights turned off upstairs in the house. She knew it was time to head inside. Besides, she was feeling the wine.

"Until next time?" she asked after downing her glass. The bottle was close to empty as well. She picked it up to take with her.

"Want me to walk you home?" Geo stood and then held out his hand to help her up.

She accepted his offer, and the heat from his touch stirred her insides.

Wow. She could have fallen into his arms. Let him draw her in and then lean down for a slow, sensual kiss as if they were a couple.

The wine. It had to be the wine.

Riley shook the thought out. She stuttered. "I-I think I can … I can manage."

Geo smiled. He squeezed her hand before letting go. "I hope we meet again soon."

He didn't seem to notice her reaction, the effect of his touch on her. She wiped her lip. "I'm sure we will."

"Stop by the hunting shack. Come see the changes I made."

"I will," she said, liking the idea of seeing the place. She couldn't imagine it being fixed up. If it was just Geo, his idea of fixing it up could be adding more boards and getting rid of the junk. Halfway to the trees, she turned around. He was still standing where she left him. "Hey, do you know who Maggie is?"

Geo turned his eyes upward as he thought. He shook his head. "No, I don't think so."

"She might be a little girl in the neighborhood. Hangs around here."

"Can't say I remember seeing anyone. Why?"

"Just wondering."

Riley waved goodbye and left through the trees.

Chapter 7

The warmth inside the house welcomed Riley in, but not like the heat from Geo's hand. How could such a touch make her insides tingle with pleasure?

She removed her coat, hung it on the hook, and then kicked off her boots. She continued to think of him. His eyes, the way he looked at her, all brought a smile to her lips.

A stranger. Yet not a stranger. Dad knew him. Geo had a down-to-earth aura, like he'd seen plenty in his life. He served our country. The community. He carried the edge of someone who'd seen good and bad in this world.

She shuffled into the kitchen. Shannon and Conner stood by the island snacking on carrots. They noticed the empty wine glass in her hand. She set it down on the counter. The wine bottle was still in her coat so she went back to retrieve it.

"All day wino?" Conner asked when she returned and set the bottle next to the glass. His words came out like a sneer. She let it go. They were under stress.

Riley grabbed a handled glass from the cupboard and turned on the faucet in the sink. She watched the water flow between her fingers as she waited for it to turn cold. She wanted to see Geo again and learn more about this man who lived in their hunting shack. He'd been living nearby and she'd never noticed or seen him before. He wasn't the type to forget with his cool yet casual demeanor. He acted like nothing would faze him.

"What's up?" Shannon watched her with an amused expression.

"Why?" Riley stalled for time.

"You've been staring at the water."

Riley jerked her finger away. She filled her glass and turned off the faucet.

Conner left the room, leaving the two of them alone.

She turned around and leaned against the counter next to the sink. "Shannon, do you think somebody tried—killed Dad?"

"That's ridiculous." Conner's voice boomed from the hallway.

Damn, he heard her.

He entered the kitchen again.

Shannon glared at her husband for a second and then refocused on her sister. "Why do you ask?"

"He didn't leave a note."

"So?" Conner opened the refrigerator door with more force than usual.

"There are others who don't believe he killed himself."

Conner stopped looking in the refrigerator to stare at her.

"Oh yeah? Like who?"

Riley kept her mouth shut. He didn't need to know that one of them was his own daughter.

"Is that what the detective said?" He quickly pulled out a carton of almond milk before shutting the door. He set it on the island while glaring at Shannon as if she was hiding something by keeping her sister's conversations from him.

"No, it wasn't the detective," Riley said. "It just seems odd. Not like Dad."

"He killed himself. Get over it," Conner snapped.

Riley gasped. The sharp words hit her like a whip. She couldn't even respond. Shannon had the same reaction. Both stared at him, shocked by his cold behavior.

"Don't look at me like that." He held up his hand. "All this goddamn wasted time is making everyone jump to conclusions. Let's just bury the old man and get the will read. Move on."

Riley's eyes widened even more. The tension in the air thickened like smoke—suffocating and harsh.

"Conner, what the hell is wrong with you?" Shannon shrieked. Her face paled.

He placed both hands on the counter and lowered his head as if to calm down, readjust his behavior. He got himself in control and raised his head again.

"I'm sorry." He pressed his fingers against his forehead. "I'm sorry."

Riley wasn't going to forgive him. Everyone was stressed. She got it. But he went overboard.

She left the kitchen, done for the night.

In her bedroom, she dressed in her pajamas—old yoga pants and a tee shirt. She jumped onto the bed, landing with her butt centered on the mattress. She lay back and stared at the white, textured ceiling, numb.

Conner made his point with everyone being jumpy. In normal circumstances, Dad or Mom would be their rock, the ones to keep them in line when tempers heated or feelings were hurt. On the other hand, the three of them were adults and should be mature enough to respect one another.

She checked her phone. Gary had called. He wouldn't be at the office anymore so she speed-dialed his cell phone. He answered on the third ring.

"Hey, Gary."

"Hi, Riley. Any word yet when the funeral will be?"

"No. We made the arrangements today. Everything's set to go, except for the date."

"I don't think we can change the time of the interview again. I'd make sure you can get back. He wants the person to start right away. Jackie's last day is the end of the month."

"There's plenty of time."

"I wouldn't be so sure. By the time you're promoted and Jackie leaves that doesn't leave a lot of time for training."

"I know the job. I've been doing it for the last six months."

"And Rita's been doing the job as well. Her interview is Tuesday."

"Oh." His news did put a little twist on timing. "I should be okay to come back. However, just so you know, I'll need to fly back after a day or two, to be here."

"That's expensive."

Well, what else was she going to do? She had to be at her dad's funeral. Riley bit her lip. She scooted upward to sit against the pillows. "Hey, do you think I could do the interview over the phone? Skype?"

"Ask HR."

"Who do I call?"

"I'll find out and text you the information."

"Great, thanks."

In today's world, an off-site interview wouldn't be an issue. But where she worked, the firm carried old-fashion attitudes and this was one of them. They wanted to meet the person before hiring. It made sense if a person came in off the streets. But she was an employee, and they knew firsthand how hard she worked.

A light knock sounded on the door and opened slightly; it hadn't been latched. Shannon poked her head into the room.

Riley motioned for her to come in while she finished her conversation with Gary. Shannon waited by the door until Riley placed her phone on the nightstand.

"I'm sorry about Conner's behavior."

"It's not your fault. You don't need to apologize." Her sister's shoulders slumped forward as she leaned against the door. The dark shadows under her eyes were more prevalent than before.

"He's been a little tense lately. Something is going on with his work. He won't tell me, but I don't think it's good."

Riley patted the bed for Shannon to sit next to her. She moved over, giving her room.

"I've heard him arguing a lot on the phone. Whenever I'm around, he tells them he has to go or he walks away, going into another room for privacy."

"We're all uptight. He's not the only one under pressure."

"Your promotion?" Shannon asked as she snuggled in.

"Yeah, my promotion." Her excitement for the job wasn't there.

"You mean the one that's going to make you work even more than the gazillion hours that you do now?"

"I don't—" Riley stopped. She wanted to defend herself and the job but couldn't. Shannon was right. She'd be working more than the sixty plus hours that she did now. Having to take care of six investors was a handful. They depended on her.

Shannon sighed. "I hope the pay is or will be good."

"I'll be able to buy a house now. Maybe then I can find the right guy and have a relationship."

Her sister stared at her with skepticism.

"What?" Riley tilted her head toward Shannon. "You don't think I can settle down?"

"Not if you're working all the time. Marriage takes two people."

"You were fortunate not having to work." Riley reminded her.

Shannon rested her head back against the pillow and stared at the ceiling. "I'm not so sure if that was smart on my part."

"Why?" Riley shifted.

The lines on her sister's mouth creased with worry. Her

eyebrows knitted together. "What if we're in financial trouble?"

"He's been in that position before. You always came out of it." Riley grabbed her sister's arm and hugged it. She sensed her pain ran deeper than normal. Again, it could be the stress of their situation.

"True. We've been through hard times before." Shannon lowered her eyes, doubt written on her face. "Sometimes I wish he had a more stable job instead of buying and selling businesses."

"You might not have the life you live now if he didn't. He's done quite well."

"I'm not so sure if it's worth it." She placed one of the toss pillows on her lap after it almost fell off the bed. She stared at it for a moment and then hugged it to her chest. She changed the conversation. "Anyway, I came to tell you that it'll be just the two of us hanging out for the next few days. Conner's taking the kids home so they won't miss any more school. His parents will watch them. He's flying to New York on business."

"That's probably a good thing," Riley said without much enthusiasm. "It'll give us a chance to dig through the office."

Shannon tapped her thigh. "All right. I'm tired."

"I hear ya, sister. I hear ya."

Riley motioned for her to turn off the light before leaving. Alone, she reconfigured, crawling underneath the covers to nestle in. Instead of creating a mental list of what she had to do the following day, she replayed her night with

Geo. She savored the memory of them sitting on the bench and enjoying his wine. She fell asleep dreaming of his smile.

The next morning turned hectic fast. Shannon packed the kids' bags, and Conner loaded the car to head home. Riley helped with breakfast. Yesterday she promised Flynn that she'd make him pancakes with the crisp edges. He shoveled his five large pancakes into his mouth as if his fork were a conveyor belt. Delana ate hers like a dainty princess, and little Elise wore more of her bite-sized pieces than she got into her mouth.

"Auntie," Delana said after drinking her orange juice.

"Yes?" Riley plopped another pancake on Flynn's plate.

"Will you tell Maggie I have to go home? I'll play with her later, when we come back."

"If I see her I will."

Delana rolled her eyes. "You should. She lives here."

"Here?" Riley looked around the kitchen. "Maggie?"

"Who's Maggie?" Shannon asked as she heard the last part of the conversation. She went to the sink, grabbed a washcloth, and rinsed it out.

"My friend," Delana said.

"Oh." Shannon, preoccupied, swooped over to Elise and wiped her face. She stopped, wrinkled her nose, and then asked, "What's her name?"

"Magdalene E. Scott," her daughter said.

"What does the 'E' stand for?" Shannon lifted Elise out of the chair and told her to hold up her hands.

"Edith," she said.

"That sounds like an old name."

"She is old, but not. She said that Grandpa misses us."
Shannon stopped cleaning Elise's hands.

The spatula froze in Riley's hand. She turned, catching the surprise on her sister's face. She leaned against the counter to watch how this went.

"Maggie also said that Grandpa can't wait to be with Grandma," Delana said after eating the last of her pancakes. The conversation was nothing out of the ordinary to her. "First he wants to make sure that we're okay."

"*What* are you talking about, Delana?" Shannon's voice rose an octave. "Who have you been talking to?"

"I told you," her daughter said with annoyance. "Maggie."

Delana looked to Riley for help. Shannon caught the exchange and straightened. Her lips pursed together in motherlike scorn.

Riley stepped in before Shannon had a meltdown. "Everybody done here? Delana, go get cleaned up. You too, Flynn. Time to go. Get your stuff from upstairs."

The two scurried off while Elise found a chunk of pancake on the floor.

"Ahh!" Riley yelled out and pointed a finger at the three-year-old to stop her from putting the food in her mouth.

Her sister swiped it out of her daughter's fat little fingers.

"What the hell is she talking about?" Shannon glanced over at Riley, wiping Elise's hand again. "Who is Maggie?"

"I think Maggie is her imaginary friend. When I went outside to get her to come in, to do her homework, she was playing in the cemetery. She seemed to have a friend with her."

Shannon frowned. "And what the hell was she doing playing with someone in the cemetery?"

"We used to," Riley reminded her. A neighborhood boy would hang out with them in the newer section, next to the cedar trees. He liked Shannon and used to bring them pop and candy from his dad's store.

"Mother of God," her sister said as if having enough. "What is this place doing to us?"

She patted Elise on the butt and told her to go find her shoes.

"I thought you said that Delana has an imaginary friend she plays with at home."

"She did and it was Barney."

"The purple dinosaur?"

"No, not from TV. A boy."

"Does she play with any real friends?"

Shannon glared at her. "Of course."

She picked up more pieces of pancake off the chair and floor. "Really, Riley? Pancakes today?"

"That's what aunties are for," she said with a grin. "Let Conner handle the sugar highs."

"You're terrible." Shannon giggled.

"You wait on those kids all day long. Let Conner take his turn with them."

Shannon groaned from her throat. "He's not always good with being patient. He's gone from bad to worse. Too preoccupied with work."

"Hopefully it'll change soon. Once we get back to normal."

Chapter 8

After Conner and the kids left that morning, Riley decided to tackle Dad's office. She stopped at the door in the hall and stared down the stairs to the basement for a second before flipping on the switch. Going down to Dad's hideaway was always special, but this time she hesitated. No longer when she peeked around the door would she hear him chuckle and motion for her to come in for a visit. This was her space now. She had the dreaded task of figuring out his finances and business. A deep sigh escaped her. Digging through his personal papers wasn't on the top of her list to do while home, but it couldn't be delayed. Her feet clunked down the stairs.

The basement was part original house and part addition. The new area gave him the space he needed for an office. Dad had done an impressive job with blending the two sections. In the old part with the low ceiling, he managed to squeeze in an ornate Irish bar and a poker table. She remembered him having a few of his buddies over on occasion to play poker until late in the night. One or two would stay over, having had too much to drink.

The new basement included the laundry room, a bathroom, and Dad's office, which was another four steps down to accommodate the higher ceiling he wanted.

Growing up, they weren't allowed in the basement. It didn't stop them from sneaking down on occasion to have a drink at the bar when their parents weren't home. They stayed clear of the office, knowing Dad's fury would be worse if he found out they were in there. Even now with the door closed, she struggled with going inside.

Riley swallowed hard, braced herself, and turned the knob. The door creaked open, and she jumped when the cold air seeped out as if thankful for the escape.

For god's sake, there was nothing there to hurt her. Of course, the room would be cold with the door closed and no heat.

Gain a pair of balls.

She flipped the switch to turn on the lights. The office was true old-style with the dark wood panels, beamed ceiling, gas fireplace, and a huge mahogany desk with a green leather chair. Dad's haven. The place where he worked. No one bugged him down here—his way of getting what he needed done. He summoned her a few times to talk to him about his investments or finances, but she never touched his books or his business.

As she gazed about the room, staying near the door, she wondered if Dad had known he wasn't going to live much longer. Six months ago, she signed papers to be his power of attorney. He gave her authority if he became ill and couldn't take care of the trust and everything else that related to money. He talked to his girls, on a conference call, to make sure they agreed with his decision to put her in charge—whether he was incapacitated or dead. His concern was more with Shannon. She would still get her part of the inheritance, but Riley would manage the trust and finances, including distributing the funds accordingly. She could sell, designate, or do whatever was needed as long as Shannon received her portion.

He also wanted to make sure no one else had any influence, keeping it to one person. He specifically made it known that he did not want Conner's business dealings to affect their inheritance. With Riley having more financial savvy than her sister and less likely to be influenced by Conner, she was the better fit. Shannon agreed without batting an eye, having full trust in her sister.

Riley walked over to the gas fireplace and flipped the switch.

Poof!

She jumped back when the sudden burst of gas ignited into flames. She should have checked the gas line first, like checking the damper in the fireplace. Dad liked working in the cold. She didn't.

Walking over to the desk, she turned on the green shaded light before sitting down. The leather chair crunched as her butt sank onto the cushioned pad. Nice. She smoothed her hands over the ornate arm rests before pulling the chair in.

The back of her neck prickled. Someone else—a presence—hovered in the room. A loud snap made her jump again. Thinking logically, the walls must be adjusting to the heat from the fire. But when a breeze brushed her arm, she jerked her limb back and rubbed the sudden coldness away.

"Don't freak me out, Dad," she said as if his spirit lurked around her.

At that moment, the light from the sun beamed into the room, coming from the egress window, as if giving her a smile. Little specks of dust floated in the sun's rays that extended past the desk and over to a table where a stack of books rested next to the Tiffany lamp. When Dad took a break or needed quiet, he always liked to read. She'd have to go through the books later on to see what kept his interest in his final days.

The dismal situation kept her mood down, and she forced herself to perk up, get the work done. However, being in the room was so weird. She glanced at the papers on his desk and then the ones at the top of the cabinets to the side of her. All were parts of him—his life. She felt guilty, having no business going through them.

You don't have a choice anymore.

Squaring her shoulders, Riley opened the drawers in the desk and the cabinets to take a cursory look. Nothing struck her as being out of the ordinary. She grabbed the pile of papers from the right corner of his desk and set them in her lap. She leafed through the stack, hoping to find his bank statements or charge-card bills. The pile consisted of old notes and ripped out articles from newspapers and magazines.

She worked all morning, leafing through each paper to see if anything stuck out as being noteworthy. More articles, household bills from the grocery store and hardware store. A doctor's bill. She stopped and peeled it away from the pile. A statement for x-rays and bloodwork. Nothing about what for or any results. Another thing she'd need to look up. Finding a notepad and pen, she started a list of people and places to call and what tasks she had to do within the next few days. First on the list was finding her dad's checkbook.

She opened the center drawer to his desk again. Supplies. No checkbook. She checked the other drawers and then the file cabinets to the side of the desk. Her elbow hit a pile of papers stacked precariously on the file cabinet behind her. The top layer fell to the floor. Picking them up, she spotted the blue, leather-bound checkbook lying on the carpet next to the cabinet and grabbed it. Why in the hell would he leave it there?

Yes. Her first task completed. She crossed it off her list. She opened up the check register and flipped through the pages. His handwriting was slanted and neat like it would be for a written ledger. Every section was filled in and tallied.

Her dad paid some of his bills the old-fashioned way, being from the checkbook age. At least she convinced him a few years ago to make electronic payments for most of his monthly bills—like the utilities and lawncare.

Footsteps tapped against the stairs. She guessed Shannon headed down.

Riley looked up as her sister stuck her head through the doorway.

She hung on to the doorframe with her fingers as she leaned in. "You up for some food? You hungry?"

Riley glanced at the papers spread across the desk. "What

time is it?"

"Two."

"Wow." She sat back in the chair, sore from being hunched over the desk. No wonder she hurt, including her eyes.

Shannon stepped inside. "I'm tired of cleaning."

"Dad pays someone to clean."

"No, not that type. I'm going through his bedroom to see if he left any note or an attempt at one."

"Oh." Riley's voice dropped to a whisper. She wasn't sure if she'd like being the one to find the note. Now she understood Shannon's need for a break. "Yeah, we should eat."

She placed her hands on the chair's arm rests to help her up and stretched her back as she stood. Her spine cracked loudly.

"Any luck down here?" Shannon asked while sauntering around the room. She stopped to examine one of the pictures on the wall—a cabin on the lake with mountains in the background. "I remember this picture. I was with Mom when she found it at the antique store in Stillwater. She was in awe, wanting to be there, on the porch, sipping coffee, and enjoying the view."

Riley smiled. "Dad always agreed with her that it'd be a lovely place to live. But we all knew he'd never leave this house."

Shannon chuckled. "I think that's why she always called it their dream cabin."

How true. Another reason why Riley couldn't see their

dad committing suicide. He loved this place. He wanted to die here—peacefully—not in the shed.

Her heart lurched. He always thought he'd take his last breath with his daughters by his side. She pinched her lips together to keep from crying.

Shannon turned away from the picture and walked across the room toward the desk. She noted the papers spread out.

"Did you find anything of interest here?" She picked up a receipt from the local hardware store.

"Dad's finances, from what I can see, are in order. His bank account has plenty of money to keep the bills paid for more than a year … I think. I'll dig deeper to make sure, but at least we don't need to panic about money not being available or having to use our own."

"That's a relief," Shannon said and put the receipt back on the desk. She wandered around the room. She'd visited the office fewer times than Riley. She picked out a book from the bookshelf, read the title, and then replaced it.

"Since you're over there, could you turn off the fireplace for me, please?"

She did, flipping the switch. With a smaller poof than before, the fire went out.

"Conner thinks we should sell this place right away. We're in a seller's market right now."

"Sell?" Riley tripped on the rug as she walked around the desk. She looked over at her sister, wondering why selling was coming up now.

Shannon was occupied with the pictures on the mantel. She seemed deep in thought when she said, "I've been tossing around the idea."

They'd talked about selling before, in general, but … yuck. It was too much to think about now.

Riley glanced about the office as she waited at the door for her sister. "It's hard to think about losing this place."

"I'm assuming you don't want to live in this house, do you?" she asked, stepping away from the mantel.

Move back here? Lose her promotion? Her job? Riley crossed her arms. "No, I guess not."

"Conner and I have our house in Milwaukee. We don't need another."

"I … true." She wasn't sure what to say.

Shannon brushed past her and headed for the stairs. Riley turned out the light and followed behind. She—they—didn't have enough information to make any decision. "I don't think we can just put it up for sale. This is going to take time, getting all his finances in order."

"I thought that's why he put it in a trust, so it'd be easier for us."

"Yes, it makes it easier, but we still have to go through everything, like the trust, to understand how it works and read the will so we can follow his wishes. Not to mention, I need to get his regular bills and accounts in order."

"Well, how long will that take?"

"I'm guessing it'll take a few months to fully understand what's going on, what he planned." They reached the hall and made their way into the kitchen.

"Okay. But we should think about it." Shannon went straight to the refrigerator. "I'm famished. Sandwiches?"

"Works for me." Riley was glad her sister let it go. She always remembered the rule of waiting to make decisions before doing anything drastic after a loved one died. As much as she liked to get things done and off her list, making decisions about selling a place that Dad loved was unthinkable, at least for now. They'd deal with it, but not today.

Shannon whipped up the turkey sandwiches while Riley set plates and napkins on the counter. She opened two beers. They were eating when the doorbell rang.

She stopped and looked at her sister. Shannon left her half-eaten sandwich on the plate and went to open the door. Riley cocked her ear to listen as she finished her last bite.

"If it's not too much trouble, I'd like a word with you and your sister, Mrs. Doyle."

She recognized the detective's voice and pictured his pretty eyes and face. Riley bet a lot of females hung on that man. Ones who were eager to help him out in any way possible.

She heard Shannon say, "Of course, Detective Torrence. Please, come in."

Riley drank a swig of her beer to wash the sandwich down. She hoped no meat or bread stuck between her teeth.

Shannon entered first. Her expression was strained. Riley saw why. By the detective's somber face, this wasn't pleasant news.

"Detective." Riley greeted him with some caution. She rose from the stool and wiped her hands with the napkin before shaking his hand.

He nodded to her. "Ms. Walsh. I'm sorry to bother you." He made his stance just inside the kitchen doorway. Dark circles shadowed his eyes, as if he'd been up all night. The pleasantries were brief.

"What's up?" Riley braced herself.

"Can I get you anything to drink?" Shannon, always the hostess, stood between the two of them.

"No, thank you." He placed his hands together, rubbing them as if to shake off the cold. "I stopped by to tell you that we've received one of the preliminary results from your father's autopsy—from the coroner's office."

Riley held her breath. Her fingers turned white as she pressed them against the cold granite.

"In our questioning, you stated that Maxwell Walsh had Stage 4 lung cancer." He paused as if giving them time to prepare. "Is there a reason why you thought this to be true?"

She glanced toward Shannon, not understanding why he'd ask. "We were told he had Stage 4."

"Did the doctor tell you?"

Her arms tingled with cold. Riley had meant to call the doctor but procrastinated.

"Conner let us know. He'd been in touch with the doctor," Shannon said.

The detective raised his eyes, curious. "Why would he be in contact with the doctor?"

"He-he knows the doctor." She stumbled over her words.

"Isn't that data private?"

Riley swallowed hard. He was right. Why would the doctor tell Conner? "Well, maybe Dad told him."

The detective wrote in his notebook, giving them time to pause.

Shannon's jaw hardened as her defenses kicked in gear. "What's your point, Detective Torrence?"

He shifted from one foot to the other. "Based on medical records and the autopsy, the coroner confirmed Maxwell Walsh had Stage 1 non-small cell lung cancer, which is curable. According to the doctor, he didn't have the type of pain you previously described."

That explained why he never brought it up in their conversations. Riley felt better that she hadn't missed something. But on the other hand, a new set of questions raced through her head. Why would he kill himself? It didn't make sense.

Her voice stuck inside her throat. She couldn't speak.

Shannon came to the rescue. "Why did he commit suicide then, if it wasn't the cancer?"

Detective Torrence puckered his lips and shook his head. "We're looking into it."

He gave them each a hard stare, one of those deep looks that made Riley uncomfortable.

"Why are you looking at us like we're guilty of something?" She called him out, refusing to give him the satisfaction of seeing them squirm.

Shannon's hand went to her heart. She paled.

The detective remained silent as he looked to Riley. He continued to watch her, see if she would crumble under his intimidating stare. After a few seconds, he said, "If you hear anything different or if you find anything, please give me a call."

Riley let out her breath—not that she had anything to be guilty about. A stream of questions raced through her head as she tried piecing it all together. She gasped when it struck. "Detective, do you think something else happened to our Dad?"

He kept silent.

"Please, detective. We need to know. We'd like to help." Shannon batted her eyes at him like an innocent baby doe.

"The case is still under investigation. We are looking at different situations. Murder is one of them."

Seriously? Murder? This was their dad. A man who lived a full life. Riley couldn't imagine anyone wanting him dead, but the way the detective reacted … there was more to this than what they'd been told.

I … sorry …, detective," Shannon stumbled, unable to speak. Her hands trembled. She rubbed her forehead as if trying to make sense of the latest news. "We're still overwhelmed."

Riley slid off her stool and told her sister to sit. The shock of Dad's dying had hit them both hard. A possible murder? She turned numb.

The detective's face softened and he took a step toward Shannon as if wanting to console her. He corrected his action, removing any emotion from his expression. He returned to his notepad and opened it to a new page. He cleared his throat. "If you don't mind, can we go over a few more questions?"

"Of course," Riley said. Deep down, she wished he'd leave. Her head hurt. She grabbed Shannon's hand for support.

The detective asked who their dad had been in contact with, if anyone threatened him in the last few months, if he mentioned anything to them—personal or business. Where he hung out. If he'd been away on business. Most of the questions he'd asked before, but now with a different twist to reexamine what they'd heard or seen.

Detective Torrence shifted, probably tired of standing. Riley asked if he wanted a chair but he declined. He glanced about. "Is Mr. Doyle here? I'd like to ask him a few questions as well."

"He left this morning," Shannon said. "I'm not sure if he'd have anything different to say."

"Where did he go?" He frowned.

"Home. He's taking our children to his parents' house for the week. They'll drive them back and forth to school so they don't miss too many days."

"When did he leave?"

Shannon shrugged. "Nine this morning?"

Riley bet Mr. Detective wasn't asking to see Conner for standard questioning. His brows creased together and his jaw tightened as he scribbled on his notepad. She studied his face. Did he know something they didn't? Was her brother-in-law a suspect?

She didn't want to ask. Nor did she want him to start questioning them about Conner. If he did, Riley would have to tell the detective about her brother-in-law's odd behavior, especially the anger, which would cause more "investigating."

Detective Torrence put his notepad away. Now he was in a hurry to leave. "Please let me know if you think or hear of anything else." He looked to Riley. "Will you sign a consent form for us to discuss your dad's financial information with the lawyers and investment firm?"

She nodded. "Of course."

"I'll be right back."

He returned a few minutes later with the form and she signed where needed.

After the detective left, the house turned cold. A layer of goosebumps swept across Riley's arms, making her shiver. She went to her bedroom and grabbed a hoodie to wear. When she came back to the kitchen, Shannon slid off the chair and tossed the rest of her sandwich in the trash. She kept her beer.

"How you doing?" Riley was concerned. Her sister looked awfully pale as she leaned against the back counter by the sink.

"Well, I guess I should be looking for a note again," she said with a grunt. "I have to say, I feel better knowing he didn't have Stage 4 cancer. Now I can stop second guessing what we could have done to prevent it."

Words Riley thought earlier on. They were on the same page.

Shannon took a swig of her beer. She played with her bottle. "Do you think someone did this to Dad?"

She noted how her sister couldn't say the word. She shrugged. "We should think about Dad in a different light. Dad was a businessman. He owned land. He rented. He invested his money. From the people I know in the business world, they didn't get where they are today by being Mr. Nice. Most are shrewd. There is a possibility."

Shannon pulled away from the counter and her breath cut short. "Dad's lawyer died. What if it wasn't a heart attack?"

She paced around the kitchen and almost turned into the wall instead of the doorway—lost in thought.

"We can't jump to conclusions," Riley said to keep her sister from going too far off the path. "Let Detective Torrence figure it out."

Her cell phone rang. She took it out of her pocket. Gary. She debated on whether or not to answer it.

Shannon set her beer down and headed for the bathroom. Great timing.

"Hi, Gary." Riley answered the call.

"What the hell is going on?" He asked between gritted teeth. No greeting, right to the point.

"Why? What do you mean?" She left the kitchen and headed for the den.

His voice lowered. "The police are here asking questions about you. Something about your father."

"What?" Her voice cracked. She just signed the damn form. "Why do you think it's about me?"

"I saw them come in. I had been talking with Jane near the reception desk. They're with the boss now in the conference room."

"Wow, that was fast. I signed a consent form so the police could talk to the firm about Dad's account."

"The goddamn police are here, Riley. You got people

talking. They know it concerns you."

"Oh." Riley's mouth went dry. She got it. She began pacing in front of the fireplace. This wasn't what she needed with the promotion coming up. People at the office liked to start rumors. And Joe Abernet, the boss talking with the police right now, was always concerned about the firm's reputation. "Is he mad?"

"Can't tell."

She imagined Gary stretching beyond his cube to see inside the glassed-in conference room near the front.

"He's not happy. I can tell that."

"Is his neck red?"

He paused for a moment. "Hard to tell. No ... not red."

"Good. He's not mad."

"Yet. Why are they here?"

Riley took in a breath. "They need to do a little more investigating ... if someone ... like a murder."

"Oh great."

She stopped pacing. Did she hear him right?

"I mean, I'm sorry. Shit. Your dad was murdered?"

"I didn't say that."

"So, what does this mean for you? Oh shit." His voice quivered. He whispered, "Are you a suspect?"

"No. I was there—in Arizona."

"You could have hired someone to do it."

"Gary!" Riley growled.

"Are they going to come and get me?"

"You mean if they'll ask you questions? Probably. We

worked late that night and grabbed a bite afterwards at the Mexican restaurant."

"Oh yeah, I remember."

She pictured him on his computer, checking the date, as he asked, "Which reminds me, can you still come home?"

"Yes."

Dammit, she forgot to go online and get her plane tickets. They probably doubled in price since she last checked the prices.

"Are you sure you can?"

She frowned. "What do you mean?"

"You know, how in murders you can't leave town."

"I'm not a suspect," she said again.

He made her think. Detective Torrence wasn't happy that Conner left town. Did she need permission? She better check. Shannon was out of the bathroom.

"I have to go, Gary."

"Police?"

"No, sister. Keep me posted."

"Fine."

Riley hung up. She slid her phone into the back pocket of her jeans. What if Gary was right? What if she couldn't leave town? She'd miss the interview. No promotion. And if people around the office started talking, or the police kept showing up, she could lose her job.

Fuck sticks.

Wait. Would this fall under the Family and Medical Leave Act? They wouldn't be able to fire her. But she really needed the promotion. She needed to get back, interview, and do some damage control.

Riley went back to the kitchen.

"Who was that?" Shannon asked over her shoulder as she washed the dishes.

"Gary. The police are there."

"Why are they—" She shut her mouth, knowing.

"They're not wasting any time."

Shannon's expression changed. Riley could guess what swirled in her sister's head. If her sister's co-workers were being questioned, the police had to be questioning people she knew too. Neighbors? School?

The doorbell rang.

Now who?

"Your turn," Shannon said.

Riley walked down the hall to the door. Geo waited. He stood in front of the side glass panel to the left of the door. He was about to ring the doorbell again when she opened it.

"Hi, Geo."

"Hi," he said with a sheepish grin. He held two bottles of wine in his hands. When she noticed, he raised them up. "I only thought it fitting to bring more over. These are from my special batch."

"Well, come in. Special batch?"

"Aged in whiskey barrels."

"I like that. Take your shoes off. Come join us in the kitchen."

"Us?" He seemed disappointed.

"Just my sister. The others left this morning." Riley

shut her mouth. Should she have said anything? Now he knew they'd be alone in the house.

She took the bottles from Geo so he could take off his coat and shoes.

Once in the kitchen, she introduced him to Shannon.

"I hear you're the one who lives in the old shack." She shook his hand while discreetly checking him out. When she smiled, Riley knew he passed his first inspection with approval.

"I am. It's not that bad of a place."

Shannon turned her head so only Riley saw her when she mouthed "Nice." Her eyes turned downward to check out the solid, muscular body underneath the sweater and tight jeans. Her sister approved of what she saw. Riley widened her eyes, telling her to stop.

"Let's try this wine of yours," Shannon said, brushing away the earlier conversation.

Riley was already looking for the corkscrew while her sister grabbed three glasses.

"Let me get this," her sister said. "Why don't you go on into the den. I could go for a nice, warm fire tonight."

Really? Riley rolled her eyes. She said to Geo, "Follow me. We'll get the fire started."

"Works for me," he snickered.

She cringed, realizing the innuendo in her words.

The wood was stacked in the box, the fire starters in a bucket, and the matches in a tin can. Dad never moved them.

She liked Shannon's idea. The den was the perfect place to relax with a fabulous wine in hand. Riley sat in the chair, and her sister curled up on the couch. Geo picked a small stool to sit near the hearth.

He seemed at home, familiar with the place, like he belonged.

"Did you come here often, to see Dad?" Riley asked.

"Sometimes here. Sometimes my place. The bar. Out in the fields. I saw your dad a few times a week."

"What did you talk about?" Shannon's face brightened. "Who was our dad when we were away, living our own lives?"

"We talked about many things." Geo sat with his legs slightly apart and his upper arms resting on his thighs. He swirled the wine in his glass, thinking back. "Your dad liked to pick my brain. We talked about the business a lot—growing grapes and next steps. We talked about the hunting shack, more so when I remodeled it. The town. You girls."

"Us?" Shannon raised an eyebrow.

"All good things. All good," he promised.

"What did he say about us?"

He became silent and gazed around the den as if trying to recall a conversation. He laughed. "One thing he told me was not to lie to either one of you. He, your dad, could never get away with telling your mom one. She'd know, according to him, even before it came out of his mouth. And you two are just like her."

His words struck Riley. He was right, in a way. Dad could never keep a secret for long. If something was happening, he would have mentioned it, like being in pain. She still had to call the doctor.

Geo raised his glass. "To your dad. He was a great guy."

"Cheers," they said in unison. They were too far apart to clink glasses, but the gesture was there.

One of the logs fell. Geo set his glass down on the coffee table. He grabbed the poker.

"Did you hear that Dad's cancer wasn't as bad as we thought?" Shannon asked.

Riley saw his arm jerk when he fixed the log. He had voiced his suspicion earlier to her. She knew about it, but Shannon didn't. She hoped he thought about his response to her question. By his slight hesitation, he did.

"Yes, I heard."

"Geo used to be a detective," she reminded her sister.

"Oh yes, that's right. And what are your thoughts?"

"Your dad didn't act like someone with Stage 4 cancer. The signs weren't there. And based on our conversations, he still had fire in him, talking about the future."

He gazed at Riley as if checking to make sure his response was okay. She smiled and then coyly watched him work the fire. Geo didn't carry a typical cop-type attitude. His presence was calm and casual. She knew a few cops who hung out at the bar that was across the street from Sikerte Investment Firm. They had different attitudes—cocky with an edge of hardness. Cops, and probably detectives, had a lot of shit to deal with and wore an invisible shield, masking their emotions, in order to handle different situations. Geo didn't have that hardness. She still couldn't decide on the right word. But he was reserved in a way, as if he'd seen more than enough, learned from it, and wanted to move on.

"You seem to know Dad the best. Do you think someone wanted to kill him?"

Riley came back to the conversation, shocked by her sister's question.

He took it in stride. "I can think of a few people who had been angry with your dad. He was tough when it came to business."

"Who would be that mad at him?"

Geo shook his head. "I'd leave that up to the police to figure out."

"Why?" Shannon didn't like his answer. "What if you know who it is?"

"I've been interviewed by Detective Torrence as well. I don't want to start rumors or hurt any reputations."

Bravo. Riley liked how he handled the situation—calm and with reason. What impressed her the most was that he didn't downplay the questions. He answered her with honesty.

Shannon settled down. "I suppose you're right."

Time to change the subject a bit.

"I started going through my father's papers," Riley said. "I see your lease is up in the spring."

"March 31." Geo sat, facing them instead of the fire, ready to talk. Is that why he came over? To find out what they had planned? Whatever they decided would affect him.

And the wine affected her. The higher alcohol content from the wine being aged in an old whiskey barrel kicked her ass. She sat up, straightening her back to stay focused.

"Do you want to keep your vineyard here?"

He nodded his head. "Yes, I'd like the opportunity to stay." He rested his upper arms against his knees with his wine dangling in front of him. "The vines are healthy, and I had a great harvest last year with the help of your dad."

"He always loved getting his hands into new things," Riley said with a smile. But she was still baffled. "I can't believe he didn't mention you or the business."

"The business is mine." Geo's jaw tightened. "I signed a contract to rent the land from your dad. I was fortunate that after a time, he took an interest and became my mentor."

Riley blushed with embarrassment. "I'm sorry. I didn't mean to apply that … it was his."

She wished she could take the words back.

"However, I did purchase land a few miles from here. Ten acres. I can move my vineyard if needed, but I prefer to stay. Here. I've grown fond of the land and the soil is perfect for growing grapes. And, I like living in the hunting shack."

"Oh," Shannon groaned. "You can have that place."

"Shannon!" Riley looked at her sister as if she should keep her mouth shut.

"Well, it always gave me the creeps." She shuddered.

Riley rolled her eyes.

Geo laughed. "Don't worry. I won't take it to heart. Just think about it. I'd like to continue renting both house and land. However, if you decide to sell, please keep me informed. I'd be interested in purchasing the land I rent and the shack, if possible."

"Why not all?" Shannon asked.

He looked at her as if she was crazy. He raised his glass and swept it across the room. "You think I could afford this house and all the land? Plus the shack?"

Sitting back, Riley took a different approach with him. "Do you think we should sell?"

She tucked her legs underneath her and waited for his response. She observed how his expression drooped, not liking the idea.

"I hope you don't. I'd miss seeing you here." He stared into her eyes as if hoping his interest in her showed through.

Riley blushed. She got his message and her heart fluttered.

"This is a fantastic wine," Shannon said, oblivious to the exchange as she reached for the bottle and poured herself more.

Her sister must be feeling it. Riley smiled, amused and impressed at how quickly the alcohol affected her.

Geo's face brightened. "The whiskey gives it that extra bite. But a forewarning—it'll knock your socks off faster than normal wine. Higher alcohol content."

"I'm fine with that." Shannon handed her the empty bottle.

"I'll be back," Riley said and went to throw it away in the recycle bin. They had left the other bottle in the kitchen, and she went to grab it. She stumbled. Holy crap—the alcohol hit her. They didn't need anymore.

Too late. The other bottle was uncorked, allowing appropriate time to breathe.

Returning to the den, she came into the middle of their conversation about grapes. Riley, content to sit back, kept quiet and enjoyed the extra kick in the wine. Out of the corner of her eye, she watched and wondered how Geo could be so mellow. His future rode on their decision. But there he sat, near the fire, like he lived for the moment. Mom would have approved. She would have noticed his warmth and kindness.

Riley looked into her glass, away from him. Once they buried Dad, she'd go back to her life in Arizona. And if they sold the house, she'd have no reason to return to Wisconsin. Geo would get on with his life. She would get on with hers.

When her sister asked him how he managed to be in the wine business, Riley paid more attention.

"It was actually a bet. I tried brewing beer to keep me occupied after I left the force. I had some friends over to try the first batch I made. I didn't think it was bad, but they couldn't drink it." He laughed. "If I recall, they compared my beer to soup with hops included. They pleaded with me to stop making beer. They told me to go make wine, and so I did. But this time, I did my research. I went to Italy and toured their wineries. I visited Napa Valley and Sonoma to learn the trade. I came back with a lot of information. Today, I sell my grapes to the wineries here in Wisconsin and Minnesota. For my personal label, I make cabernets, table reds, Malbecs, and ..." he raised his glass to show the whiskey-barreled wine, "my favorite."

"Here's to the best and strongest wine ever." Riley raised her glass.

"I totally agree." Shannon hiccupped as they toasted. She

stared at her glass. "Do you make any whites? I usually don't drink reds because they stain my teeth."

"I produce two whites, one close to a Riesling and the other …" he flapped his hand back and forth, "I guess something like a Chardonnay. I'm still perfecting my whites."

"I'll test your whites, any day," Shannon offered.

"I'll take you up on that."

"You perfected the reds," Riley said and took another sip of her wine. Boy, was she relaxed. Her head swayed, too heavy for her neck to hold. She let it fall to the back of the couch. No cares. No worries. She was like Geo that night.

They continued their conversation—light and reminiscent of their days growing up. After a time, Geo stood. "Ahh, you mind if I use your bathroom?"

"Of course not," Shannon said. When he left, she leaned toward Riley and whispered, "He's handsome."

"Yeah, so?"

"You could date him. He's got eyes on you."

"Shannon," she scolded. "That's a little awkward. I can't hit on a guy while mourning Dad."

"Why not? Life goes on," she said. "There's something about him that I like. He may be just the one for you."

"You're a silly woman." Riley made a face at her. "The wine is talking."

"And look who made it."

Geo came back into the room. He emptied the second bottle, pouring it into their glasses, filling his last. He checked the fire, throwing another log on before settling down on the floor next to the hearth.

"Don't you want to sit on the couch or the chair," Riley gestured to the open seats. "Be a little more comfortable?"

"I'm fine, thank you." He changed the subject right away. "What about you, Riley? I know you work for an investment firm. Are you an investor?"

"No, I work in the office."

"She's up for a promotion," Shannon said. "Managing the office."

Geo raised his eyebrow. "I'm assuming this is a good thing?"

"Yes. I'm hoping it'll be enough to finally buy a house."

"In Arizona?"

"Yes. Arizona." She felt bad saying the words, especially when his face fell with disappointment. But she had worked hard for the last two years to get to this point.

"Congratulations." His voice didn't carry enthusiasm. He stroked his beard and said, "Your dad always thought you'd come back here. He missed you."

Riley had difficulty responding to his question. Guilt overcame her.

"I'm sorry." Geo raised his hands as he realized what he said. "Don't get me wrong. He was very proud of you. He just missed his little girl."

"Hey, what about me?" Shannon didn't want to be left out.

"He loved your phone calls. He would drop everything when you called. If he was with me, our time was up."

Shannon beamed. 'I tried calling him every day."

"I miss him," Riley said with her eyes down. She played with the fringe on the blanket that covered her lap.

"Well, there's one thing you should do while you're here."

"What's that?" Shannon asked.

Riley raised her eyes as well.

"You should honor your father by going to the charity ball, a costume party, next Friday night."

"Oh yeah." Riley remembered her dad talking about it. "Bill Johnson, the one who owns the event center."

"The Barn?" Shannon asked. "Isn't that the name of it?"

"Yes, that's the one," Geo said. "Your father was a big advocate for Bill's charity to help students with their college loans. Your father had planned on attending. He was a friend of Bill's."

"And a generous donor." Riley had seen the amount on the check he wrote.

"You said costume? We'll have to dress up?" Shannon perked up. "That sounds like fun."

"Yes, it's usually the talk of the town."

"What the hell would we dress as?" Riley drew a blank.

"You don't need anything extravagant," Geo said.

"What if Dad's funeral is Friday?"

"It won't be. Everyone will be at this event, including the funeral director and the new caretaker at the cemetery."

"There's no possible way." Riley's feet unfolded from underneath her as she sat up in the chair. She thought about the timing. Fly in to Arizona on Monday, interview, stay for a few days, and then fly back. Well, she could make it work. But what if there was a second interview? That could cause an issue.

"Riley, you can come back late Thursday night or early Friday morning," Shannon said. "We'll probably be here for at least another two full weeks. Possibly a month."

"A month?" Her voice quivered. She didn't have the vacation time. Her boss wouldn't understand. She'd be demoted or they'd give her crap work as punishment. Luckily the booze kept her from flying off the couch and panicking.

Shannon and Geo continued discussing the event. The festivities would be a nice break for both of them. Riley still thought it wrong to dress up for a party when they mourned their dad. Shannon liked the idea, more so for representing Dad.

"Riley, we'd be supporting students, helping them continue with their education at the University of Wisconsin. They need our help."

"Dad already donated the money." She tried reasoning with her sister. He'd done his part.

Shannon's direct stare was mom-like with the arm wings up.

Yes, they would go.

Chapter 9

Riley lay in bed with the blanket over her body and her legs out to keep cool. She wanted to sleep in but her head hurt. The wine affected her more than she cared. Her thoughts rambled and tumbled over the hangover, thinking about all the things she needed to do. Top on her list was to buy plane tickets to Arizona and then back again to Minneapolis/St. Paul. She had four days—max—to assure Joe that she was the right person for the job. He wouldn't be happy when she requested the last of her vacation time, but he'd get over it. A death in the family wasn't controllable. She had the funeral to attend, figure out his paperwork, and of course the reading of the will. Once she returned to Arizona, she'd have time to really look at Dad's finances ... when she wasn't working her ass off, playing catch-up, and taking on more responsibilities.

A tall order to handle, but possible. Riley wouldn't have to stay a month like Shannon predicted.

Yes, it's doable.

She needed coffee. Her body refused to move. Chilling

with Geo and her sister the night before was exactly what they'd needed—to relax. How long had they stayed up, talking? Riley knew it had been after midnight before he left.

Her head went up. Did he sleep over? They had talked about it, offering him the couch. Riley's head fell back to the pillow. No, he decided to leave.

After another half hour in bed, Riley managed to get up. She shuffled to the kitchen.

Shannon paced around the counter. She was on her cell phone with Conner. His voice was loud, angry. She held the phone away from her ear as he shouted loud enough for Riley to hear from across the room. She cringed, feeling bad for her sister.

Riley opened her mouth to yell at Conner to keep it down, but Shannon frowned and put her finger to her lips to keep quiet. She then rolled her eyes and shook her head in frustration. While her sister talked, she poured her coffee and listened. Conner came through clear as a bell. He wanted the reading of the will to take place soon. His lawyer contacted Dad's firm to get the final details. They refused to work with Conner or his lawyers.

Again, that anger coming out. Riley didn't understand why the will was so important to him. Like everyone else, she wanted everything to be settled and done but not at warp speed.

Eggs sounded good for breakfast. Her stomach was a little queasy and food would help as she continued to feel the effects of the alcohol. She opened the refrigerator door, scanned the contents, but couldn't remember what she went in there to get.

This might not be a productive day.

Oh yes. Eggs. Riley held up the carton with one hand and with the other she pretended to hold a pan and made a flipping motion for omelets. Her sister nodded and left the room.

When she returned, the ham and cheese omelets were done and on their plates at the counter island.

"Ugh." Shannon set her phone on the farther end of the island. She looked as rough as Riley felt. The conversation had been a tough one … or it was the effects from the night before. She rubbed her face, something she never did. "He wants you to sign papers to give him permission to handle the will."

"Why does he want to handle it?"

Shannon pulled her goldish-red hair away from her face, tucking it behind her ears. "He wants to make sure everything is taken care of the right way. He doesn't trust Dad's lawyers."

Riley frowned. "They've been handling his affairs for years. There's never been a problem—ever. Dad knew all the partners. Golfed with them. I don't get it. Am I missing something?"

"Not that I'm aware of." Shannon dug into her omelet.

Being the one responsible for Dad's finances, Riley wanted to think smart and not make rash decisions. This was one of those times. "Conner will be back soon. Let's wait. I'd like to talk to the lawyers myself about our situation."

"What do you mean?"

"I'm not sure what happens to the trust or other finances if Dad committed suicide or if it was murder. All of his assets could be frozen."

"Oh," Shannon gazed up from her food. "I didn't think about that. It could take even longer to clear everything up."

"You got that right."

"Are you sure we have enough cash?" Shannon hesitated when she spoke. "I don't think we, Conner and I, can cover any additional costs."

"We shouldn't need to worry. I'm listed on Dad's checking account. I can use that to pay the bills. I don't think they'd freeze everything, but I'll call to find out."

Shannon used her left hand to hold her head up while she finished her omelet. This wasn't like her. Something bugged her.

"What's the matter?"

She shook her head, frustrated. "I don't know. Conner's changed in the last year. He's been getting angrier."

Riley frowned. "You've said that before. He's not hurting you, is he?"

"Oh no." Shannon's eyes flew open. 'He's never hit me."

"Abuse can happen in other ways too." Her last relationship was an example. Ted. Handsome, rich, and cunning. Their first dates were wonderful and he reeled her in. When she became hooked on him, he started cutting her down and telling her that she wasn't worth anything. Riley shuddered at the memory, still too fresh in her head, how he made her feel worthless. Gary came to her rescue, seeing Ted's dark side, and nabbed her away for the weekend. He got her out of the situation and made her think more clearly. His words, almost exactly, were "What the hell are you doing, girl? Ted's a fucking asshole who's sucking the life out of you."

He was right. She'd let the relationship go on for too long. When she and Gary returned from their weekend, she dumped Ted. The guy tried coming back, but two of her burly friends threatened to smash his pretty face if he ever attempted to see her again. That was the last of him.

However, Shannon's situation was different with Conner. They'd been married for twelve years now and produced three beautiful children. He always treated them with respect. Riley asked, "What's happening now?"

Shannon sipped her coffee. "He's always snapping at me. He's very distant at times, shutting me out of his conversations, going off here and there without telling me." She played with the diamond ring on her finger. Three-carat princess cut with a row of diamonds for the wedding band. Five carats total?

Riley wasn't a good guesser. She only knew it sparkled like the lights on a marquee whenever her hand moved. "Do you think he's in over his head with his business?"

"I'm believing he may be," Shannon confessed. "I'm seeing him sweating more, especially when he's arguing on the phone."

"And yelling at you." Riley didn't like the change in Conner. She bit her fingernail, thinking of him in a different light. Should she be careful with him? What if he wanted Shannon's inheritance to pay off his debt? Is that why he wanted his lawyer to take care of Dad's will?

The guilt of being untrustworthy churned her stomach. This was Conner they were talking about. But Dad gave her a big responsibility. Way more than what she expected. When they talked about his finances—the three of them together— Dad's request made sense now that the agreement between them took on a heavier reality. She should stay here. Take care of things.

No.

She needed to head home. Her promotion was on the line. Dad kept enough money in his account. They could wait a few weeks.

Riley cleaned the kitchen while Shannon made a list of what she needed for their costumes. Earlier, she'd found Mom's sewing machine buried in a closet in the craft room. Together, she and Shannon got it threaded and working. Her sister loved to sew—perfect to keep her occupied. However, Riley guessed it also gave her an excuse to delay going through Dad's belongings. Instead, Shannon would go shopping and buy what they needed.

"You want to come with me?" She gathered her list and purse.

"No, I'll stay here," Riley said. "I'll work on the office."

"Don't you want to pick out your feathers?"

"Feathers?" She wasn't sure if she should be scared or not. What was her sister concocting for her to wear? A Big Bird costume?" She didn't look good in yellow. "You better be teasing me."

"I'm not. You'll like it. Don't worry."

"You better be right," Riley yelled before her sister shut the door.

Alone, she called the lawyer's office, and when no one answered, left a message. She made a few other calls before walking to the mailbox at the end of the driveway. White and gray clouds billowed across the sky with darker ones on the horizon. Normal temperatures were in the fifties, but this morning turned out to be well above average. She looked on her phone; the weather app showed rain with a chance of thunderstorms for both today and tomorrow. She could use some sun. The one thing she loved about Arizona was the sunny, hot days.

They had forgotten to check the mail so the mailbox was crammed full. Ads, magazines, donation requests, bills, and sympathy cards. Ugh. She contemplated going for a longer walk but decided against it. She had to buy her plane tickets and wait around for the lawyer's office to call back. Calling Gary was on her list as well. She wasn't getting as many emails from the office. Riley hoped everything was okay. She'd get the scoop from him on what happened when the police were there, if they talked to him.

Returning to the house, Riley opened the sympathy cards. She sat in the den at the table—Dad's desk. There were over a dozen cards from friends and businesses that he knew. Some sent money. She wrote down the amount in the card for when they wrote thank you notes later on. She placed the checks and cash in a separate pile to deposit later.

The doorbell rang.

Flowers from an aunt in Boston.

A basket of three peace lilies with a little ceramic dove in the middle. Dad would have liked it.

A brew of emotions stirred when she envisioned the plant next to his casket. Riley let out a sob. She had no idea where it came from, but her insides shook when the convulsive gasp came out. A stream of tears followed. She didn't feel sad or like her heart ached from grief. This came from nowhere, as if saying she hadn't cried in a while. She cursed herself for letting a plant trigger the reaction. Spotting a box of tissues on the coffee table, she stood and grabbed them. Ten minutes passed before she could pull herself together.

Riley sat and analyzed the last few days and what happened. She grieved for Dad, extremely hurt to lose him so suddenly, but this was different. Was it learning his cancer didn't kill him? That someone could have murdered him? Or was it selling the house? Riley glanced about the den—the stone fireplace, the cozy blue-striped couch, the red chairs, the chandelier ... all were perfect. The thought of losing the place, and a piece of Dad and Mom, rattled her.

Frustrated, she stood and gathered the used tissues into her hand. She walked to the kitchen and threw the pile away, not wanting to cry or think about it anymore. After a drink of water, she headed down to the office and concentrated on one of the piles in the corner of the desk. So far, nothing of importance. Her back and shoulders ached from sitting too long. At work, she was always bouncing about, going from one office to the next. Riley stretched and yawned. Time for a walk to wake up a bit. She placed her hands on the desk and pushed down as she rose out from the chair.

Click.

A thin, narrow pencil drawer opened from the underside of the desk. Inside, a set of keys on a silver ring lay in the compartment. One of the keys appeared to be for a house—she assumed a spare for the shack. The other two keys were small and unique. The gold key could be for a safety deposit box at a bank, while the silver one was round like a security key. That one, she had no clue to what it could be for. Riley examined each one more closely, to see if anything on the keys hinted at their purpose. All three had numbers but nothing else.

She set the keys down and examined the hidden compartment. She pushed the drawer back into position so it locked in place. Riley tried opening it again but couldn't find a latch. Prying the crack with her fingernails didn't work either.

Son of a bitch.

Riley spent fifteen minutes trying to figure it out. She crawled under the desk to find the drawer but found no indication of one. She retraced her steps by sitting down on the chair. She repositioned herself to center with the blotter and then sat up and pressed her hands down on the top of the desk.

Nothing.

She tried again.

No luck.

She smoothed her hands over the top and found the places that were slightly raised before pressing down. The third time was the charm. The drawer clicked open. How sweet, finding a secret compartment. Now she wondered what the keys unlocked. If hidden, they must be important.

Her phone rang. She jumped as if she'd been caught doing something bad.

Silly girl.

The call was from Detective Torrence. He asked how they were doing, and if she'd found anything unusual. After the small talk, he told her the good news. The coroner's office released Dad's body.

What a relief. They could finally schedule the funeral.

After she hung up with the detective, she decided the keys could wait. She placed them back in the drawer and closed it. They were in a safe place until she figured out what they were for.

Riley called Shannon and repeated the news to her.

A patch of sunlight came in through the window. She smiled. Dad must be glad to be coming home. Or Mom. Peeking outside and gauging the break in the clouds, she deemed this the best time for a walk before it rained. Fresh air first and then she'd figure out the keys.

Upstairs, she donned a pair of Wellies and a lighter pink coat, which she believed had been Shannon's in high school. Riley admired herself in the mirror. Her hair turned out super curly today with the humidity in the air. Surprisingly, the rusty strands weren't frizzy. Picking a pink coat might not have been the best choice as it clashed with her hair, but she liked how the belt cinched and fit her form. The length was right too, not cutting off her longer legs. Shannon would throw a fit if she saw her younger sister wearing *her* coat. Too bad she wasn't home.

Riley left the house through the front door and locked it behind her. At the end of the driveway, she glanced across the grassy knoll toward the horizon. The southwest sky was dark and headed in her direction. The distant clouds were impressive—a dark, grayish blue that rolled like an ocean wave. She guessed the rain would hit in thirty minutes or more.

She walked along the road and then turned right on the country road that bordered the front side of the cemetery. It curved left into the woods toward their little town. Dad owned the land on the other side of the road. Round bales of hay lined the open field, ready to be stored or sold as animal feed for the winter months. The farmer who rented it had a good crop.

Beyond the cemetery was the driveway to the hunting shack and the patch of land where she assumed Geo's grapes grew. If she walked the driveway, she'd be able to catch a glimpse of the property before cutting back to Dad's house. She stayed to the left of the driveway, nearer to the black iron gate that closed in the cemetery. Every so often, she glanced over to the cemetery to see if Geo happened to be there, next to his grandfather's grave. The tucked-in homes of the dead seemed peaceful in the gated community.

Her heart skipped when she thought about Geo. His warm, gentle face with those blue eyes made her tingle. How different he was compared to the sharply dressed men she was used to. She wondered if he used to live in the city before, being an investigator … or detective. Was there a difference? She couldn't remember which one he said.

Detective. Yes, detective.

She came to the more private part of the driveway where the woods separated the shack from their dad's house and lined the property. She spotted the path that forked in two directions. One led to the cemetery and the other led to the house.

Riley ignored the path and headed toward the hunting shack that was just beyond the hill. Geo did say she could pay him a visit to see how he remodeled the place. She glanced around the mowed lawn. All the tall weeds and compiled junk were gone from the yard. She climbed the hill like she used to, instead of taking the driveway, which curved around to the side of the house.

Standing on the hill, she admitted Geo was right. She couldn't believe what she saw. The shack had been transformed into a home. The weathered shingles were now replaced with a new gray steel roof. Four new iron posts lined the front porch. Each one, shaped like a tree, gave the place a unique flair but nothing too wild. Two red rocking chairs with a white table dressed the porch and made the butterscotch yellow siding pop. He kept the same color as before. Not a fan favorite of hers, but he made the different colors work. She doubted if she could have been as creative.

"Riley." Geo walked around the side of the house, using the steps and sidewalk. He carried a walking stick, the length a little taller than his shoulder.

"Hi," she said. A gust of wind whipped across her face and a strand of hair went into her mouth. After pulling it out, she continued, "I hope you don't mind that I came to see the place."

"Not at all. You're invited anytime."

She noticed his limp and how he used the stick to balance himself. She frowned and stepped down from the porch. He didn't look injured. "Are you all right?"

He shook his head and seemed annoyed at the stick. "I injured my leg and it acts up when the weather changes."

Riley understood. Her wrist did the same thing after she broke it as a kid. She pressed her hand on the spot. Today it didn't bother her. Weird.

Geo stood beside her and faced the shack, like her. He rested his hands on his hips. "It's a little different. Isn't it?"

"To say the least. Did you rebuild?"

"No. The base was solid—the foundation and walls. Only the roof had to be totally replaced."

He continued to stare at the place with a proud gleam in his eyes, as he should.

A wind gust pushed her toward him. Riley strained to keep from raising her hands to steady herself against him.

He turned his attention back to her. "Care to join me for lunch?"

"As long as I'm not imposing."

"I have plenty." He motioned for her to head up to the house. "Just in time too, with the storm coming."

"Wow," she said while walking across the level wood planks on the porch. "Dirt, cobwebs, piles of junk, and uneven floor is how I remember it."

"Wait until you see the inside." He opened the door and held out his hand for her to enter.

A warm golden glow emitted from the open rooms when she entered. Riley's jaw dropped.

Home.

Her first and only reaction. This was home to her.

Wood, steel accents, and leather made the place cozy and welcoming like a cabin. Antique pictures of different lake scenes hung on the walls with an occasional metal sculpture to complement them. An old red wagon sat in the corner with two pillows and a blanket ready for use. A neat stack of wood waited inside a copper bucket next to the stone fireplace. The leather furniture cozied up to the fireplace, offering a comfortable place to sit and relax. Geo's style was simple but well thought out.

She turned to the kitchen. A counter and cabinets separated the two rooms. An antique table with four chairs was centered in the middle of the kitchen. No dirty dishes in the sink or junk on the counters. Nice and clean.

"Unbelievable," she managed to say, in awe of the place. She stood between the two areas, drinking it in.

Geo's hand rested against her lower back as he moved around her. The power of his touch charged through her like a current of electricity, tingling her senses. The house was forgotten. Riley swayed and had to brace her legs to stay upright. When his hand slid from her back to her hip, his fingers cascading over her ass, her insides went into a tizzy. She bit her lip, shocked at how she turned hot between her legs.

127

"Look around. See the rest of the place, while I get lunch going," he said and headed to the kitchen.

Didn't he feel it too?

"Feel free to check upstairs."

Riley forced herself to push her feelings aside. Her hands trembled as she slipped off her boots and placed them near the door. She was glad he left so he wouldn't see how much he affected her. He must not have felt the same way. Disappointed, she brushed her hands down her hips to sweep the remnants of his touch to the floor. He was her dad's renter. Nothing more. She lived in Arizona. He lived here. She inhaled a deep breath.

The house. Look at the house. That was why she came here.

The stairs were to the side of the door. The bathroom was straight ahead. She peeked inside, surprised to see a full bathroom. Part rested underneath the staircase. A claw tub, modern toilet, and sink. She loved the large, black, metal-framed mirror. Oh, and a small chandelier hung from the ceiling. Who would have thought?

She couldn't wait to see the upstairs. The loft looked down on part of the living room. The small area held a cozy leather chair, ottoman, and a small table with a Tiffany lamp. She recognized the dragon fly shade on the lamp, identical to the one on Dad's desk in the den. A perfect little reading nook on a cold, dreary day. Today was one of those days.

Another nook at the back of the loft led to three doors. The door to the right opened to a bedroom-turned-office.

Thin-planked car siding covered the walls and slanted ceiling. A newer L-shaped desk was centered in the room with a web-backed chair behind it and near the window. She walked across the tan plush carpet to see outside. He had an awesome view, being able to see the vast skyline, rolling hills, and his vineyard. She'd probably do more gazing out the window than work if this were her office.

Back in the nook, she opened the door on the left, which held his bedroom. A huge four-poster bed dominated the space. She loved the fluffy white comforter and pillows and how they contrasted with the black iron frame. But white? For a guy? Impressive. There was enough room on each side of the bed for end tables and tall lights with green shades. Again, simple cabin comfort.

From the bedroom, she entered the bathroom.

"Oh wow." She fell in love. Ceramic tile enclosed a huge walk-in shower. Inside, two shower heads poked out from the sides and one rain showerhead dropped from the ceiling. A blue panel made of glass bordered the walls. She flipped the switch next to the opening. Sure enough, the panels in the shower lit with a soft glow.

She'd love to take a long shower in it. Nice touch. They needed that at Dad's house.

Riley turned off the light. The other door in the bathroom led out to the loft. She went downstairs to the kitchen where he continued to prep their lunch.

"You did all this on your own? This place is awesome."

"I'm glad you like it." He smiled at her and then went back to placing dinner rolls on a plate. "I still have a few things I'd like to do, but I'm pleased with how it's turned out."

"I could easily live here."

Geo's gaze turned to her. He smiled as if thinking about the idea.

Riley leaned against the counter. She gazed at the ceiling, then to the copper tiles in the kitchen, and then out to the living room where he blended planks of old and new wood. "What made you think this place was worth fixing up?"

"You just need to see beyond the roughness to the beauty underneath."

No doubt, the place cost him money. She didn't see any bills in Dad's checking account paying for it. Nothing indicated any receipts for new items.

"How—" she wasn't sure of the right way to approach the subject. She circled her finger around the air in front of her. "How did this all happen? Financially?"

"I used my own money. The older decorations and some of the furniture came from my grandfather's place, after he died, or pieces that your dad gave to me. Most of the work came by the way of labor. I had plenty of time."

And he paid rent. Every month. On time. The lease combined both house and land one year ago, according to the copy of the lease agreement she found in the cabinet. However, the rent for the house was four hundred dollars, much lower than what the place was worth, and now it made sense.

Riley rubbed her temple. Another complication. If they sold Dad's property, Geo would be pissed. She would be if she were him. All this work, his labor. She'd have to see if they could split the property and let him buy what he rented. She nodded, liking the idea.

"Penny for your thoughts?"

"I'm just floored. You're very talented. What did my dad think?"

"He loved it." Geo beamed again. "He offered advice, gave me ideas, and put some hard labor into it. Not to my liking, he'd be here at five o'clock in the morning ready to work. Max liked hammering nails to relieve his frustrations."

Alarms sounded within her. "Frustration? Did he say from what?"

Geo was about to answer when a bright flash from outside lit the kitchen. A loud crack of thunder boomed over the house, rattling the pictures.

"Jesus!" Riley jumped and found herself next to Geo.

"Shit almighty." He went to the kitchen window and gazed out as the sky darkened into night. The storm hit. Rain pelted the window.

She joined him at the window. "I'm glad we're inside. Safe."

Another flash of lightning ran along the clouds and charged to the ground. This time, the lights in the shack flickered. Another bolt of lightning with a loud bang cracked the sky. The lights went out. Riley grabbed Geo's arm.

"It's okay. It happens a lot," he assured her. He wrapped his arm around her waist. "The electricity is one of those things I still have to work on."

He gave her a gentle squeeze and then let go. This time his

touch was soothing. Her fear of the heavy storm overrode the initial spark. Besides, this was the afternoon and they weren't in a relationship.

Geo left her to retrieve a long-barreled lighter from the drawer. He lit the candle on the kitchen table. Next he moved to three candles on the counter by the stove. "Candles are a necessity here. I've had electricians come out, but we can't find the problem."

The glow of the candles softened the effects of the storm outside. Geo went to the living room and lit the ones around the fireplace and on the coffee table.

The pot on the gas stove rattled as steam escaped from the lid. Riley grabbed the spoon on the counter, lifted the lid, and then stirred the beef stew.

Her throat constricted. Beef stew was one of Mom's go-to meals. Comfort food. While her mother used stew meat, Geo had cut up chunks of steak. The aroma of the beef, carrots, celery, onion, and tomato filled her nose and smelled delicious.

"I think it's done," she said over the pounding of the rain on the steel roof. The thunder continued to roll across the sky and shake the ground. "I don't ever remember lightning and thunder in October."

"Two years ago?" He squinted as if in thought. He came back to the kitchen. "Yeah, two winters ago I remember thunder in January. Like now, it scared the hell out of me."

"I can imagine. You wouldn't expect it."

Geo grabbed two bowls, spoons, and napkins. She

used the ladle resting on the counter to scoop the stew from the pot. She filled the bowls and then placed them on the table.

"Wine?" He held out a red. "Looks like we may be here for a while."

"Why not." The whole setting—the hunting shack, the candles, the storm, and being with Geo felt right. She stepped back, disconnecting herself from her other chaotic life. The job and the promotion, along with the worries and stress of the funeral were thrown under a rug.

Her world stopped, and Riley, for the first in a long time, enjoyed it. She sat down at the table as Geo poured the wine. The windows rattled, the rain pelted, and the thunder rolled overhead. The symphony continued while they ate their food and the candle glowed between them.

"This is so good," she said after taking another bite of stew. The buttery sauce had a touch of burn from one of the spices, which helped warm her insides. "You like to cook?"

Geo shrugged. "I don't mind it for the most part. I hate the cleanup."

"Are you a messy cooker?"

He turned silent as he thought about it. "No ... well, maybe."

"I bet you're not," she stated. His house sparkled. If he did make a mess, he probably cleaned soon after making it.

They talked about the renovations to the hunting shack, what he did first, and how it came together. She liked his voice and how it lowered into a sexy drawl on occasion. Riley sensed there was more to this man than appeared on the surface. He seemed restless, as if struggling on the inside. She wanted to know whatever she could about him to help.

"Why did you settle here?" She had dropped the subject before, in their den. She finished her wine. Geo, the attentive host, refilled her glass. He did the same with his. A droplet of wine trickled down the outside of her glass. She wiped away the drop with her fingertip and then licked it with her tongue.

When Geo didn't respond, she raised her eyes to see what was wrong. He had fixated on her as she sucked on her finger. Riley blushed, knowing what other act must have popped into his head. She stammered. "I-I've met your g-grandfather ... he was the caretaker ... here at the cemetery." She sipped her wine to help wet her tongue. "You came here because of him—to help. But why did you move?"

"I ... eh." He hesitated.

Now she cornered him.

"I'm sorry," she said but didn't mean it. "Did I get too personal?"

He saw that she challenged him and his eyes sparkled. Riley couldn't hold back her smile.

"My sister and I would come here to the haunted shack and play truth or dare. We'd confess who we liked at school, which boy we wanted to marry."

Geo rubbed his hand across his chest. The light blue shirt contrasted with his tan hand. A working hand with rough skin. He asked, "So, more truth than dare?"

"I'd say you're correct."

"Okay, what do you want to know about me?"

"Truth?" Riley asked, referring to the game. She took a sip of wine and leaned against the table to wait for his response. The flame from the candle grew brighter.

He leaned in as well, ready to play. "Truth."

She went easy on him for this first round. "How did you injure your leg?"

"I chased a guy who stole a woman's purse. He pulled a gun out of his pants and shot me in the thigh before I had the chance to move away."

"What?" Riley shrieked. "You were shot at?"

"Goes with the job."

"Wow." She hadn't expected that answer. "Did the woman get her purse back?"

Geo laughed. "No. I don't think she ever did."

"A small price compared to her life." Riley couldn't imagine.

"The woman was lucky. He was on parole for rape."

She agreed. "How many times have you been shot at?"

"Shot at? Many times. I've only caught two."

"Caught two? What?" Her eyes widened. "You've been hit twice?"

"First one was to my leg. The shot messed up my thigh, reason for the limp when I've been on it too much or the weather changes. I can usually tell when it's going to rain. The second time, I was hit in the shoulder, chipped the bone."

"Another purse robber?"

He shook his head. "I was caught in a drug fight down in Miami. That one almost took my life."

"Oh." She made a face. Robbers. Drugs. Bad

neighborhoods. He had a rough job. "This place has to be like a safe haven for you."

"In a way, you're right. To answer your first question, I came here to avoid a third bullet. Three times, as they say, and you're out. I didn't want to take the chance."

"Did you live in a bad neighborhood?"

He shook his head and gazed down at his wine glass. "I worked in a bad area."

"What did you do?"

"My job."

She frowned at his lame response.

Geo coughed and took another sip of wine. He shifted and rested his back against the chair as if forcing himself to be casual. He didn't like talking about it. "Like I said before, I was a cop for two years and then a detective for three. Before that, the army. I've seen and been through a lot."

"And now you're a grape grower."

"Less dangerous."

"How true." She thought about her job and the financial wizards who could do wonders with money. She shuffled their papers and created order out of their chaos when the stocks changed. It was all hard work, but not the type of job that would make the world a better place, like helping people in times of trouble. Her work was far from being dangerous. She'd never done anything heroic like Geo. She heard about people who completely changed their lives after being close to death. Is that why he remained so calm and didn't let the little things bug her?

Geo snapped his fingers.

Riley came back, realizing she zoned out on him.

Staring him in the eyes, she said, "First off, thank you for your service. Second, you have to be proud, knowing you helped save people's lives. Third, you brought peace to families. As tough as it was for you, the job had to be rewarding in a way."

He acknowledged her with a nod. "Good with the evil."

His demeanor changed and focused on her. It took Riley a second to realize that he was ready for her turn. A slight smile curved on his lips. "Truth or dare?"

"When my sister looked at me with a smile like the one on your face, I always picked dare."

"What would she make you do for dare?"

Riley laughed. "She came up with some crazy but fun things—like climb on the roof of this place and act like a monkey."

He contemplated it for a bit. "I'm not sure if you'd like my dare. But what will it be? Truth or dare?"

Her heart flipped. Would it be a kiss? She'd dare him for that one. But his expression warned her of something more. Wanting to stay in her comfy spot at the table, she decided on truth.

Geo leaned across the table again. "What do you know about Conner?"

She wrinkled her nose at the odd question. She guessed he would ask her about their plans for the estate and how it would affect him. This was an easy truth.

"Well ... let's see ... Conner's married to my sister. He's a nice guy—most of the time. Seems a bit angrier lately, but we've all been out of sorts." She drew a blank. "What do you want to know?"

"Who does he work for?"

"Himself. He's into exports. Business transactions. Selling and buying companies."

"Like …?"

She shrugged. "I really don't get into his business. He keeps his work private and doesn't talk too much about the details. Not that I'm around them a lot to hear about it. I know he's provided for his family. My sister is happy. Kids are happy. They live in Milwaukee. I live in Arizona."

"That's it?"

Riley blushed with embarrassment at her lack of knowledge. "Work keeps me away from them. I'm pretty tied up with my job. When I do talk to them, it's more about the kids and what they're up to. Not Conner."

"You said he's a nice guy most of the time. Has he changed?"

She nodded her head, thinking back to his outburst in the kitchen when they discussed Dad's lawyers or his anger toward the detective and police. How her sister was concerned about his behavior, even at home. "One thing Shannon did say is that one of his business deals fell through. He's down on his luck now. But like the stock exchange, he's always bounced up again. He gets through it."

"Any idea who he's been in contact with? What type of deal?"

Riley's alarms went off. Geo questioned her like a detective on a case. "Why are you interested in my brother-in-law?"

Geo turned quiet for a moment as if deciding whether or not to tell her.

"Truth," she said.

He gave in. "He'd been seen around town with your dad, a few days before he died."

"Maybe he was asking for advice on what to do. They've talked business before."

"Do you think your dad might have been involved in Conner's acquisition?"

In the files she raked through, she hadn't seen anything. "Not that I'm aware of."

Riley began to see a pattern in his questioning about Conner. Geo didn't believe Dad committed suicide.

Her eyes popped. Had Dad been involved in a deal that went out of control? If he was killed, did Conner know about it? Is that why the detectives kept asking question?

Geo's phone rang. He moved to get up and the flame from the candle flickered, threatening to go out, but then settled into a gentle wave after he left.

She couldn't sit anymore either. While he took his call in the other room, Riley gathered their dishes and took them to the kitchen sink, she followed with the silverware and the empty wine glasses. A clap of thunder drew her attention to the storm. The rain continued its downpour, just as her mind scattered with twenty different thoughts as she processed what Geo had said. When he returned to the kitchen, she spun around and leaned against the counter. "Do you think whoever did business with Conner could have killed my father?"

He hesitated in his step and response. "Well … the men that Conner is dealing with are dangerous. If your brother-in-law owes them money …" He bobbed his head. "They'll get their money. One way or another."

Riley swayed. The idea of Conner being involved in a bad or dangerous deal seemed unbelievable. He was smart. He wouldn't put his family in jeopardy. She stared at Geo as he watched her. He stayed quiet, giving her time to absorb his words.

She swallowed hard. "How do you know?"

"I was a detective—it's been my experience that owing large amounts of money involves dangerous people."

"But you're retired. Did my dad say anything to you?"

"No, unfortunately not."

"Then how can you make any accusations against Conner and lead me to think he's a bad person? What happened to innocence until proven guilty?" Her voice rose an octave higher as she spoke.

"I'm not accusing him of anything," Geo said and remained calm.

He watched her. She didn't like it. Her eyes lowered. She needed to think.

Shannon. Her heart swelled with concern for her. Riley needed to make sure her sister was all right.

Was she home? Was she busy working on their costumes? Riley dug out her phone from her back pocket. She sent her sister a text to find out where she was and to tell her she'd be home later. Her hands shook.

"You all right?" Geo moved closer and placed his hand on her shoulder.

Riley turned away. She pressed her lips together, afraid of what emotion might come out if she said anything.

"Talk to me." His other hand went to her other shoulder as he stood in front of her. When she kept her head down, he placed his finger underneath her chin and raised it up. "Who were you texting? Your sister?"

She nodded. "I told her where I am so she's not worried."

Geo stepped back to give her breathing room. "Is she home?"

"I'm not sure."

"Riley," he said to keep her attention.

Oh boy, seeing his serious blue eyes, she gathered he was about to tell her more news. She held her breath.

"That was Detective Torrence on the phone a few minutes ago."

Her prediction was right. She coaxed him on when he hesitated. "And …"

"They have enough evidence. Your dad was murdered."

At first his words didn't register. She stared into his eyes to see if he joked. He was serious. "How … how can you say that?"

"The autopsy report's been released."

A chill raced up her spine and sent goose bumps across her arms. She stood, frozen in her spot beside the counter. "What …?"

"The examiner found fingerprints on his neck. Your dad died from strangulation, not by hanging himself."

141

Her head clicked on different picture frames, trying to piece his words together. "Are you saying someone made it look like he hanged himself?"

He didn't have to respond. She wasn't expecting him to as she filtered through the information. Not that she liked the idea either way.

Riley slid to the floor; her knees gave out.

Geo dropped down and took Riley in his arms as the tears fell like the rain outside.

Chapter 10

Geo walked Riley home after the rain stopped. The low-hanging clouds continued to thin out as the storm passed. He held her hand as he led her through the woods and helped her avoid the puddles. His fingers fit perfectly as he kept a firm grip around hers, offering support and strength. She needed it. The news of Dad being murdered hit her harder than she expected. Probably more than he had expected as well. Detective Torrence warned them earlier, saying that they were investigating. Now it was confirmed.

She wasn't sure how she felt about it. Yes, she'd cried her eyes out in front of Geo. He held her as she curled into a ball and wept. The tears hadn't been in grief, but more out of anger that he had died because some horrible person wanted him dead. He wasn't able to fulfill his wish to die of old age with his daughters next to him.

Reaching the back yard, she spotted the black Taurus belonging to Detective Torrence. She looked to Geo. "Is he telling my sister?"

"I'm not sure."

"Does he know that I know?"

He nodded. "He wanted me to tell you."

Geo stopped before they reached the back door. He took her other hand. The glow from the back-porch light touched his face and showed the worry under his eyes. She could only imagine what she looked like. Her eyes felt swollen and puffy from crying. Riley hoped she didn't look like a racoon with smeared mascara. She wanted to rub under her eyes again but that would mean she'd have to let go of Geo. Her vanity could wait.

"Listen," he said. Riley turned her attention to him. "I asked Torrence if I could tell you so you'd be more at an advantage when your sister finds out. I figured she was going to need the support. Torrence will be asking her questions about Conner."

He sent her a look that stated it wasn't going to be easy for Shannon. Riley got it. If they asked about their life, his business, what she knew, her sister was going to freak out. Geo was right to tell her first so she could be there to help.

Riley made one request. "Make sure he doesn't push her too far."

"I'm not going in."

Her head jerked up. He'd been her support this afternoon. Now he was leaving?

"This isn't my time. It's yours."

Geo squeezed her hands before he let go.

She breathed deeply to brace herself.

"You've got this." Geo leaned forward and wrapped her in his arms. She soaked in his warmth. When he pulled back, he waited to make sure she was okay.

Riley nodded. She had no choice.

Once inside, she found them in the living room. Shannon knew. She looked as white as the couch. Her hands clutched her stomach. Relief lit her eyes as Riley rushed toward her.

"Did you hear?" Shannon's voice crumbled when Riley went to sit by her.

Riley found her sister's hands and held them tight.

"I heard." She glanced toward Detective Torrence, greeting him with a nod.

He acknowledged her with a look of compassion before lowering his head to give them a moment of privacy as they hugged each other for support and assurance that they'd be okay.

"I can't believe it," Shannon whispered in her ear. "Why?"

Riley had no answer. She turned to the detective. "What can you tell us?"

The detective briefed her on the evidence they found, exactly Geo's words. He couldn't give them details, only that his death changed from a suicide to a murder.

"He asked for records, permissions," Shannon said, speaking to her sister. "I told him he'd need to talk to you. He meant *my* records."

Riley turned off her emotions even though she burned with pain on the inside. Now it was business.

The detective also needed permission to talk to their father's bankers and the accountant.

No problem. She'd cooperate fully with the investigation.

More questions about her, what she had been doing at the

time of his death. How often she managed his finances. Riley bit her lip. She'd answered the same questions when he'd asked before. Why would her responses change now? She had to keep in the back of her head that this was his job—to collect evidence, information. Her nerves frayed, sparking at the end. She kept her grip until Detective Torrence focused on Shannon.

Same questions for her sister. Shannon was more poised when answering. He slipped in questions about Conner and his whereabouts. At first, Shannon didn't notice the shift in direction, moving from general to more detailed information about her husband's work. The more he tried to dig, the more her sister's hands shook when she couldn't answer half of them.

Riley had enough. She shot the detective a look that warned him to back off. She steamed. "My sister doesn't have the information you want, detective. Why don't you ask Conner?"

"We intend to," Detective Torrence said and closed his notepad.

Riley walked the detective to the door, letting Shannon recover from the shots fired at her.

"You were pretty brutal to her," Riley told the detective before he left.

"No, I really wasn't," he said. "I could have taken you both in."

She raised her eyes to meet his. He wasn't so handsome anymore.

"Just remember, we're humans with feelings. Don't

forget yours." She shut the door on him.

"My god, what the hell was he after?" Shannon cried out.

At first, Riley thought she was talking to her. She was about to respond when her sister spoke again. She was on the phone with Conner. Her voice turned low yet sharp when she hopped up the stairs to the bedroom. The door closed behind her.

Riley went into the kitchen and plopped on the stool at the island. She shook with cold. The chill vibrated the backs of her arms, her shins, and her joints. She still wore her jacket, but it did nothing to keep her warm.

The refrigerator turned on, the hum of the motor like a loud cat purring. Oddly, the sound calmed her a bit as her heart slowed down to a normal beat.

She should call Gary. Work.

But why? What could he do?

Work seemed so out there—in a different world.

She still hadn't bought tickets for her flight.

"Why are you sitting here in the dark?"

Riley jumped at Shannon's voice. The kitchen light popped on, blinding her for a second.

Her sister didn't notice she had scared the shit out of her— or she ignored it. Shannon walked to the cupboard, found a glass, and filled it with water from the sink. She drank a full glass before saying, "Conner will be here tomorrow."

"Is that good or bad?" Riley wasn't sure if her sister's sharpness was the result of the news or the conversation with her husband.

"Beats me," Shannon said as she joined her at the counter. Dark circles had formed under her eyes from crying. Her normally smooth skin was tight and wrinkled, as if she had lost a layer of softness. They were both under stress.

"Why is this happening to us?" Shannon rubbed her temples.

Riley couldn't answer. Dad always said things happen for a reason. He'd say, "You might not realize it at the time, but eventually you will." Usually he was right. But this time? She didn't get it.

Shannon placed her forehead on the counter. With eyes closed, she said, "I ... I just don't know what to think."

Riley was right there with her. She rested her head against the counter, one ear down in order to see her sister at eye-level. "In a way, I'm glad Dad didn't commit suicide."

Shannon's eyes were still closed. "Conner thinks it's bullshit."

"What is?"

Her sister turned her head and opened her eyes to find Riley's face in close proximity to her own, surprising her. She recovered and continued their discussion. "He thinks the police will be all up in our asses. He was pissed that Detective Torrence asked me questions about him. He told me not to talk to him or anyone else about our business."

A chill ran through Riley, from the back of her neck and down her spine. Resting her head against the cold counter didn't help, but she was too tired to raise herself. She was perfectly fine having their conversation in the awkward position.

"I guess I can understand his point of view," Riley said. "But there is a difference between cooperating and being a jerk. I don't see anything wrong with telling the detective or the police what we can. If it would help catch whoever did this— killed Dad—I'm all for it."

"Same here," Shannon said.

She let out a heavy puff of air that made Riley flinch as it hit her face.

Both laughed, letting go of some stress.

"I suppose." Shannon raised her head from the counter. She pushed her hair away. "What do you want to do? Eat or drink?"

"Both." Riley sat up. Now with work back in her head, she had to make decisions. She really didn't want to go back to Phoenix. Her heart wasn't into the interview or heading back to her apartment for a few days, only to return again. Until then, she thought the change of scenery might do her good, but not now with Conner at the house. Her sister would be alone with him. What would he do or say to manipulate Shannon into doing something she shouldn't? One that could jeopardize the estate or their inheritance.

Riley's heart sank. She couldn't leave.

"I'll be back."

"Where you going?" Shannon asked as she opened the door to the pantry and walked inside.

"I'm going to call Gary and HR to cancel my interview."

"What?" Shannon stepped out of the pantry with two potatoes in her hands. "Why?"

"I can't see leaving now."

149

"But you'll lose your promotion. Right?"

"Yeah, for now."

Shannon placed the potatoes next to the sink. "But everything is set up."

"I can't leave here. Not now."

"Why don't you interview by phone?"

"I tried but they refused. They want me in person. Being fair to the other candidates."

"Seems backward in today's world."

Riley agreed. "You're preaching to the choir on that one."

"I can hold the fort down for a few days so you can go."

Her dear sister. Always willing to help. Always wanting to make it better. No wonder that she was a great mom.

"Thanks." In her heart, Riley couldn't leave. She was in charge of Dad's finances. They had a funeral to attend. A murder to be solved. "I'm staying. I'm not going to leave you alone."

"Conner will be here. I won't be alone."

The exact reason Riley wanted to stay.

Chapter 11

Riley sat on her bed and stared at her phone. The nervous churn in her stomach, as she prepared to tell Gary she was canceling the interview, also made her palms sweat. He took it well, by which she guessed he was in shock at the news. She gave him time to process what she said, knowing that on the other side of the line he was tapping his pencil on his desk.

"Let me see if I can change the date. Give you another week."

"No, Gary. I'm fine. Let Rita be top runner for the job." She dried her hands on her jeans.

"But you're better. The advisors want you."

"There will be other opportunities."

She didn't know if another opportunity would arise. Her boss, and others, wouldn't like to hear that she dropped out. They were the type of people who would make her regret the decision by giving her more work. Lucky for her.

"Did the police talk to you?" She was curious. "Have you heard any other news?"

"They questioned me. Not a lot though. Mainly what I was

doing on that night."

By his tone, he didn't seem upset or that it had been a big deal. Her stomach settled.

"They are now investigating my dad's death as a murder."

"I had a feeling that was the case. I'm sorry to hear." He seemed more understanding about why she needed to stay.

They talked about other work news before hanging up. Next, she called their HR Department to tell them to cancel the interview. The person took the call in stride. This wasn't personal to them, like with Gary, making it easier.

"There you go, Rita," Riley said to the phone after ending her call with HR. "You can deal with the long hours and additional stress."

There went her plans for buying a house. Down the drain.

Oh well.

Riley released a long breath. The pressure was off. Now she could concentrate on the funeral and the estate. She gained another week, her remaining vacation time, to do what she needed in Wisconsin before heading back to Arizona.

She looked for Shannon and found her in Mom's sitting/sewing room. Her sister's head was down in full concentration as she worked on the costumes.

"Shouldn't you be going through Dad's bedroom?" Riley asked.

"I want to get these done in time. Your costume is, mine's not."

"I see," she said. "Ms. Procrastinator."

"You bet," Shannon agreed without any guilt. She went back to placing the thin paper pattern on top of the dark blue fabric draped over a card table.

Riley let her be—if she said more, she'd get pulled in to help. She wasn't a seamstress. Instead, she liked to bake and cook. Mom let her make cookies and bars on Saturdays to have on hand for the rest of the week. She loved trying new recipes and testing them on the rest of the family. Most of the time, they liked her creations.

Baking. When was the last time she baked anything? Or really cooked a meal? In Phoenix everything was fast food or restaurant eating. The deli at the grocery store was also a favorite spot to pick up something quick to eat. Who wanted to cook after a long, hard day at work? Now she had time.

Screw the finances and the estate. If Shannon could procrastinate on her duties, so could she. Which should it be? Baking or cooking a good meal? Riley decided to make a homemade dinner with dessert.

They needed a guest.

Geo was the first person who came to mind. She sent him a text, asking if he'd like to join them for dinner. Within a minute he responded back. A smile rose on her lips as she read that he'd love to join them. Her heart skipped. Her energy rose a level as she got into her new task. She went to the kitchen, found Mom's well-used recipe book, and then sat at the counter to plan dinner and make the grocery list.

She drove to the grocery store in River Falls. The wind turned brisk as a cold front moved in after yesterday's storm. She zipped up her jacket as she speed-walked across the parking lot. Glancing up at the sky, she realized how low the clouds hung, as if threatening snow. Good ol' Wisconsin weather—hard to predict.

Inside the store, Riley stopped for a second to gain her bearings. Normally, she only needed a basket as she hit the deli section. This time, she grabbed a large grocery cart and strolled along the aisles. Riley stopped in the section with all the cereal. A whole fuckin' row. Who could make a choice? Cinnamon donut flavored? Chocolate peanut butter? Even the healthier cereals promised to taste like dessert. Riley shook her head. After spending five minutes perusing the cereals, more out of curiosity than wanting to buy, she made her way to the next aisle.

A stocky woman with short brown hair recognized her and smiled. She hesitated at first but chose to address her. "Riley? Riley Walsh?"

"Yes," she said and stopped pushing her cart.

"I'm terribly sorry to hear about your father. A murder? My gosh. Terrible, terrible news."

Riley swallowed hard. The word was out. That was fast.

"If you need anything, please let us know. Bud and I can help. Your father was a great man."

"Thank you. I will." She still had no clue who the woman was, and the name Bud didn't ring a bell.

The next aisle was the same. This time an older couple stopped her. The man shook her hand. The woman hugged her. These were people who genuinely cared and wanted to show their support. Riley almost lost it. She forced herself not to cry.

Another aisle. Two more women.

How many people did Dad know?

She was relieved when she turned the corner and saw no one in the next aisle. Two college-aged students were in the snack aisle, trying to decide which potato chips to buy. They ignored her. Riley wasn't so lucky in the dairy section. She caused a small gathering, mostly women, who gave their condolences and offered help. She brushed away the tears as she continued on with her shopping. She found the remaining items on her list through blurred eyes.

The checkout clerk, an older man, greeted her like he'd normally do each shopper. As the items from her cart were beeped through, he said, "I played poker with your dad. I see him in you. Good man."

She nodded and bit her lip.

The man ignored the next shopper and helped bag her groceries.

"He'd come here and talk with the other farmers on occasion." Riley made a face. He explained, "The men sit at the coffee pit, over there." He pointed in the direction near the entrance where three older men in flannel shirts sat drinking coffee. "They prattle while the women shop."

Riley smiled. She hadn't seen that one coming.

"You try to have a good day. Let me know if you need anything."

"Thanks," she said. "I appreciate it."

And she did. A grocery store full of strangers offered their support. Here, people cared for each other. For an odd reason, one she couldn't explain, she suddenly felt angry at her work. Not once had her boss asked if she needed anything. He sent an email; two sentences to offer his and the firm's sympathy with no personalization. Two of the financial advisors sent her separate emails, hoping she'd return soon. No one asked if they could do anything to help her. They continued on with their lives.

Even if they offered help, Riley doubted if they would follow through. But these people here at the grocery store would help in a heartbeat. Maybe that's why Geo decided to move here. She could easily understand. There was something to be said for small towns.

Back home, Riley found Mom's old apron—a simple, homemade pink-cotton cover with ties at the neck and midsection. She wrapped the two ties twice around her waist so the tails didn't hang low and get in the way. Next she turned on the old-style radio with an extended antenna and found a local classic rock channel. She was ready to roll.

The dinner menu included a hearty salad, little meatloaves with cheese and barbecue sauce, and herbed potatoes roasted in the oven. For dessert, a chocolate, flourless cake. She started with the cake.

Shannon entered the kitchen and her nose went up in the air as the first wave of chocolate wafted from the oven. "Oh my god, that smells awesome."

"I hope it turns out."

Her sister gazed about the kitchen and pressed her lips together as if to hold back any comments.

Riley scanned the room. The counter spaces were full of bowls, spoons, cutting boards, spatulas, spices, tin foil, butter, and everything else. She had a mess on her hands. "Don't worry, I got this."

Shannon, like Mom, cleaned as she cooked, while Riley waited until after she finished baking or cooking.

"What's the occasion?"

"Geo's coming for dinner."

Shannon's curiosity rose. "All this for him?"

"No—" Riley paused when she turned on the oven light and peeked inside to check on the cake. So far so good. She guessed another three minutes. "Well, yes. I suppose in a way. I was thinking about our dinners growing up, when Mom made us home-cooked meals. I thought it'd be nice for us to have a homemade meal."

"Getting a little domesticated?" She looked over her shoulder from the sink and smiled.

"No, nostalgia." She ignored her sister's hidden comment and helped to clean a portion of the counter while waiting for the cake. Besides, she needed the room to make the meatloaves.

Once the cake was done, Riley shredded the cheddar cheese and put half in the bowl with the meat mixture. She molded the individual meatloaves and coated each one with a thick layer of barbecue sauce before placing them in the oven.

"Do you want me to leave?"

"Huh?" Riley was busy coating the small potatoes with olive oil. She registered what her sister asked after seeing the smirk on her face. She got it. "No, you can stay."

"Are you sure?" Her smile grew. "He likes you. This could be your chance to get *closer* to him."

Riley tried hiding a smile. The attraction toward him was different from what she experienced with other guys. Most times she went for the physical attraction, finding herself in bed with her date too soon, before deciding if she liked him. Not dating a lot, with too many spans in between dates, she was ready for a good romp. But Geo was different, and she didn't put him in the category of her past men.

Shannon interrupted her thoughts. "Anything going on between the two of you?"

"No, not really. He's a nice guy." Her heart beat faster thinking about him. She wanted to know him. His calmness soothed her as if saying to her that life wasn't all about living in a big rush. He enjoyed what he did. Riley couldn't say the same about her job. Putting out fires, one after another, didn't give her a chance to sit back and think.

Her sister wiped down the island with a wet washcloth. "You should give him a chance. Go out with him."

She made a hesitant noise. "I'm not into long-distance relationships."

"You could stay here."

Riley's head shot up. "What do you mean? Stay here?"

"Why not? What's keeping you in Arizona?"

"All my stuff. My job. My car."

Shannon made a face as if asking whether or not she was serious.

Now she had to defend herself. "My life is out there, dear sister. My friends are out there."

She remained silent.

Riley didn't keep too many friends. She had a limited social life because she worked a lot. If she wasn't working, she was at the fitness center working out.

Shannon placed her hands on the counter and stared at her. "When was the last time you watched the sun rise?"

Odd question, Riley thought. "Here, it's almost impossible. All these clouds and the storm."

Her sister shook her head, sighed, then went to set the dining room table.

A month ago, Riley had watched the sun rise, on the way to work. She'd seen beautiful sunrises.

Damn her.

Life in Arizona wasn't perfect. But what would she gain by living here? She'd have to start over again, like Geo. He was successful but that was different. He needed the land. Her line of work required being in a city. She'd have to find a job in St. Paul or Minneapolis and that'd be a commute.

The doorbell rang.

Her heart skipped a beat.

Geo.

Shannon came into the kitchen as Riley wiped her hands on the apron. Her sister reminded her to remove it, signaling with her hands. Riley slipped the fabric off, tossing it on the floor in the pantry, and then smoothed out her hair as she went to answer the door.

Dressed in a blue, sharp-fitted shirt with white cuffs and a pair of black pants, Geo took her breath away. She didn't want to take her eyes off him—the way his shag cut hung in curls at his shoulders and his five o'clock shadow gave him a sexy, rough-edged look. He even smelled like heaven, fresh yet not overpowering.

"Please, come in," she said and stole another whiff of his scent as he passed. "Perfect timing."

It really wasn't. She wished she had time to freshen up, straighten her hair, put makeup on, and dress better.

Geo removed his shoes and coat. He lifted his nose to the air and breathed in. He placed his hand on his stomach and smiled. "Smells wonderful in here."

"And it's almost ready." She took his coat and hung it in the closet. She showed him into the den while Shannon finished setting the table.

"Oh," he said and took a step back toward the door. "I brought the wine."

"I thought your coat was heavy," she commented. The coat was the same one she'd seen him wear before, and she was aware of the deep pockets.

He held up two bottles. Riley glanced at one of the cabs, not recognizing the label.

"One of my test blends."

"Oh," she exclaimed. "I can't wait to try it."

"And for backup, I brought an award winner as well. If I recall, you liked it the last time."

"You bet I do," Riley said with more enthusiasm than

she intended. She blushed.

"Did I hear wine?" Shannon came out to greet him.

"How could I not bring the wine?" His smile showed perfect teeth.

"Follow me," Shannon said. "Let's get the first one opened." She cast a glance toward her sister, giving her a nod toward the bedroom.

Riley was grateful. She slipped away to freshen up. Black yoga pants and a purple lace tunic would do—quick, easy, and comfortable. She fixed her hair, putting it up in a loose bun. She debated on makeup and decided to add a touch of mascara and eyeliner to draw out her eyes, and lip gloss to give her face a touch of color.

Shannon gave her an approving look when she returned. They enjoyed their first glass of wine while waiting for dinner. Riley went in and out to check the food, not wanting her meatloaves to burn. The food was done. Shannon must have heard her pulling out the pans from the oven because she came into the kitchen. "I'll serve. You sit with your guest."

Riley agreed. She went to the den and had Geo follow her to the dining room. He pulled out her chair and helped her sit before taking his place at the end of the table. The salad was already at the table, and she let him start.

Shannon came out with the rest of the meal.

"Meatloaf?" His smile widened. "I haven't eaten meatloaf in ages."

Riley's heart skipped, pleased with his reaction. "I can't guarantee the results. It's been awhile since I actually cooked."

"You don't like to cook?" He seemed surprised as he eyed

the spread of delicious food, ready to eat.

"I do. But when you're one person, it doesn't make sense to cook a ton of food."

"I hear you," he agreed while digging into the salad. "It's a perfect reason to start a family, or invite great friends. Thanks for letting me join you."

"So … no kids of your own?" Shannon asked and glanced at Riley.

"None yet."

"Family?" Shannon passed the potatoes to him.

"An aunt out in Boston. Three cousins. That's about it."

"Well, here's to starting families and being with friends." Shannon raised her wine glass to toast.

Riley didn't dare look at her sister. If Geo caught on to what her sister was doing, he didn't seem to mind. He dug into the food. She wondered if they would be a perfect match if they dated.

When they had lunch at his place, she felt connected to him, like they'd known each other for a long time. Conversation came easily to them, with no awkward silences. And when he touched her … she tingled again, thinking about it.

She stole another glance at him. Why hadn't they kissed yet? They were close to touching lips once. Did he decide she wasn't worth it? Was he not interested? Her eyes widened, hoping she wasn't the issue.

Shannon coughed and caught Riley's attention. Her sister glared at her as if seeing the panic rise inside her, telling her to stop it.

"Great potatoes," Geo commented as he took another bite. "Love the rosemary on them."

"Thanks," Riley said. Besides, this wasn't the time for dating. She was mourning her dad. Geo was being respectful.

"I hear the wake and funeral will be on Sunday." He stopped eating and glanced up when they turned quiet. Riley was surprised that he knew. Shannon just scheduled the date that morning. He wiped his mouth on his napkin. "I'm sorry. I shouldn't have brought it up at the dinner table."

"Oh no, you're fine," Riley said to assure him that he did nothing wrong. "You're right. We're set for Sunday."

"Is there anything I can do? Help you out?" He looked to her and then to Shannon.

Riley hadn't thought about it, with her sister making the arrangements. It seemed as if everything was in order.

"We're going to keep the wake and funeral to one day. Both will be at the building inside the cemetery. After, we'll open the house to visitors."

"You'll need food. People helping," Geo said. "I'm on it." He leaned over toward Riley. "Can you make about two hundred of these little meatloaves?"

She laughed. "Two hundred?"

"We'll want to make sure there're leftovers." Geo helped himself to another half. "Did you arrange for protection?"

Both of them stopped eating. Riley looked to Shannon and then back to Geo. "For what?"

"A precaution." He glanced up to see them both staring at him.

Shannon asked with hesitancy, "Are we in danger?"

"It's hard to say," he said between bites. He swallowed his food and took a sip of wine. "Like I mentioned before, it's a precaution. Your father's murder has been in the news, so you'll get curious people who might attend. And if you're opening your house to visitors, you'll want to make sure no one tries to take advantage of your situation."

"Oh," Riley said in unison with her sister. She never thought about it from that perspective. She heard of thefts occurring when the family attended a funeral, but this was a small town, almost rural Wisconsin.

"I suppose we should ask if someone could be here at the house." Shannon bit her fingertip as if thinking who she could ask.

"I'll take care of it," Geo said and added, "If you'd like. I can talk to Detective Torrence and make arrangements."

Riley stared at her potatoes. If Conner's business partners, the ones he might be in trouble with, were angry, how much of a threat would they be to Shannon? Or the kids? She looked to Geo. "But really, should we be worried?"

"Scared no. Cautious yes."

She set her fork down. Murder did have consequences. She never thought she'd be this close to one.

Shannon took a drink of wine. She sat a little straighter and said with a professional manner, "Geo, do you think my husband's business is involved?"

He checked with Riley as if determining how he should respond. She shrugged, only enough for him to see.

164

Geo didn't answer fast enough. Her sister said more pointedly, "The police are asking a lot of questions about him and his partners. I need to know if I should be concerned about the safety of my children."

Riley's skin prickled, uncomfortable with how the conversation turned. This wasn't supposed to be a drill or a time for serious discussion. This was dinner. However, her sister didn't act angry or scared, but more needing information to decide what her next move should be.

"Honestly?" Geo paused. He shook his head. "I can't say. You'll need to talk to Detective Torrence."

Shannon didn't catch on, but Riley noticed how he *couldn't* say. What information was he privy to? After their truth or dare session at the hunting shack, with him asking her about Conner, she had a bad feeling about what he wasn't telling.

Riley finalized the subject. "Geo, we'll talk to the detective about security for the house. We'll also see if he has any additional information for us."

"Sounds like a plan," he said and seemed relieved.

Shannon took her cue and changed the subject. "Are you going to the charity ball?"

"I'm not."

"Oh, why not?" Riley asked too quickly. She tried to hide her disappointment.

"I'm not a party kind of guy."

"It's for a great cause," Shannon said. "I hear it's quite the occasion."

"I went last year." Geo smirked.

"Out with it." Riley wanted to know what happened.

"I went with Max, your dad. He had a few women vying for his attention."

"Women interested in Dad?" Shannon made a face.

"He was quite the handsome man."

"What did he go as last year?" Riley asked.

"Errol Flynn, the swashbuckler." Geo laughed. "And he enjoyed all the attention from the ladies. I felt like a third wheel."

Her dad mentioned the event. He didn't provide too many details. She'd be interested in seeing these ladies who hung around him. Whether they had known Mom. She said, "Shannon's making our costumes."

"And with that …" Her sister placed her napkin on the table. "I need to get back to my sewing before Conner and the kids show up tomorrow. Unless … you want me to clean up."

"No, go." Riley waved her hand.

She was glad to spend time alone with Geo. He cleared the table while she put the dishes in the dishwasher and cleaned the kitchen. Shannon had taken care of most of the mess earlier, so there wasn't too much to do. With the second bottle of wine, she and Geo retired to the den.

"A fire?" He headed toward the fireplace.

Riley's face lit up. "I love the idea. Can you start, and I'll pour the wine?"

While he went to his chore, she darted to the bathroom to freshen up. Rejoining him in the den, she saw that he had turned on the small, ornate, green lamp at Dad's desk. Her heart turned heavy with grief.

"I'm sorry," Geo said as if thinking he had done something wrong. "I turned the light on so I could see."

"Oh no, you're fine." She smiled to break the sudden sadness. "I had one of those memory moments in time." She brushed away a tear. "I'd get so excited, seeing the light on, which meant that Dad was up here and not in his office."

Geo swept over to her and gathered her in a hug. "If it's any consolation, when I turned on the light, I felt the same way. When we'd come to the den, he'd always turn that light on first."

Riley half-laughed to cover her sob. "Even though he could easily flip the switch to the chandelier, he'd stumble his way over to the light. I noticed you had the other one at your place."

He squeezed her a little harder. "He thought it'd look good on the table. I can bring the light back if you'd like."

"Oh no." That wasn't her intent. "I … I just miss him."

He let go of her, and they sat on the couch. "Come. Let's toast."

Geo handed her the first glass she had left on the coffee table. Riley swirled the wine around to see the legs form on the glass. She placed her nose to the rim and inhaled, getting hints of pepper and cherries.

"Here's to your dad." Geo held up his glass.

"May he rest in peace." She did the same.

He raised his glass again. "And here's to a fantastic dinner."

"Thank you."

"And to good company."

She leaned against the back of the couch and placed her

feet on the coffee table. She noticed he waited for an invitation. "Please make yourself comfortable. Sit back. Relax."

He held up his finger and then left to add another log to the fire, now that the smaller logs started to burn. He returned to the couch. This time, he sat a little closer. The heat from his body radiated toward her, making her want to snuggle into him. She refrained and thought about what she could say to keep her mind off touching him.

"Starting tomorrow it's going to be even busier, more chaotic, with the kids here and Conner."

"If you need a break, don't hesitate to come over." He tipped his head back and closed his eyes. "You can hide out with me."

"I'll probably take you up on that offer." She wanted to run her hands down his neck to smooth out his trimmed beard. For some reason, the short neat hairs looked soft to touch.

"I hope you do."

His thigh touched hers. Nothing else mattered in that room anymore. The pleasure, so simple, awakened her senses. All she could think about was him being so close.

She scrambled for conversation. "How long do you think this will take?"

"What do you mean?" He opened his eyes and turned his head toward her.

"The investigation. Finding out who killed Dad."

"A week. A month. A year. Longer. It all depends on the evidence, if they can charge the person and then how he pleads. After that, if he pleads not guilty, the trial has to take place."

"Uff," she made a noise, not wanting to think about the timeframe. "Finding out who killed him would be nice. Give us closure."

"I've seen my share of crime and gruesome murders. I've been able to push the emotion aside—just do my job. But with Max ..." he shook his head and lowered his eyes, "He was my mentor."

Geo raised his hand and spread his fingers apart, wanting to hold her hand. She didn't hesitate and wound her fingers around his until their hands clasped together. He tucked them between their legs, keeping a tight grip around hers.

"I'm sorry." Riley felt bad for him. In his expression, she saw he grieved as well. Her heart strings pulled toward him.

He emitted a slight laugh. "You don't need to feel bad for me. My loss doesn't compare to yours."

"My dad played a part in your life." Riley blew out a long, slow breath. "You know I'm in charge of his estate."

Geo nodded. "Max had mentioned it a few times." He squeezed her hand. "He said I'd be dealing with you if I didn't stop being so stubborn."

"Stubborn?"

"About my future."

She tilted her head in question.

"If I could see myself staying here. Make the most of my vineyard and grapes. If I wanted to expand."

"What do you want to do?"

Geo let out a short grunt. "I'm not sure if there's a choice

169

now."

"Not necessarily." She pressed her lips together. She shouldn't have said that. It slipped out. He was right. Things could get messy. What if they decided to sell the estate? He'd be out unless the new owner allowed him to stay. Could they write in a stipulation requiring the new owners to lease the property? Or could they sell a portion of the estate?

"Are you selling the place?"

She glanced over at him. He didn't seem upset. "Did someone tell you that?"

"No one, really. It's not too hard to figure out. Your sister has her life in Milwaukee. You live in Arizona. This place would be a pain in your asses to maintain long distance."

Riley frowned. What a depressing thought. She twisted slightly, facing him directly. "You could buy the estate."

Geo laughed. "As I said before, I can't afford it."

"Umm," she said, not liking his response but getting his point. Dad did own a valuable piece of property. If it were sold, she'd be able to buy a really nice house in Arizona.

They stayed quiet, deep in their own thoughts. The fire crackled and one of the logs fell. Geo jerked and leaned slightly to see around the dried flowers decorating the coffee table. He hesitated as if thinking he should add another log to the fire. Instead, he relaxed and stayed with her.

She heaved a heavy-weighted sigh. "I feel so lost

without him here."

"I know." Geo gave her a head hug, placing his on her shoulder and then rising up again. "I do too. I could always bounce ideas off of him. I valued his opinion. I would have done anything for him." He shook his head. "I never saw it coming. Never."

"I hope Detective Torrence can solve his murder right away. Tomorrow, not two months or two years from now, would be nice."

"Even if it means the person who murdered your dad could be someone you know?"

Odd question. But she supposed this was a small town.

"Of course," she said.

"Would you be ready for it?"

She stared into his solemn blue eyes to determine what he meant or if he knew something that he couldn't say. Or did he still believe Conner was involved in the murder? She started to question him when he let go of her hand and sat up. He tapped his palms against his thighs.

"It's late. I better go."

Riley sat up. She didn't want him to leave but didn't feel right asking him to stay either. She feared it would come out sounding too desperate. They took their wine glasses to the kitchen. Geo wanted to say goodbye to her sister, and they found her hunched over the sewing machine.

"See you around." He raised his hand to her.

"You're leaving? Already?"

"Yep."

She got up from the chair and walked over to give him a

hug—so like her sister. People always liked her hugs. They were drawn to her. Geo didn't seem to mind either.

"You can come around here any time," Shannon said and winked at Riley from over his shoulder. "We love your company."

Riley made a face at her sister. She quickly changed expressions when Geo spun around.

They left her sister and walked to the front door.

Geo struggled with his jacket. She helped by holding the sleeve so he could put his hand through it. He placed his black scarf around his neck and turned toward her.

"Remember, you can drop by anytime. Day or night if you need an escape or help."

"Thank you."

Geo placed his hand on her waist. "I mean it."

Riley blushed. His gaze showed the sharpness to the blue flecks in his eyes. He leaned in and kissed her. Full, soft lips danced with hers. A tender kiss. She swayed, ready for more. Their bodies touched, sending a bolt of desire through her. Shocked by the intense desire of wanting him, she pulled away.

Okay, this is bad. I'm falling for him.

"Good night, Riley."

"'Night," she managed to say. With her fingers, she caressed her lips, wishing his lips were still on her mouth. When he reached the driveway, she was able to find her voice again. "Thank you for bringing the wine."

Geo turned and walked backward. "The pleasure is mine."

He smiled, bowed, and turned around again. She watched as he disappeared around the corner of the house and headed toward the cemetery.

In no rush, she closed the door and then leaned against the wall. She replayed his kiss in her head, wanting to enjoy the moment for a little longer. His lips were like a true lover's, wanting to savor the feel, the taste of their mouths together. She wondered what he would be like in bed. She bet he'd be strong, supple, and firm.

When she opened her eyes again, Shannon stood in front of her.

Riley jumped and cried out, more at being caught than being scared by her sister.

Shannon rocked on her heels with a smirk on her face.

"Stop it." Riley tried swatting her sister on the ass, but she moved away too fast as she trotted back to the sewing room.

Chapter 12

Riley woke to the slam of a car door. And then another. Conner and the kids were here. Early. She leaned over and looked at her phone. 11:00 o'clock.

"Shit!" She'd slept in late.

She swung her legs over the bed. The cold floor creaked underneath her bare feet as she headed to the bathroom. The air chilled her skin, more than expected, and her nipples popped against her tee shirt. Last night the news forecasted the weekend to be typical for the fall—a little breezy yet sunny and no thunderstorms or rain. This was like winter weather in Arizona.

The front door opened with a loud bang. The blare of the kids' voices called out for their mom and announced their arrival. She assumed Shannon went to greet them because they were all talking at once. Riley smiled, picturing her sister giving hugs and kisses to each one. It made Riley wonder if she'd be a good mom, be able to handle the chaos of raising a family. Would Geo be great with kids?

She grunted, annoyed for thinking it.

Time to get ready. She'd missed most of the morning and was late.

Leaving the bedroom dressed in jeans and a light blue blouse, she was about to head for the kitchen when Conner's angry voice stopped her. She guessed, hearing Shannon's lowered voice, that the discussion's heat level was more than casual.

Riley hesitated in the hall. The kids were upstairs. Should she go help her sister and break up the conversation? Or go upstairs and say hi to her nieces and nephew? She listened a bit more. Shannon's voice stayed steady and in control. Conner's wasn't so steady. He growled like a dog with its teeth bared. Her sister might need her help.

Damn it.

Her stomach growled. Riley needed coffee and food.

She inhaled a deep breath, braced herself, and then walked into the kitchen like she was oblivious to their argument.

"Hi, Conner." Her voice squeaked as she tried being cheerful.

He glared at her with cold steel eyes. She almost retreated out of the kitchen. Seeing her sister's welled eyes and flushed face, Riley made the right choice. She played dumb to diffuse the tension.

"Those kids are going crazy upstairs. I bet they're glad to be out of the car." She patted Conner on the shoulder as she swept her way toward the coffee maker. "I bet you are too."

Dumb thing to say but it took the focus off Shannon.

He said, "They slept on the way here."

"Ah, another reason for their being full of energy now."

175

She kept her back to them as she grabbed the coffee pot and poured the hot black liquid into the empty cup next to it.

Conner tapped his fingers on the counter. Riley forced herself not to glance over her shoulder. She felt the lasers from his eyes piercing her back.

"I need you to sign these."

She turned to face him as he slid a document across the counter toward her. Riley's heart skipped a beat when she realized what he was asking her to do. "Why?"

"Your father's new lawyer will not talk to my lawyer about a deal Maxwell and I put together."

Made sense to her. She sipped her coffee, trying to be casual. "What deal are you talking about?"

"It's none of your business."

Riley raised her eyebrows. Really? A warning bell went off in her head. She tightened the grip on her mug. "Well, I think it is."

"Your sister and I can handle it," Conner said as he placed a hand on his cocked hip. "It's the lawyer that's fucking with us."

Shannon went for the coffee and snuck in a sideways look as if telling her to be careful. Riley offered a slight nod and then glanced down at the papers. She scanned the document. The Walsh sisters would be giving Conner's lawyer control of Dad's financial dealings.

Huge red flag. Riley sucked in her breath. She tried keeping a poker face, not wanting to blow up—not yet anyway. What was he trying to pull? She took a couple of sips of coffee, giving herself time to think. She then set her mug on the counter so he wouldn't see her hand shake. She said, "Dad's law firm has been great to work with. And I actually think the new lawyer is doing a great job as well." First pitch completed: defend Dad's firm. She took a breath and then threw out the second pitch. "But even if we wanted too, we can't sign those papers. Everything is under investigation, now that it's a murder and not suicide."

Conner's nostrils flared as he stared at her. "What do you mean you can't sign it? Investigation, my ass. You can do whatever you want."

Was he not listening? "Conner, we're not going to make any changes now." She thought of a different tactic. "Besides, we haven't completed the reading of the will."

"You have every goddamn right to do what you want." His hands flew up into the air in exasperation. He took two steps away from the counter and pulled his arms in, crossed over his chest, to think. He looked to Shannon. "When is the reading of the will?"

She turned to Riley.

"I believe it's Wednesday morning … no, afternoon."

Conner shook his head and rolled his eyes as if disgusted with the two of them. "Why in the hell did you wait so long after the funeral?" He opened the refrigerator and pulled out a beer. "I have work to do. I can't be coming back here every couple of days to hold your hands." He pointed the beer bottle at Shannon. "And you need to get home. Take care of your kids."

Tears rolled down her sister's cheeks as she stood

motionless. Riley wasn't sure why she wouldn't defend herself.

"For chrissake," Conner spouted as if he had enough. He pointed to the papers and then walked out of the room.

Shannon brushed away the tears after the room went quiet. Her arms cradled her middle as if she had been punched in the stomach. Riley didn't blame her. Conner's anger surprised her. The depth of it. She had never witnessed him being so snarly.

"Are you okay?" She went over and hugged her sister.

"Yeah," Shannon said in a faltering voice.

The front door slammed shut, making them both jump. Soon the car sped down the driveway. At least they had a break.

"I'm not about to be bullied by him," Riley said and grabbed the papers.

"I hope he didn't take the beer with him."

She glanced up at her sister and laughed. "Having him get pulled over by the cops might not be a bad thing."

"We can't afford it. An open bottle?"

"True."

Shannon left the kitchen. Riley went back to the papers. She verified what she read earlier when speed reading. It was what she thought. He wanted his lawyer to have full control of all finances, including the trust. At the very end of the two-page, small-print document, they were also giving Conner control of selling the estate and handling all business dealings. Fat chance in hell.

"I can't sign this, Shannon," Riley said when she heard

her sister return.

Shannon held the open beer bottle in hand.

"I can't either." She took a swig of the beer. Her sister's expression changed from that of a meek woman in tears to one hard and cold. She set the bottle down. "We can never let Conner's lawyer gain control."

"What's going on with him?"

"I don't know and I don't like it. It's different this time." Her lip trembled, teetering back to the meek side. "He's become a stranger—not the fun-loving man I married."

Riley's heart fell.

Shannon lifted the beer and guzzled half the bottle—so unlike her. She set the beer down, hitting it hard on the counter. She wiped her mouth. "Boy, I needed that."

"I guess," Riley commented, sticking to sips of her coffee.

Staring at Conner's name on the document, she knew he wouldn't give up. He would be persistent about getting her to sign or forcing Shannon to sign. Wait. Riley remembered her sister's signature wouldn't matter. Smart move on Dad's part. Had he known Conner would try to get involved?

"I'm not sure what to do, Riley." Shannon leaned over. "I don't like him this way."

"Neither do I," she said and swallowed hard. "Has he ever threatened to hurt you?"

Shannon shook her head. "Oh no. Never."

What a relief.

"He's a good man." She stared at the counter. "He used to be caring. He used to be loving. I can't let that go because of one bad business deal."

"Is it bad enough that he could lose his company?" Riley tried understanding, wanting to justify his behavior. "Is he afraid?"

"He's obviously not afraid. You saw his anger."

"Toward us. But we don't know what's going on with him."

Shannon blew out her breath, causing her bangs to puff out. "I don't even know if we have money in our checking account. Or savings. He doesn't share our finances with me."

"Ohh, that's bad." Riley cringed.

Shannon shrugged her shoulders. She stood again, grabbed a tissue out of her pocket, and then blew her nose. "He takes care of all the finances. That's what we've been arguing about. I'm trying to get him to tell me what's going on."

"Can you do some digging on your own?"

She raised her eyes to meet Riley's. "I guess I can. I never thought to snoop around. I feel guilty even thinking about it."

"You have a right. This is your life too."

"And if we are broke—I'm okay with it. We'll get through it. Unfortunately, I can't help him if he won't let me."

Riley nodded. "Just be careful."

She picked up the document from the counter. At first, she hadn't planned to do anything with it, but seeing the papers ready for signatures made her nervous. What if he forged her signature? Or worse, forced her to sign?

Gripping the document from the top, she made one straight tear down the middle until she had two parts.

Shannon gasped. "What should I say if he asks?"

"Tell him you don't know where the papers are." She tore the halves again. "I'll be responsible. He can ask me."

Conner would be pissed. No doubt about it.

Chapter 13

Riley was on her third cup of coffee and finished eating two slices of toast. Her head felt better, clearer after all the wine from the night before.

The noise upstairs turned louder. Toys were being thrown around. She looked up at the ceiling and had an idea. "Let's get them outside so they can run."

"I could use fresh air," Shannon agreed. "Sun's out." She checked her weather app. "A little on the cool side, but they'll warm up as they play."

They gathered up the kids, who were more than happy to play outside. The first thing they did was run through the fallen leaves in the back yard. Riley found a rake in the garage and used it to make a pile for them to jump in. The kids screamed and laughed. They stayed in the yard until Elise fell flat on her face as she tried keeping up with her sister and brother. She cried at the top of her lungs. Riley was in flight mode, ready to help, but Shannon held her back. She nodded for her to watch. After two loud wails from Elise, Flynn ran to help her.

"He's such a good boy," Shannon said with a smile, showing her proud mom moment.

"And she knows how to manipulate him." Riley caught how her niece milked it.

They moved on to the cemetery. Riley and Shannon found a spot in the sun to stand as the kids raced around the headstones. They were alone, no other visitors were seeing their loved ones, so they let them explore within the gated community.

Tomorrow they'd be at the cemetery for a different reason. Riley glanced over to the family plot again. They hadn't come to dig the grave yet, which surprised her. Usually the graves were dug on Fridays or early Saturday mornings, even for a Sunday funeral. In a way, she was glad. Soon enough their mom and dad would be inside their permanent resting place.

Now she'd have four people to talk to when needing guidance. As a teen, she would sit on the edge of the family plot, next to her grandpa, and tell him about her problems and worries. When finished, she'd picture Grandpa sitting in his chair and giving her a sympathetic chuckle. He'd say, "You'll find your way, kiddo. Now that you've got it off your chest, you'll be fine. Handle it as it comes."

She needed a conversation with him and Grandma soon. Her troubles were piling up. She needed to get them out of her system—have a heart-to-heart with the dead.

Riley looked over at the house, half hidden in the trees. Mom and Dad's home. Dad loved that house. He loved the land. How sad he lost out, not being able to live a full life and see his grandkids get married and have their own babies.

She wished she'd talked to him more. What were his plans for the future? Did he want to travel? Add a gazebo to the backyard? He mentioned building one before. But no, she'd been too busy at work, always thinking she'd call him back, but some other fire would distract her and make her forget.

"I'll be glad when the funeral's over," Shannon said, bringing Riley back to the present. Her sister drooped as if a weight hung on her chest. "Soon we'll be back to our normal lives."

Riley glanced at her. The way she said it didn't sound too convincing. "What's wrong?"

"Nothing."

"You could've fooled me," she said with a grunt. "I can think of a dozen things that are wrong."

Shannon shoved her hands in her coat pockets. "Can we really go on with our lives like we used to?" She gazed toward her kids but didn't see them as her thoughts were heavy. "How can life be normal when someone out there is guilty of murder?"

Her sister was right. They had a long road ahead of them. She wondered what people in town thought now, if they were gossiping about suspects.

As if reading her mind, Shannon said, "I feel like everyone's going to judge me as if I'm the one who is guilty."

"You haven't done anything wrong." She couldn't say anything about her sister's husband. Different story.

"I can't shake thinking about Conner's being involved

in some way, shape, or form."

Riley asked, "Do you think he knows what's going on, and he's not telling the police?"

She didn't respond. The situation was hard on her. Her face showed signs of stress. Her sister's usual creamy smooth skin was tight and dull. When she spoke, she put thought into it. "I think he's got something up his sleeve. He might have a part in it, but I'm not sure what."

"Did you hear or find anything?"

"I thought about it last night in bed." Shannon scratched her neck. "I learned Dad's cancer was terminal from Conner. He said that Dad told him, instead of me, because he wanted his son-in-law to take care of us. Conner made a big deal out of it, which I thought was odd. Why would he do that?"

Riley tried her best to help. "Had he been misinformed? Or did he assume?"

Shannon gasped. "Or … did Conner lie? Did he want us to believe Dad had terminal cancer to justify the suicide?

"Jesus Christ," Riley said under her breath.

"I'm just ill." Shannon held her stomach. "I can't stand this—not knowing. He's my husband. I love him. I'm stuck—no torn—between wanting to believe he's innocent yet, at the same time, cringing when he's around, in case he was involved."

"Oh, Shannon." She didn't know what else to say. Instead, she moved closer and put her arm around her shoulders. Her sister swayed. Riley guided her over to the bench and they sat.

What a mess. "I just want you and the kids to be safe."

She shook her head. "I don't think he'd do anything to

185

harm us."

Riley played with her sister's hair, pulling it into a pony tail and then letting it go. The tresses flowed around her fingers like silk. "What the hell do you do to your hair? It's so soft and shiny."

Shannon laughed. "I rinsed it with beer."

"I wish I could get mine shiny."

"Yours is hopeless. You got Dad's hair."

"Screw you." Riley nudged her sister. She was too tired for another round of deep conversation. She guessed her sister felt the same way.

The rumble of a diesel engine and then the sight of a yellow digger caught her attention. As she predicted, the tractor turned in to the cemetery. Riley hit Shannon's side with the back of her hand and nodded her head toward the road.

"Delana. Flynn. Elise," Shannon yelled as they stood. "Let's go. Now."

The two older kids ran toward them. Both had bright rosy cheeks from running around the older plots. They were giggling as they raced each other.

"Elise," Shannon called out.

The little one sat on her knees on top of a grave. She seemed mesmerized by the headstone, lost in thought.

"I'll go get her," Riley said as the tractor drove close to the fence line to avoid them. "Come on, Elise. Are you hungry?"

She shook her head. Her bottom lip went out as her eyes rounded with sadness.

"What's the matter?" Riley crouched down.

"Delly said Maggie died being sick. Really sick."

Maggie. Riley glanced at the headstone and read the name.

Magdalene E. Scott

She brushed away the wet leaves covering her birthdate.

Born March 29, 1892 - Died March 30, 1902

Ten years old. Riley shuddered.

"Come on, sweetie. Mommy's waiting." She held out her hand for Elise to take. Her niece accepted, placing her chubby hand in hers.

"I like her," Elise said as they walked out of the cemetery.

"Who?"

"Delly's friend."

"Delana's friend ..." Riley tried thinking about whom she referred to.

The dots connected.

Maggie.

Of course.

Great. Now Elise saw ghosts as well. Shannon wasn't going to be happy.

Later, as the kids ate soup and grilled cheese sandwiches, Riley stood with her sister at the counter and nudged her. "I know who Delana played with at the cemetery."

"Who?" Shannon grabbed another half of a grilled cheese sandwich from the plate and began nibbling on it. "You mean Maggie?"

Her sister waited for more information. Riley couldn't help but smile.

"Well, who is she?" Shannon became impatient.

"Maggie is a ghost."

She snickered. "A ghost?"

"The gravesite that Elise sat at … Maggie's grave."

Shannon stopped eating mid-bite. She gave her the are-you-kidding-me look.

Riley raised her hand. "Born in 1892 and died in 1902."

"Oh shit." Her sister finished chewing the food in her mouth so she could talk. After drinking water from her glass, she said, "Delana told me that Maggie was her best friend—ever." She laughed. "And she told me that her friend wore funny clothes. And boots—not tennis shoes."

"So how come we never saw her?" Riley asked. "We grew up here. Why now?"

"Maybe she was and we didn't know," Shannon suggested. "There were a lot of unexplained noises around the house." She made a face. "But why would my child connect with a ghost?"

Riley couldn't resist. "You warned your kids about talking to strangers. Did you forget to warn them about ghosts?"

She giggled. "I guess so. I'll add it to the list."

Shannon's back turned rigid. She shoved the last of her sandwich into her mouth and began cleaning up. Riley didn't catch on until she heard the front door open. Her sister must have heard their car drive up to the house.

"Can we go watch the tractor?" Flynn asked as he tried to see the digger from the kitchen window.

"No," Shannon said and moved him away. "He's busy now and doesn't need to watch out for little kids."

"I'm not little." He scowled.

"Not now. Can you take Elise upstairs and read her a book? She needs a nap."

He started to protest again, but she stopped him. With drooped shoulders, he went to help his younger sister out of the chair. He had her follow him out of the kitchen.

"You go help too." Shannon shooed the older one off.

"Hello, girls." Conner came through the door.

The smile on his face and the change in attitude shocked them both. They stood, not knowing what to say. Riley glanced over at Shannon as she continued to watch him with a cautious eye.

He held two bags of groceries in his hands, and he set them down on the counter. With his hands free, Conner swept over to Shannon and gave her a quick kiss.

Her sister wiped her lips with the back of her hand when he moved away. Riley's eyes rounded in disbelief. Did Shannon realize what she had done? Luckily, Conner didn't see. What a situation. If Conner was guilty, she had a right to turn against him. But if innocent, she'd need to regain her trust in him. Could she?

Conner opened his arms to the both of them. He sang while twirling his fingers. "Our troubles are going to fade away."

Was he on Plan B? Hopefully it was better than Plan A, the one giving his lawyer control.

"Well, what is it?" Shannon asked when he waited for them to become as excited as him.

Conner straightened and announced, "I have a buyer for

the house."

Riley swallowed hard. She glanced at Shannon, who looked at him, dumbstruck.

He grabbed his wife's shoulders and squeezed them. "A company that I've been working with is interested in buying the place." He kissed her on the forehead and then beamed as if he had answered all their prayers to everything. When Shannon continued to stare at him, he looked to Riley. "Don't you get it? I found a buyer. We can dump this place and settle the estate in no time."

Riley tightened her hands into fists as the anger pumped through her body. How dare he?

The fire rose to a near-explosive level. She took three short breaths to stay in control. This was not his house to sell. This was their dad's house. Her house. Shannon's. She snapped. "Who said we want to sell?"

"Yeah, right." Conner brushed her off. "You can't handle your own life. How do you expect to manage this place?"

Just like that, he dissed her. Riley's face burned as red as her hair. She came forward, ready to punch him.

Shannon quickly stepped between them. The way her jaw set and her eyes warned said to back off. Riley forced herself to ease up. She shook out her hands to release the anger boiling inside her. Let her sister deal with him. The asshole.

"Let's talk about this tomorrow." She placed her hand on Conner's chest. "I'd like to get the funeral over. Agreed?"

"Of course. Of course," Conner said and gave her a hug. "I'm sorry. I'm pumped, excited. Let's talk later." He glanced at Riley and then back to his wife. "Alone."

She wanted to ask him more questions. Why would a company be interested in buying the estate? People were meant to live here and make happy memories. Unless, of course, the company thought to tear everything down and develop it. But why here?

Riley squinted at Conner as he put away the groceries. It didn't make sense. This place was too far from I-94 for businesses to be interested in the property. She didn't think the small town would want to expand, especially with River Falls not too far away. Houses? Or something else?

She started to ask Conner what he was up to when Shannon gave her another stare-down. She respected her sister's wish and let it go. Instead, she grabbed a bottle of red wine from the rack in the corner and left the kitchen.

Time to get out of the house. She didn't want to leave her sister alone with him, but he was in a good mood. And his parents were coming in this afternoon for the funeral. They'd be staying with them at the house.

After putting on her coat and boots, she ducked her head into the kitchen again and motioned for Shannon to call her if needed. After getting the nod, she went outside toward the cemetery. Riley stopped when she saw the tractor in the family plot. She noticed it was Henry who was there to dig Dad's grave. He offered a sympathetic smile and a weak wave to acknowledge her presence. She waved back and hurried away. She couldn't watch.

Pivoting to the back of the yard, she found the path leading to the hunting shack. Now seemed right to visit Geo. She needed time to think about how to have a conversation with Conner so he didn't blow up at her. To be fair, she should hear him out first and then decline the offer.

Dad would be furious if he knew what was going on. The thought of Conner going out to find a buyer … This was her problem, not Conner's. If they decided to sell, she'd find the right buyer. And poor Shannon—she didn't need tension between her and Conner while trying to get ready for the funeral. She also had to play host to her in-laws. Not to mention, she needed time to mourn. The estate and proposed sale could wait for a few days.

The hunting shack was quiet. No lights on in the house. She stepped onto the porch and peeked into the window. Geo wasn't home.

What a fucking day. And to make matters worse, she forgot the corkscrew to open the wine.

Now what?

She decided to text Geo.

I'm here.

In less than a minute, he responded. *Where?*

Your place.

Be there soon.

She sat on the rocking chair off to the side of the porch. The cold seat soon warmed underneath her as she rocked back and forth. The floor creaked in rhythm to her feet pressing down. The sound comforted her and reminded her of when she'd sit on her grandma's porch as they drank iced tea. Back then, the two of them would listen to the birds sing and the water lap against the shoreline on the lake.

Yes, Wisconsin was a beautiful state. Each day the leaves brightened with color. The rolling hills and woods created a perfect picture of country living. When was the last time she actually sat down and let time pass? Why didn't she do this in Arizona?

As she continued to rock, the tension in her shoulders relaxed. Living here, at the estate, wouldn't be so bad. The small town was a perfect place to settle down. The winters were brutal, especially now since she hadn't lived there in a while. But she missed seeing the ground sparkle white after a fresh coating of snow. Even on super cold days, the crisp air could be refreshing, especially when the sun shined and no wind blew.

Geo's heavy-duty Ram truck turned into the driveway. The gravel crunched under the tires as he drove slowly toward the shack. He waved when he passed the front of the house and then parked near the side.

He frowned as he came up the steps. "You look cold."

Her face and hands were chilled by the wind shifting directions, coming from the side. She said, "I'm not too bad."

"You should've gone inside." He leaned in to give her a quick hug before opening the door.

No key. Unlocked. Riley laughed, forgetting she was in the middle of farm country. Few people remembered to lock their houses or cars.

"Are you all right?" Geo asked as he let her in first. He saw the wine. "Uh-oh. What happened?"

"Nothing. Really. I needed a break." They removed jackets and boots.

She made a beeline for the kitchen and set the wine down on the table.

"Do you want me to open the bottle now?" Geo cocked his eyebrow as he followed behind, keeping pace with her.

She turned red, realizing he may need to work more or that he may have other plans. "I can come back. I've … you're busy …"

"I'm fine. Today my schedule's open."

"Okay." She felt a little better. "In truth, I don't want to deal with Conner or his parents right now. They're coming in this afternoon or sooner."

"Conner will be back?" His interest peaked as he grabbed the silver corkscrew out of the kitchen drawer.

"He is back." She found the wine glasses in the glass-doored cupboard and set two out on the table. "The man irks me."

"How come?" Geo popped the cork.

"I don't know." Riley lowered her eyes, unsure if she should tell him. Selling the house would mean he'd have to leave. She tapped her fingers against her cheeks as if it would help to soften them from the cold. "I think my emotions are on overload."

"Understandable." He kept glancing over toward her. He seemed concerned yet allowed her time to figure it out.

"I saw Henry and his tractor," she blurted.

Geo made a low noise from his throat. "A hard one to take in?"

"Yeah," she said with a long breath. She folded her arms and rested her elbows against the table. He sat to the side of her, ready yet patient. He didn't touch his glass of wine, waiting for her. Riley gazed into his eyes; he was ready to listen and be with her. She started with one of her first concerns. "I'm not sure if I'll be able to handle tomorrow."

"The funeral or all the people?"

"Good point." She hadn't thought about it that way. She hated the thought of burying her dad and mom, but then it would also give her relief and the ability to move on. Having to be at her best and talking to relatives and strangers was a different story. "I'll say the people. I have no idea what to say to them. What to do. How to act. I had strangers come up to me at the grocery store. I didn't know what to say or how to deal with it."

"Did you swear at them? Piss them off? Ignore them?"

She laughed. "Of course not."

Geo placed his hand on top of her arm and gave her a reassuring squeeze. "You'll be fine. I promise."

She offered a weak smile, not believing it.

He raised his glass and said, "Here's to a very beautiful woman."

Riley bowed her head and used the wine glass to cover her face. Geo's face changed to a sour expression. He checked the label on the bottle.

"What's the matter?" Had she done something wrong?

"Really?" He motioned for her to turn the bottle around.

She read the label. A cheap brand of wine. Riley laughed. "Sorry, I just grabbed."

"Did your dad have that in his house?"

"I can't say for sure. Shannon could have brought it with them."

He squinted his eyes and puckered his lips after another taste.

"I won't care if you pour it down the kitchen sink," Riley said.

"I tell you what, I'll suffer through drinking bad wine if you tell me what else is bothering you."

Good one, she thought. "You obviously know me."

"Not as much as I'd like to," he said, looking over his glass at her.

His attraction toward her showed in his eyes and smile. Riley's heart skipped a beat. Could she fall for him? Nope, not with her leaving. However, her thoughts didn't match what she felt inside. She never intended to let him into her heart but he managed to find his way in.

Riley took a sip from her glass. She agreed the quality of the wine was poor. Geo's wines were crisp, smoky, robust, and pure. Just like him.

He nudged her leg as if reminding her that she had some explaining to do.

"Well," she said while gathering her thoughts back to what bothered her. "My sister is concerned about Conner. She's wondering if he had anything to do with the … with Dad."

"Why is that?"

She told him about Conner's anger, the papers he wanted her to sign, and the all-over sense that something wasn't right. Geo's face turned white when she told him about her brother-in-law wanting control over the estate.

"I'm glad you didn't sign any papers." He took a large gulp of wine.

"I have no intention of signing anything over to him or anybody else," she assured him. "Dad left me in charge, and I plan to follow his wishes."

"It's a huge responsibility."

"Yes." The word came out sharp.

"What else happened?"

Riley swallowed hard. He'd find out sooner than later. She should be the one to tell him. "So, this morning, like I said, he was furious and stormed out of the house. When he came back, a few hours later, he'd changed to being happy, like his life would soon turn around." She shifted in her chair, sitting up straighter. "He announced to Shannon and me that he found a buyer for the estate. A company, not a person. A company."

Geo stiffened. His eyes squinted a bit but he kept a poker face. He took it well, but then he had been in a line of work that required him to keep his emotions in check.

She continued. "He was pretty excited about it."

"And you?" He tested her. "How do you feel about selling?"

"I'm pissed. I wanted to argue with him, mainly because he wants to manipulate his way into controlling what happens."

"What did you tell him?" He smoothed down his trimmed beard. His fingers pressed against his neck.

"Shannon had us drop the subject, not wanting a fight. She asked us to wait until after the funeral to discuss it." He tilted his head to the side as if trying to figure out why. Riley helped. "She wants him to stay in a good mood and behave for the funeral."

Geo nodded, understanding. He lowered his eyes as he played with the wine glass, turning it with his fingers, taking time to think.

She imagined that he processed the new information like a detective, trying to piece all the parts together. "What I don't get is why he'd want to sell to a company? It's not like this is prime land or has easy access to the freeway."

He tilted his glass toward her. "Maybe he owes the company money."

Riley's eyes lit. "Oh, I never thought about that."

Conner was in financial trouble. If they sold, Shannon's portion of the money would probably cover his debt.

"Oh boy," she moaned. A whole new bag of worries flowed through her. If he expected to use the money for his debt, Shannon would be left with nothing. An ice-cold shiver raced through Riley.

"Come," Geo said and held out his hand. "Let's get you warmed."

She let him lead her to the living room and to the couch. He found a blanket and placed it over her.

"Mind if join you?"

"Of course not." Riley remembered she had imposed on him. "Wait. I should go. You need to work."

"It's Saturday." He sat down next to her and pulled her in as if to make sure she didn't have another excuse to keep them apart. "Relax. I can tell your nerves are shot."

She leaned back and he winced. Riley shot up again.

"It's fine. Lean back. Snuggle in."

"What happened?" The pain continued to show on his face.

"My shoulder is acting up. I overdid it yesterday. I could use this too."

Riley relented and melted into him as he wrapped his arms protectively around her.

"You comfortable?"

She nodded. He had no idea how comfortable he felt. She could do this every night.

Her eyes widened. Should she be doing this? She was about to change her mind when he said, "At times I get numbness in my shoulder due to nerve damage. You pressing against it with your back actually helps."

Riley doubted him, but she stayed. He kept a tight grip around her waist, and she held his arm close against her. His breath was like a warm summer breeze against her neck. She closed her eyes and focused on his touch. How their bodies melded together. How clean he smelled—fresh with a hint of mint.

Her phone went off. She jumped. Geo jumped.

They had fallen asleep.

Riley dug her phone out of her back pocket. A text. Shannon asked if she would be coming home for dinner.

"I need to go." She shifted. With reluctance, she peeled the blankets off.

"Everything okay?" Geo rubbed his eyes. He looked around as if to gather his bearings.

"It should be. Conner's folks are there. Dinner."

She tried getting up but sank down again.

"Sorry." She regained her balance.

"My pleasure."

Riley raised her head. Geo's face came close to hers. He didn't waste time and took advantage of their closeness. His head leaned in. Too late for her to do anything but to kiss him.

Warm. Tender.

When his tongue slid into her mouth, Riley brought her hand up and placed it against the back of his neck. Everything inside her woke with excitement. Geo responded as well. He pulled her hip into him. She felt his urge, wanting more.

Her phone went off again.

Geo backed away, ending the kiss with a few light kisses as if to seal the first one in place. He smiled and said in a low, husky voice. "I know. You have to go."

"Back home." She couldn't get any other words to form. She gazed out the window to pull herself together. The sun sank toward the tree line. Night came faster these days.

"You want me to walk you home?" he asked when she put her boots on.

She shook her head. "I'll be fine."

Riley didn't want to leave. She wanted him. The sweet

spot between her legs ached with desire, wanting to be fulfilled.

This is so wrong.

He pulled her back, grabbing her arm. He kissed her again with more hardness, as if wanting her to know he felt the same way.

"See you tomorrow?" She wanted to make sure he would be at the funeral.

"Of course."

Riley turned and disappeared down the path into the woods.

Chapter 14

Everyone seemed to be in a good mood when Riley returned from the shack. If anyone looked in from a window, they'd see a happy, normal family. No one would guess a murder had taken place or the husband was in near financial ruin. As they say, looks could be deceiving.

Riley waited to greet Conner's parents until they sat down at the table. She didn't know them too well, but they were decent people. They had gained weight and aged a bit more since the last time she saw them. Two years ago? Mrs. Doyle always wore a smile on her face. Mr. Doyle was like Dad, always dabbling in projects. Both were retired teachers.

Shannon served stuffed chicken breasts, mashed potatoes, and butter-roasted carrots for dinner. They needed to eat a hearty meal before tomorrow's funeral. The food tasted fantastic. Riley kept to herself. The conversation focused on the parents and the future trip they were taking to Germany. After dinner, Riley excused herself to work in Dad's office. She took her dessert with her.

She sat in Dad's leather office chair. The slice of pecan pie with the generous dollop of whipped cream called her name. Conner's mom brought seven pies for tomorrow and one for tonight's dessert. If she remembered rightly, Mrs. Doyle's pies won ribbons at the local fairs. Riley smothered the top of her slice with the whipped cream before taking her first bite. Heaven.

Halfway through, Riley set the plate on the desk and opened the secret compartment. She placed her hand deeper into the drawer and found Dad's appointment book. She flipped through the pages. His last entry was on the morning he died. No, wait. She turned the page to the next week. He scheduled a meeting with Satchel Casing, Inc. Conner's name was written underneath it. Dad wrote the word "front" underneath his name. Enter through the front door? Another name? She grabbed her phone and opened the browser to look up the company. They used a very basic website. She scrolled down. They made iron and steel casings to fit around engines and motor components. The company didn't look like much. Was it one of Conner's investments?

Footsteps came down the stairs. By the sound, her sister was coming to visit. Riley slid the appointment book into the secret compartment next to the keys— the ones she still had to figure out what they were for. She didn't want to tell Shannon about the item, in fear she'd say something to Conner.

"Hey." Shannon stopped in the doorway.

Riley grabbed her plate to finish her dessert. "Awesome pie."

"I hear you. I'm glad I don't live too close to them or else I'd be fat. That woman loves to bake." She leaned against the doorframe. "I thought I'd come check on you. Make sure you weren't avoiding me."

"I'm not avoiding you," Riley assured her. "Come sit."

Shannon left her spot by the door and walked over to the chair on the opposite side of the desk. The "visitor" chair. They always liked to sit there because it was made out of calf skin with the hair, spots, and all. Later in life, they learned it was fake, but Dad had told them how the cow stuffed himself inside the chair. She plopped into it and automatically petted the hair. "Hopefully we're not crowding you out. I should've asked whether it was okay if his parents stayed here with us before inviting them."

"I'm fine with it," she said. "I'm giving you a little space and making sure I don't get in Conner's hair. I don't think he'll be as angry or act out with his parents being here. I actually think it's a good thing they're staying with us."

Shannon pulled her hair back, away from her face. A habit she did when stressed or tired. "Well, we're all set. I called the funeral director and everything is ready to go. The flowers were delivered. In fact, I saw the van there, at the stone building, this afternoon. After the small service, we'll walk through the cemetery, behind the casket, and in a procession to the plot."

"Sounds great. And then, I assume, everyone will be coming over here afterwards."

She nodded. "Once the kids pick up the toys in their room, the upstairs will be done. Main level, we only need to clean the bathrooms since the maid came on Thursday. And down here, no one's allowed."

The maid. Another person Riley needed to deal with. Another life in her hands. Luckily, the woman owned the company and cleaned other places as well. At least she'd be able to pick up another client after Riley sent her a notice stopping service.

"The time's here, Riley. Mom and Dad are going to be together."

"Six feet under."

"Who would have thought we'd be at this point in our lives." She leaned forward in the chair and stared at her hands. "I thought they'd live forever."

"So did I."

They sat in silence for a moment before one of the kids screamed upstairs. Riley believed it was Elise, the youngest. Soon she began to cry, calling out for Mommy.

Shannon dropped her hands to the side arms and pushed herself out of the chair. "Duty calls."

"Be a good mommy."

After she disappeared from the room, Riley opened the secret compartment again and took the appointment book out.

Satchel Casing. She flipped back to previous weeks. No mention of the name, but there were a few loose pieces of paper between the pages.

She caught Geo's name at the end of August. Two o'clock meeting with him, Dad, and his lawyer. She went back a few more pages. Two more dates. Both of them were crossed out. She made a mental note to ask him what those appointments were about. Otherwise, nothing else seemed to be out of the ordinary. But then, she wasn't a detective.

Thinking of him, Riley called Detective Torrence and told him what she found. He'd be over within the hour. She figured tonight worked better than tomorrow for giving him the book. She placed it in an envelope, not wanting any of the loose papers to fall out and be missed. She set it on the desk.

Upstairs, she went into the kitchen to wait for the detective. She did a quick glance around to get a feel for the mood. Elise clung to her mom's leg, Flynn drank a glass of milk at the table, and Delana sat at the island with her colored markers and coloring book. Riley was glad Conner wasn't around. She heard him talking in the living room and guessed him to be on his phone. The TV blared in the den. The distinct ticking of a wheel came from the TV.

Ah, yes. Wheel of Fortune. His parents must be watching the game show.

The night before the funeral. No fanfare, only normalcy.

"Auntie," Flynn said. "Auntie."

"Yes?"

"Will you play a game with me?"

"What would you like to play?" She hadn't spent a lot of time with him. He had an hour before bedtime.

"*Trouble.*"

"Go get it. We'll play here."

"Yesss!" He pumped his fist and then ran upstairs.

A flash of headlights shined through the window.

Detective Torrence's car pulled into the driveway.

Shannon looked up from her phone in silent question.

"Detective Handsome."

"You knew he was coming?" Shannon smoothed her hair down.

"I asked him to."

"Oh." She straightened her blouse. "Why?"

"I have a book for him." Riley waited by the door. He left his car running as he got out and sprinted to the door. She opened it before he could knock, hoping Conner wouldn't hear they had a visitor.

"Thanks for coming," she said and invited him inside.

Detective Torrence glanced about as if looking for someone else. She guessed Shannon by the way he adjusted his coat. Riley gave him a treat by motioning him into the kitchen so he could see her. The detective's eyes lit up. She was right about his interest in her. What surprised her more was to see her sister smiling back. She liked him. No wonder she primped. Granted, he was super attractive—no denying it. With the issues she had with Conner, the detective could be a fantasy lover for her. An escape.

Riley smiled as the two exchanged pleasantries. She then remembered the reason for his visit. She left the two alone to go downstairs into the office. She grabbed the envelope with the appointment book.

"Here it is," she said, returning to the kitchen. She handed the envelope to him.

Delana tugged on the detective's coat, grabbing his attention. She rattled off questions at him. "Are you a cop? Do you wear a uniform? How come you're not wearing one now?"

Detective Torrence answered all with a smile. When she gave him a break, he asked her what she was drawing. She showed him the picture. He looked closer, seeing something.

"That's a pretty picture."

"Not really."

"How come?"

"It hurt my grandpa."

The kitchen turned quiet. Riley stepped closer to see what she had drawn. She braced herself, thinking it would be the rope around his neck. It looked more a red rock.

Detective Torrence glanced toward Shannon. She picked up his silent signal. "Delana, how'd it hurt Grandpa?"

"It cut his cheek."

"Ouch," Shannon said. "What is it, sweetie? A rock?"

"No," she lifted the paper to look at her work. "A sleeve ring."

Riley repeated the words in her head. A sleeve ring …

Shannon figured it out. She raised her hand and pointed to her wrist. "A cufflink?"

"Yeah, a cufflink." Delana patted her wrist.

"How do you know it cut him in the cheek?" Detective Torrence asked.

"It scratched him. Right here." She ran her finger down the side of her face and across her cheek toward her nose.

Detective Torrence coughed to cover his surprise.

"Can I have the picture?"

"Let me sign it." She took a blue crayon and signed her name before giving it to him.

He turned serious. "Did you hear someone talk about what happened?"

"Maggie." Delana pointed to another picture she had drawn of a girl in pigtails and a pinafore dress. "She told me."

He looked to Shannon. Her eyes were as big as two balloons and her face flushed. When she didn't respond, he looked to Riley.

"She's a permanent resident of the cemetery."

His expression blanked, not understanding.

"A ghost," Riley mouthed and moved behind Delana so her niece couldn't see her hands floating out to her sides.

"What's going on in here?" Conner's sharp tone broke their conversation.

"Mr. Doyle." Detective Torrence greeted him. He didn't offer his hand.

"You're here on business, I assume?" Conner's chest puffed out. His hands went to his pockets.

"Yes, I am."

Mr. And Mrs. Doyle joined them. Their curiosity kept the detective busy when they asked him about what happened, if there were any suspects, or if he had any clues to help with the case. He stayed patient and answered their questions. When the older couple began arguing a point between them, the detective took the opportunity to excuse himself and hurried out the door.

Riley wished she had a chance to talk to Detective

Torrence about the drawing before he left, but she understood why he made his escape. The Doyles would keep him there longer than he intended.

"What did he want?" Conner asked her sister.

"Auntie gave him an envelope," Delana said as she moved to a blank piece of paper to draw on with her markers.

Riley cringed, hearing the words come out of her niece's mouth.

Conner twisted his head around. His eyes bored into her like lasers.

She debated but then decided to tell him the truth. "I found Dad's appointment book. I thought they might be interested in it."

Conner's face turned red. The veins in his neck popped. He glanced at his parents and then checked himself as if knowing he had to stay in control with them around. He took two hard breaths and then asked, "Why? Did you find something in it?"

"No, nothing out of the ordinary that I could see." Curiosity overtook her. "However, he had an appointment with Satchel Casing. I suppose I should call them. Tell them what happened to Dad."

"No," Conner stated. "I can do that for you."

"Why? Do you know who they are?"

"Yes." He was blunt and offered no other explanation.

Riley refused to let it go. She stepped back, creating more space between them. "Who are they?"

Conner glanced to her, to his parents, and then to

Shannon. They were all waiting for his response. "They are the ones wanting to buy the estate."

She wasn't expecting his response. A dozen questions raced through her head. Why would Dad be interested in selling? Why would a company that made steel casings want to buy the place? Were they working out a deal?

As if reading her mind, Conner said, "Your Dad scheduled a meeting with them before his death. He planned to sell the place."

Riley's head spun. She leaned against the wall for support. Why didn't Dad tell her or Shannon? He would have talked to them about it. She should have found paperwork or notes in his office. Unless his lawyer handled it? But he was dead too.

Son of a bitch.

Riley became more confused each day.

"Auntie!" Flynn's anger showed that his patience had timed out.

She shifted her attention to him. He had set up the game at the table and waited the entire time. She couldn't say no.

Chapter 15

The minute the alarm went off on her phone, Riley's heart fluttered, fast as a fly's wings.

Funeral day.

She went through the motions of getting ready. She showered, straightened her hair, put on makeup, and then dressed in a simple A-line dress—black with a white collar. At first, she put on pumps with three-inch heels but remembered she'd be walking in the cemetery. She switched to her lacy black ankle boots.

After breakfast, she and Shannon went over to the stone building at the cemetery to meet the funeral director and make sure that no last-minute details were needed. While he talked to her sister, Riley glanced around the room. She hadn't been inside the place since she was a little girl. Stained glass windows lined the bare limestone walls with two sections of wooden folding chairs. The altar was raised and to the side. Dad's casket was centered below the wooden cross hanging from the back wall. Surrounding him were the dozens of flowers and plants sent by relatives, friends, and business partners. Her nose tickled from the scent of so many blooms confined to one area. She did like how the roses, lilies, carnations, and other flowers brightened the stone building and made the place less tomb-like.

Riley walked up to the closed casket and placed her hand on the cold steel. Inside Dad rested in his best suit, the one they'd taken to the funeral home a few days earlier. Mom, in her urn, was placed next to him on a table. She'd join him later.

A picture of the two of them, taken a few years before Mom died, sat on the table next to her urn. The photo had been enlarged to fit an 8 by 10 frame. She picked up the picture and smiled. If she recalled, they had been at an Irish wedding. His hair was red and curly, while her long, wavy locks were dyed auburn. Both were smiling and relaxed. A happier time.

"You ready?" Shannon came up from behind and stood next to her.

What a loaded question. Seeing Mom and Dad buried? Finding out who the murderer was? Taking care of the estate? Figuring out what to do with her job, especially now that she lost the promotion? Being with Geo? Finding love?

"I guess," she responded.

Shannon placed her hand on the casket as well, almost in the same spot Riley had recently placed hers. Her sister smiled. "He gave us a good life."

Riley's throat constricted. The words barely came out when she said, "Yeah."

Her sister hugged her. They stood in front of Dad, having their moment with him before turning to the pink urn on the table.

"I can't believe her ashes are still intact, safe in the urn."

"Hey," Riley said, taking some offense to her comment. "I know how to take care of Mom."

Shannon squeezed her shoulder. "And how many times were her ashes in the room when you were *doing* it?"

At first, Riley didn't get it. She then laughed. "Once. Twice."

"You're bad," Shannon said and wiped a tear that fell to her cheek. "Come on. Let's head back to the house."

At the house, they shut the doors to all the side rooms on the first floor so visitors would stay in the main areas of the house. Aunt Pam and Cousin Deb arrived first to watch the place and keep people where they should be. As promised, Detective Torrence provided two plain-clothes detectives to help keep everything under control if needed.

They weren't home long before having to gather the children and head to the cemetery again. People were arriving and standing outside the stone building as the front doors were locked. Riley looked at Shannon, wondering if they would all fit into the small space.

"We'll be fine," her sister said and hooked her arm around Riley's. "Dad wanted it here."

How true.

Riley glanced about. The kids were skipping through the cemetery. The older Doyles followed behind them. "Where's Conner?"

"He'll be coming. He's on a phone call."

Today they should all be focused on the funeral.

Conner didn't need to be on the phone. Riley shook her head with annoyance.

They had half an hour. They slipped into the side door that the caretaker had unlocked for the family's use. Shannon brought a doily she found in the sewing room, one that Mom made, and placed it under the urn. More flowers had arrived since the morning. Riley took the time to read the cards to see who sent them. Sikerte Investment Firm, where she worked, sent a beautiful arrangement of different-colored carnations. She was touched by their thoughtfulness. Gary must have pushed them into sending something. They weren't a bad company to work for, they just drove their employees into the ground the hard way.

She missed Gary. He gave her sanity checks when she became stressed at work. It seemed like a lifetime ago since she'd been there. She'd call him later on.

The pastor entered the stone building, and Shannon went to greet him. They approached the casket. Her sister called her over. The pastor stood on the other side of Dad and said a prayer, words of comfort for the family. Riley lost it. Tears fell like rain down her cheeks. The sorrow overwhelmed her as she realized the finality of the day. She would never see him again. Never get his advice.

Shannon swept over and hugged her tight. She cried as well. They stayed together as the rest of the family joined them.

"What's wrong, Mommy?" Elise whimpered and tugged on her mommy's dress.

In a hushed voice, Mrs. Doyle tried explaining why Mommy and Auntie were sad.

Shannon released first to pull herself together. Riley grabbed a tissue from the side table and blew her nose. A hand pressed against her back. She smelled the familiar scent of musk and grapes. Geo was there. His arms replaced her sister's.

"How you holding up?"

She shook her head. She couldn't say anything yet; her throat was still constricted from crying. He kept his arm around her and she felt better for it. Today was a day to be strong and be with those who came to pay their respects.

Geo squeezed her hand when the first person came through the door. He stepped back but stayed in proximity to her. Shannon stood next to her so they could both talk to people as they arrived. Conner stayed at the back of the room. He should be next to Shannon, giving her support. What a jerk.

By the time the pastor made his way up to the altar, ready for the funeral to begin, the stone building had swelled with people. Riley, Shannon, her family, and the Doyles sat in the front row. She glanced over her shoulder to find Geo sitting two rows behind. He winked at her. The pastor began with a prayer and words of hope and encouragement for all as they mourned the loss of Maxwell Walsh. When Shannon's turn arrived to read the first lesson and brief eulogy, Riley snuggled Elise in her arms.

Her sister spoke with poise and grace. A few times she stopped and used a tissue to wipe her eyes. Her sister did quite well getting through her part in the service. At the end, she thanked everyone for coming and stated how much Dad would be missed. Riley lowered her head to keep from crying. She stared at Elise's black patent shoes. Her niece fidgeted and then scooted back over to her mom when she returned to the pew.

· At the end of the service, the pastor, the funeral director, and an assistant stood in front of the casket with their backs to the attendees. They blocked their view as the funeral director opened the lid. The pastor said a prayer and placed Mom's urn in beside Dad. The lid closed as quickly as it opened. Tears fell. Noses were blown. A few sobbed and a child sang at the back of the stone building. That's what they needed to do more of— to sing and celebrate versus crying.

The pastor said another prayer. Elise's tiny hand slipped into Riley's. The little girl gazed at her with big hazel eyes as if trying to figure out why her auntie cried so much. She doubted her youngest niece would remember today. Even Delana, sitting on her other side, patted Riley's shoulder in comfort. Being consoled by two children made her cry even more. Shannon offered more tissues.

Riley gained control when the time came for the pallbearers to stand next to the casket. Two uncles, two aunts, and two brawny cousins wheeled the casket down the aisle. She and Shannon walked behind. They held each other up; all eyes were on them as they passed the attendees.

Outside, as they waited for the pallbearers to pick up the casket, Riley inhaled a deep breath of fresh air to clear her head. She continued to cling to Shannon to make sure neither one tripped across the uneven lawn toward the family plot. The six pallbearers struggled with holding the casket. She looked at her sister, wondering if they should help. Instead, Geo and another man stepped in to grab the casket in the back.

Where did Conner go? She glanced about. He had disappeared again.

The wind blew, cooling her face as they stood in front of the casket, now in place and ready to be lowered into the grave. Shannon carried Elise in her arms. Riley moved Delana and Flynn closer to her to keep them warm. They were glancing about the cemetery, especially Delana. She fixated on a spot next to the tree. Maggie?

After the final prayer, Riley placed a kiss on Dad and Mom's casket. Her last goodbye. But this wasn't a goodbye. She'd come back and talk to them, like she did with her grandparents. She'd share some whiskey and wine. Tell them her troubles.

She pulled out a red rose from the arrangement on top of the casket and gave it to the first attendee. One by one, she and Shannon handed out single flowers to those who said their last goodbyes.

The hardest part was over.

A few people mingled or wandered about the cemetery to find other graves. A handful left, finding their cars and driving off. The majority continued on to the house. Geo appeared and took her hand, tucking it under his arm to walk with her. Delana hung out with them. She waved back to the family plot. Riley looked over. A girl with brown pigtails and a pinafore dress waved back. As quickly as she appeared, she disappeared.

Riley bent down to whisper in her niece's ear. "Was

that Maggie?"

Delana nodded. She glanced back one more time and smiled before running ahead of them to catch up with Flynn.

Geo lived up to his promise of taking care of the food. A large spread graced the kitchen. Smaller tables of finger foods were set up in the living room and den. Coffee, water, tea, wine, and whiskey were available to drink. Geo walked straight to the table near the drinks. Riley and Shannon joined him. He poured out two shots of whiskey.

"Here's to getting through the service." He handed one to her and one to Shannon.

Without words, they clicked the glasses and downed the shots. The hard liquor burned Riley's throat and warmed her insides—exactly what she needed.

While the wake and funeral were about mourning, the gathering at the house celebrated his life. The attendees came to tell her and Shannon how they loved Max. He was always their go-to person when they needed any type of help. Mom had been too. Their parents kept to themselves, but they were also there when anyone needed anything.

Riley snuck into the kitchen and grabbed a chicken salad sandwich. Conner came from behind and stood next to her. As she took a bite of food, she looked twice at her brother-in-law, noticing the second time his face was flushed with anger.

He spoke through thin, closed lips. "Why are you letting that guy hang on you?"

"Who?" She glanced around the room, wondering who he meant.

"Geo." He motioned to his target with a sharp glare. His

lip turned up in a snarl.

"Why not? He's been a big help." She spotted him near the doorway, looking handsome in black pants, blue shirt, and tie. He was talking with a neighbor.

"He's a suspect, you know. He could be the killer."

She cocked her head back, surprised at his comment. "Geo? He was fine with Dad."

"Are you sure about that? Ask him about the deal that pissed Max off."

"What deal?" she asked him instead.

"You haven't run across any papers yet?"

"No." She didn't recall seeing anything about a deal or papers with Geo's name on them. But then, she didn't see any documents with Conner's name either. Did Dad have another place where he kept important papers? She remembered the dates in the book that had Geo's name crossed off. No one—neither the lawyers nor the detective—had questioned her about him, like he was a suspect. "Why do you think it could be him?"

'Why do you think he's being so … on to you like a dog in heat?" Conner said, like she was an idiot. "He wants your dad's money. Not you. Are you that stupid?"

His words stabbed into her back like a knife. She never thought about being suspicious of Geo. He cared about her—something she wasn't used to in the other men she dated.

"He's the one who has a motive for killing Max. You're falling into his trap." Conner let out a laugh and then walked away.

Riley put down her sandwich. She grew hot and had an off-balance feeling that turned her insides around. She slipped away from the living room and found solace in her bedroom. She shut the door and kept the lights off so no one could tell she hid within her room. She even closed the blinds in case someone decided to peek through the windows.

She stayed still, sitting on her bed as her mind ran wild. Geo a suspect? He couldn't be. Or could he? She thought of him with a different set of eyes. He had a lot at stake—staying at the hunting shack, growing a vineyard on Dad's property. He was settled here and had invested a lot of money into the place. If they sold, he had the most to lose.

Geo. A killer.

Riley didn't see it. He was warm, kind, and protective. Yet, he did have a slight uneasiness to him that had concerned her before. He didn't talk much about his past, being in the military or in his career as a police officer or detective. He had been shot twice as a good guy—not a bad guy.

The pit grew in her stomach. She rubbed her head. Riley liked him. She loved being with him. He made her feel comfortable, safe, and at home. The men she dated were about the sex and being curious if redheads were truly red in all places—if the curtains matched the drapes, so to speak. Geo wasn't like that. He was a gentleman, looking after her.

And the other guys, those wanting a relationship—they were more about themselves. The world revolved around them and their careers. They were too busy getting their own success stories in order. A few dumped her. The majority she dumped. Again, Geo was different. He took a step back, changed his life, and did what he wanted. He made life simple for himself, and she respected him for it. Or was he fooling her, like Conner said?

A light tap on the door made her jump.

"Riley?"

Geo. Her breath caught in her throat.

Do I open it? Ignore him?

She wasn't sure if she wanted to see him. Her insides—head and body—were a tangled mess. Let him in. Don't let him in.

She had to find out. Riley stood up, went to the door, and opened it. She stayed in the room, blocking the entrance and not allowing him in. He sensed something was wrong by the way his forehead wrinkled with worry.

"Why didn't you tell me about the deal you were working on with my dad?"

Geo stepped back and fumbled for words.

His hesitation wasn't making Riley feel any better. The door was ready to shut, and he knew to talk fast.

"Max and I were working on a deal so I could buy the house—the shack, not this house—and the property my grapes are on. Maybe even more land. I offered a price but your dad didn't like it. Yes, we argued, but it's not what you think."

She didn't care. She slammed the door on him. He should have told her about their deal from the start. If Dad and he were arguing that meant Dad wasn't happy with him.

"Riley!" Geo pleaded from the other side of the door.

The tears fell. She hated crying, was so tired of it, but she couldn't help it.

"Riley," he growled with frustration.

"Go away. I don't want to talk to you."

She failed at relationships, picking the wrong men. Why would he be any different?

Chapter 16

Shannon knocked her signature two quick raps on the door. Riley raised her head, coming out of her stupor. She sat on the floor with her back to the bed, knees up and head down. She had either fallen asleep or was too dazed to know how long she'd been in the position. She glanced at the clock on the nightstand. Fifteen minutes had passed.

Her sister didn't bother to wait for a response. She jiggled the door knob, using the pin to unlock the door. She popped her head in to search the room and saw Riley on the floor. "Are you all right?"

"No." She sniffled.

Shannon sat down next to her and folded her skirt in to make sure the fabric didn't get too wrinkled. She stretched her legs out and leaned her head against the edge of the bed as if glad for the break from everyone in their house. "It's been a rough day, hasn't it?"

"It's not over yet," Riley said, thinking about all the other stuff they had to deal with.

"People are starting to leave. I can't believe how many

people Dad knew. They were coming in like ants to a picnic."

With a tissue, Riley wiped underneath her eyes to remove the smudges of black mascara. She looked to Shannon and waited. Her sister was there with a purpose.

She said, "Geo told me you were upset."

"Did he tell you why?"

"No, but Conner did. I guess he saw Geo leave and said it was about time. He seemed pleased that he'd left."

"Did he say why?"

"Not why but he did say Geo could be the one who murdered Dad. I don't get why though …"

"Geo and Dad were arguing about Geo buying the shack and the property he's renting. I asked Geo if it was true, and he couldn't deny it." Riley shredded her tissue, the pieces falling to her lap. "Why didn't either one of them tell me about the sale before? Here I thought Geo and Dad were friends. Geo said they got along great." Riley refrained from crying again by drawing in a deep breath. Her voice cracked when she exhaled. "He lied to me."

"Hold on." Shannon raised a hand. "Friends argue. Sisters argue. People argue all the time, especially about deals and money. He may not have lied."

"He's a suspect."

Shannon turned to her. "How do you know?" When Riley didn't respond, she asked, "Did Conner tell you that?"

"Think about it. He has a motive."

Her sister let out a sigh. "No, you think about it, Riley. It's been an emotional day." After a pause, she slapped her hands across the top of her thighs. "But now, people will be looking

225

for both of us. We need to be out there."

She was right.

"Let me refresh my makeup and make sure my eyes don't look like a racoon's mask."

"Put some color on those cheeks as well." Her sister rose from the floor. "You're pretty pale, even in your little barricade."

"Shannon …" Riley caught her before she walked out the door. "Are you sure Geo isn't out there?"

"No, he left." She focused on the ceiling to think about it. "I believe it's what Conner meant by him leaving." She brushed off the back of her skirt and then straightened her clothes. "I'll make sure he's gone."

"Thanks." Riley waited until she slipped out the door before getting up from her spot. A pile of wet tissues was on the floor, so she gathered them up and put them in the garbage bin in the bathroom.

Once the last of the attendees said their goodbyes, the house turned quiet. Conner's parents went to Dad's room—where they stayed while visiting—to take a nap. Shannon retired to the den to watch a movie with the kids, and Conner disappeared once again. Riley remained in the kitchen to clean up the mess.

She glanced about, surveying the dirty bowls, plates, and cups. She filled the dishwasher and then gathered the fine china to wash by hand. If they had thought about it sooner, they could have given an item to each guest. Let them take something home as a remembrance of their parents.

"Oh well," Riley said to herself. "Too late now."

As she washed a pink bowl, she smiled. Mom always put their favorite fruit salad in that bowl. Who would be the keeper of the piece now? *Shannon? Me?* She glanced about at the other dishes she'd washed. There was only a small number they'd want to keep. Would she have room for the items in her apartment? How in the hell would she get them back to Arizona? Rent a truck? She was already out of personal days at work. And what about the other stuff? The furniture, the knick-knacks, the junk in the garage, the car ...

She'd probably inherit enough money for a good-sized down payment on the house she wanted. If they sold the entire estate, she'd be able to buy an even better house. She could be a suburbanite in Phoenix with a ranch-style house and a decent yard with a pool.

Funny how it worked. She'd get her home. A dirt yard with cactus. That's what she'd get. Her spirits fell.

Riley gazed out the kitchen window as the orange and red leaves twirled around in the air before floating down to the yard. The grass was trampled where everyone walked from the cemetery to the house, but the lawn still looked healthy and thick. She did miss how green the summers were in Wisconsin and how blue the lakes were as they sparkled in the sun. But soon she'd be leaving.

The reading of the will was on Wednesday, and they'd sign whatever papers were needed. Mr. And Mrs. Doyle were leaving tomorrow, and they would take the kids back to Milwaukee so Delana and Flynn wouldn't miss school. Conner would leave Thursday night or Friday—missing the charity ball—and Shannon would leave on Sunday. Life would go back to normal for them.

She still needed to make her plane reservation. She had to call Gary and let him know when she would be in the office—back at her old normal job.

Riley wasn't looking forward to going back. Even with the chaos here, she felt relaxed and less stressed. Of course, she wasn't running around ten to twelve hours a day like she did working at the firm. Now she had a chance to breathe.

"Auntie," Delana came into the kitchen. She opened the cupboard but couldn't reach the shelf. "Can you get me a cup?"

"Sure, honey." Riley picked out a green glass and set it on the counter. "What do you want? Milk? Water?"

"Can I have root beer?"

"You got it." She pulled out a can from the refrigerator and popped it open. The fizz bubbled out from the top. "I'm glad I was able to see Maggie today at the cemetery."

Delana nodded as she watched her pour the root beer into the glass. Her eyes lit as the idea came to her. "Can I make a float?"

Riley stopped pouring. "Sure."

She checked the freezer and found the vanilla ice cream, placing the container on the counter. She then searched and found a taller glass to use. After making the float, she slid the foamy mixture over to her niece.

Delana's eyes grew and she licked her lips. "Mom never

lets us have a treat before bedtime."

"Well, you have time. It's still early." Riley sat down next to her. She took the smaller glass and added a scoop of ice cream for herself. "I haven't had one of these in years."

"This is good," Delana said and showed off her foamy moustache. "Thank you."

Having her niece to herself, she decided to ask about Maggie again. "Is your friend always alone?"

"No, a man is sometimes with her too."

"Her dad?"

"No. He takes care of the cemetery. Leo's grandpa."

Leo? She bet she meant Geo. "I think I've seen him there too."

The man in the hat with his head always down.

"I'm going to miss her."

"Maggie?"

"Yep. I like her laugh."

Riley smiled. "I've never heard her laugh."

Delana tried to imitate it and then started giggling.

Shannon came into the kitchen and stopped. She surveyed the two of them sitting at the center island. "What are you drinking, young lady?"

Delana pulled the glass toward her as if trying to protect her treat before Mom could take it away.

"I let her indulge," Riley said.

Shannon let it go as if too tired to argue or care. She went to get herself a glass of water.

Delana leaned closer to her aunt. "She's sad."

"Your mom?"

"No, Maggie."

"Why?"

"She doesn't know what's going to happen. If she'll lose her home."

Riley wrinkled her forehead in confusion. "Why would she lose her home? How can you lose a cemetery?"

Delana frowned. "No, silly, Maggie lives here."

"Oh." Riley's eyebrows rose. "It's been Maggie making all the noises in the house?"

"She likes to play upstairs."

Now the noises made sense. As a little girl, Riley often thought someone else had been in the room with her. She was right. "Tell me, why is she sad?"

"If the bad guys come, we can no longer be here. She won't have a place to stay."

"That's not good. Everybody needs a place to stay."

Chapter 17

A hard frost settled on the lawn the next morning. The bustle of getting Shannon's in-laws and the kids ready to leave and trying to clean up from yesterday's mess happened at the same time. Riley stayed in the dining room to do a thorough cleaning, picking up what they missed from the day before. She was sidetracked and started to look at what items needed to go.

Two antique hutches stored the crystal bowls and knickknacks Mom collected. A buffet table hid the fine china and silverware behind walnut doors. They had a lot to go through—pack, sell, or get rid of. When would they get the chance to come back and go through everything?

And the table could seat twelve people. No way would she have a place big enough to keep this table. She doubted if Shannon had the space in her house either. Riley sat at the table, which was usually covered with a gold table cloth when guests came for dinner. She liked the bare wood instead and being able to see the thick legs with the fancy scroll work. Running her fingers across the top, she felt every nick and bump—each one had a story.

Their house was full of memories. And ghosts, per Delana.

What did she mean by Maggie not being able to live here? What did the ghost know about the bad people? Who were the bad people?

Craziness, she thought.

She spotted the ceramic figurine of a little girl with a flowing yellow dress in the hutch. Riley stood and went over to open the glass door to take her out. She always liked this one, especially how her brown hair flowed down her back. Shannon liked the girl wearing a pink gown with her hair styled in a bun on top of her head. Would they keep the figurines together or each take their favorite?

Riley glanced around the room at the different items. They had a lot of decisions to make.

"Daunting, isn't it?" Shannon asked after entering the room.

"When did Mom and Dad accumulate so much stuff?" Riley set the figurine back in the hutch and closed the glass door.

Shannon laughed. "That's what happens when you stay in one place for years. Instead of getting rid of it, they shoved it aside to make room for more."

"Maybe we can take what we want and sell the rest with the house."

"We'd still need to go through everything." Shannon tucked her hands in her back pockets and stared at the room like Riley had minutes before. She clapped her hands together as if remembering why she came in there. "The kids will be leaving soon if you want to say goodbye."

"I do."

They left the dining room and went to the kitchen where the kids waited, bundled in their jackets. Each one carried a backpack full of fun things to do for the trip to their grandparents' house.

Riley gave each one a big hug and kiss, starting with the youngest. She loved Elise's rosy cheeks. She'd miss her pattering about the house and slapping her bare feet against the wood floors. Next came Flynn. He pushed away, not wanting auntie germs. Even so, she'd miss playing board games with him. And Delana ... a beautiful, smart girl. Riley wished she had time to take her niece shopping and do some girlie things together.

When would she see them again?

She hated goodbyes.

Riley gave Delana an extra squeeze.

"Don't be mad at him," her niece whispered.

"Who?"

"Leo."

"Who told you I'm mad at Geo?"

"Maggie."

She should have known.

"He really, really likes you," she said with her hand cupped over her mouth so only her aunt could hear.

Riley stuttered, not sure how to respond. "Oh, d-does he now?"

"The man with Maggie thinks you should marry him. He likes you too."

"Okay, that's enough." Riley straightened, not wanting to hear anymore. She nudged her niece toward the door.

After getting them outside and into the car, the Buick drove off. Their little hands waved from the back seat.

Shannon stifled a sob. Riley placed her arm around her sister, knowing her heart broke at being away from her children. Riley was going to miss them as well. For her, she wouldn't see them for a long time. She tried calculating when she'd be able to take her next vacation. Six months from now. Too depressing to think about.

For the rest of the day, she did laundry and helped Shannon sift through the craft room. They learned Mom liked "things." Their Mrs. Pack-Rat stored extra fabric, clothes, coats, and old curtains in her room.

"Curtains." Her sister held up a ball of pink fabric.

"From our bathroom, growing up." Riley recognized the material.

"Why didn't she throw them away?" She refolded the curtains and tossed them in the thrift store pile before picking up the next item in the storage bin. A long scarf with white fluffy feathers. "Oh, I like this."

Riley made a face. "You plan on wearing the scarf?"

"No." Shannon placed the item on the table next to the sewing machine. "I can use these for your costume."

"Well … okay." Riley became concerned. "Am I going to be stared at all night?"

"As being one of the most beautiful women in the room." She flashed a smile.

"With you being the other?"

"Of course." She laughed.

Riley found a decent-sized box and transferred the thrift store items into the cardboard container. When finished, she set it next to the other five boxes lined up by the front door.

Conner passed by and she asked him if he could help and take them out to their car.

Curious, he skimmed through one of the boxes. "Nothing of value in here."

"They will be for someone needing an almost new coat or dress."

He seemed happier now that the funeral was over. After loading the car, he asked Shannon if she needed help dropping them off. She took him up on the offer, and they left before he could change his mind.

The house turned quiet. No noise upstairs. Now Riley had time to work. She went downstairs to the office and sat at the desk. She tapped her pen against the blotter. Why wouldn't Dad keep anything on those deals with Conner or with Geo? She glanced about the room. The office was very old-school with the bookshelves, the leather chairs—including the cow chair—and the dark wood panels. No place for storing additional papers. She stood again and went around the room to peek behind the pictures. No hidden safes.

What did she need to focus on now?

Geo's lease.

They had a couple of months to figure out what to do before they'd have to give him notice to vacate. Better sooner than later with the wine harvest completed for the season. For her and their situation, selling the estate would also make it easier, even if they needed to split the land and houses. She tried remembering how much land Dad owned. Two farmers rented from him. She guessed fifteen acres each. Geo said he rented ten acres. The house was on five acres, making it forty-five acres. She thought fifty. Oh yes, the apple orchard. She had forgotten about the section of trees.

Thinking of apples, her mouth watered. She loved going to the small orchard, strolling through the rows of trees and picking out the fruit for baking and eating. Dad had once thought about selling the apples as a side business. A place where people could pick their own. She forgot why he didn't go through with the plans. She always liked the idea.

She wondered if apples still grew on the trees. At this time of year, Mom would make her special apple crisp.

Riley tossed the pen on the desk. Nothing was getting done in the office.

She closed it down and went upstairs. The day turned out to be sunnier than expected, a good reason to get some exercise and take a walk, check out the orchard.

The direction she walked placed her in view of the shed where they found Dad. Seeing the yellow tape, she hesitated. From the house, the area was hidden behind the trees. Riley found herself drawn to it. She stopped at the tape that fenced in ten feet around the red building. The grass was trampled outside and inside the tape perimeter. She wondered what type of evidence the detectives found. Red roses leaned next to one of the trees that was tied with the yellow tape. The flowers curled in, starting to wilt.

Someone from the funeral might have visited the area.

The shed would have to go.

A shiver ran across her arms. She tried to figure what she felt inside. Numb? Sad? Nothing she could pinpoint. She refused to associate him with the shed and its being his last place alive. Turning around, Riley left the taped area and turned on the path, again toward the orchard.

She wasn't going in the direction of the hunting shack, but the rooftop of Geo's place peeked out from over the hill. Further up the path, around the hill, she glanced over to check for signs of Geo's truck or his being home.

Pushing him away tugged at her insides. The day of the funeral had been too high with emotions, like Shannon had said. She regretted acting out and telling him to go away. If she'd been thinking straight, she'd remember the police didn't name him as a suspect in the case. If so, Detective Torrence would have questioned her about him. However, as much as she wanted to apologize to Geo for her behavior, she was still mad at him for not telling her about the sale. He could be trying to get close to her for the place rather than a true relationship with her. She shoved him out of her mind, not wanting to think about him.

The apple trees had grown about a foot taller and wider since the last time she visited. Each row carried different apples, but she couldn't remember the names. Dad kept a list somewhere in his office. She walked up and down the rows, surveying their health. A few branches hung close to the ground. Some had split and broken. All in all, with some grooming, the trees would look good. Her foot rolled on a half-chewed apple. A few others were the same. She couldn't tell what type of animal feasted on the fruit.

Riley stuck to the middle of the orchard, finding a tree with an abundance of apples hanging like red Christmas ornaments from the branches. She picked four apples and stuffed two into each coat pocket. Taking off her hat, she dropped another six into the makeshift bag. She headed back to the house.

Shannon and Conner were home. The car still ticked as the engine cooled. Riley entered through the back door. She dumped the apples from her pockets and hat to the counter. One apple fell to the floor. She couldn't find it.

Her boots left splotches of dirt on the wood planks, making a muddy trail. She went to take them off before her sister yelled at her. Riley then grabbed a wet rag and wiped the mess off the floor. She found the apple next to the pantry door.

Back on track, Riley needed the apple corer.

Holding the first apple, she pressed down on the tool. The slice didn't go through all the way so she helped it along. Pushing too hard, one of the sharp edges sliced her finger.

"Damn it," she cried out when seeing blood.

Pissed, she tossed the corer into the sink and then pressed her finger into a napkin to stop the bleeding.

She peeked. The size of the cut was halfway across her index finger, and it continued to bleed. She went to the bathroom and found a small bandage in the medicine cabinet. No one would appreciate blood in their apple crisp.

As she turned into the hall, she noticed the light on downstairs. Riley thought she turned it off. After taking care of her finger, she went downstairs. She stopped when she saw the office light glowing, turned on as well.

I know I turned them off.

Tiptoeing, she walked toward the door to see who was inside the room. She heard shuffling and the side chair shift from someone bumping into it.

Someone is in there.

A few papers shuffled, but not at the desk. She tried remembering what other papers were scattered about. A few bills were on the corner table, a couple of old newspapers on a chair, and a letter from an aunt had fallen to the floor near the bookcase.

Careful not to make any noise, she moved closer. The floorboard creaked underneath her weight.

Shit.

The person inside did a quick shuffle. Riley had no choice but to walk in as if oblivious to what was going on or give any inkling she had been lurking in the hall. Taking a quick breath, she bounced into the office.

"Oh!" She hoped she acted surprised. "Hi, Conner. I didn't know you were in here. I thought I left the light on. I didn't realize you were down here."

He stood in the corner of the office. He held the newspaper in his hand.

"Riley," Conner said. "I came down to find something to read."

239

"Newspaper?" She tilted her head. "Isn't that from a few weeks ago?"

"Yeah, I noticed." He turned the folded paper over. "I was hoping for today's."

He tossed the paper down on the table.

Riley's eyes narrowed. What was he searching for? "I stopped the paper soon after getting here."

"I suppose," he said with a half chuckle. "I guess I'll go upstairs and use my computer."

They went upstairs together, and she turned out the lights as they went. Shannon stood in the kitchen examining the apples.

"Where did you get these?" She looked at Riley.

"From our apple trees."

Conner slipped away, going upstairs to their room. Shannon gave her a questioning look.

"I found him in Dad's office snooping around."

"For what?"

Riley shrugged. "No clue. He made up something about wanting to read the newspaper."

Shannon wrinkled her nose. "He doesn't read the newspaper."

That night they ate funeral leftovers and apple crisp for dinner. Conner left the house five minutes after eating. He informed Shannon, as he grabbed his keys, that he'd be at the bar.

"Doesn't that bug you?" Riley asked after he shut the door behind him.

"What?" Shannon asked.

"That he didn't ask you to go?"

Her sister's gaze flicked upward. She shook her head with annoyance and said, "All day I listened as he explained how we must sell this place. How we couldn't afford to maintain two homes. How you'd be back in Arizona, making me do all the work."

Riley stiffened.

Shannon ignored her reaction. "So, does it bug me that he left? No."

She excused herself to work on their costumes.

"I wouldn't leave you to do all the work," Riley shouted after her.

Her sister waved her hand as if to say "whatever."

Fine. Riley headed downstairs to see if she could figure out what Conner wanted in Dad's office. She turned the light on and headed for the desk. She stopped and changed her mind. She sat in the side chair, off to the corner, where Conner had been snooping.

She looked at the table next to her. A lamp, a stack of books, Dad's reading glasses, a crossword puzzle, and a pen. Nothing out of the ordinary. A thin layer of dust coated the top of everything. She placed her finger on the burl wood to wipe off the corner and then she noticed a line of polished wood that ran along the edges of the books. Conner must have moved them.

Leaning over, she grabbed the top book. The red book didn't come up. Shifting in her chair for a better angle, she tried the second book and found it to be attached to the third.

What the hell?

The stack of books was heavy to pick up from where she sat. Riley stood. Examining the stack more closely, she discovered they weren't real books. All had gold-lettered titles on the binder. The bottom book, and largest one, looked like a volume from an encyclopedia set. The middle one was based on a psychology theory, and the small red book was titled *The Red Shoe*. Books no one would pick up to read—or at least, she wouldn't.

Riley carried the books to the desk and then placed the stack in her lap when she sat down on the chair. Turning the stack to the side, she found a small crack between the top and second book. Her curiosity pumped up. A newly discovered secret box.

She did a quick glance around the room, wondering what other neat things were hiding about. Did one of the bookshelves turn into a secret room? She wouldn't put it past Dad to make another treasure cove behind the walls.

But first, the pretend stack of books.

Riley traced her finger around the crack. No clasp on the outside. She checked the other sides, feeling for any bumps. She flipped the stack over, taking some care with the weight heavier than expected. Nothing on the bottom except for a piece of tape to seal a tear near the corner. The tape was clear, not old and yellow from age. With care, she picked at a corner of the tape and peeled it off. A leather strip opened and revealed a lock.

Sweet.

Now where was the key? Riley drummed her fingers

across the red book. She needed a small key that fit into a thick hole. She bet it was old and ornate, like the books. Her eyes popped.

The key in the desk.

She placed the books on the floor and then placed her hands on the desk, pressing down to open the secret shelf.

The security key in the desk had the right circular shape. Her heart skipped faster. Was this the place—like a safe—that held Dad's important papers? She guessed it would hold a few papers, but not many.

The key fit into the hole. She turned it. A slight click. Nothing.

She pressed the key in deeper, jiggling it. She tried again.

The crack between the red book and the theory book popped open.

"Bingo," Riley called out, happy with her discovery.

Sitting on the floor, she tugged and opened the top. She peeked inside to find two folders. Riley curved and twisted the folders to get them out of the opening. She did so with care, not wanting to tear the papers as she struggled to pull them out. Peeking inside again, she found a few more small pieces of paper and rolled up money. Ten stacks of one hundred-dollar bills. The money would be counted later.

Riley opened one of the folders while smoothing out the curled ends. By the worn sides, the file had been in and out of the books on a few occasions.

A legal document. A land agreement. No, a sale of a partial plot of land—numbers that identified the piece of property with the county. A section of Dad's land with Geo's name printed all over the document.

Riley's breath caught in her throat.

Is this what Conner referred to? The paper was definitely a sales transaction. After reading the legal description of the property, she found the sale price on the second page. Ten acres of land and the hunting shack. In typed print: $100,000.

Her mouth dropped. What the hell was he thinking? Even she knew the price was dirt cheap. Geo couldn't be dumb enough to believe Dad would sell it for that little. Grant it, he renovated the shack, but still ...

She flipped through the next two pages. At the bottom, Dad's notarized signature filled in the line. He signed the document, not Geo. Strange. Riley's nose wrinkled. What did that mean? If Geo wanted to buy the shack and land, he'd have signed a purchase agreement. This wasn't a purchase agreement but a sale.

Riley rubbed her forehead, confused. She decided to check out the second file, hoping that would help solve the mystery of the sale to Geo.

The set of papers was torn in half. Interesting. Her curiosity grew. She placed the top and bottom sections together. Again, legal jargon. Instead of Geo's name written all over the document, this one had Conner's name. She frowned. He wanted control over Dad's finances. Wait ... Satchel Casing? The business name caught her attention. Her eyes widened. She flipped the first page of both halves to continue reading.

Conner owned Satchel Casing. Co-owner of the

company. Who was the other partner? She thought back to when she looked up the business on the internet. Conner's name was not on the website.

Riley pulled out her phone from her back pocket and searched for the website again. No names were listed. She went back to the document halves and flipped to the last page of both. Conner signed the document. Dad had not. In large letters where he was supposed to sign, he wrote "front" across it. She re-read the first page wondering if he didn't like the front page and that's what needed changing. Nope. No cross-outs.

Is that what they had been arguing about? She didn't understand why Conner would want to take charge of Dad's finances. Just like now, he kept bugging her and Shannon for control.

Riley shook her head. Dad wouldn't do this. At all. First, second, third, or fourth page of the tiny print was all bullshit. Dad had been adamant that she take control of the estate.

"Riley?" Shannon's voice called down. "Are you down there?"

"Yes, I'm here."

"Just checking." After a moment, she called out again. "I'm going to bed."

"Okay. Good night. I'll be doing the same shortly." She glanced at her watch. Eleven o'clock.

"Just so you're aware, Conner should be coming home soon."

"Thanks."

Her footsteps turned away.

Riley left the rolled money and the other small pieces of paper inside the secret safe. She kept the folders out. When she went to place the books back on the table, she noticed the top looked half-clean. A person, like Conner, snooping around would know she'd found something.

Damn it.

She shouldn't have brushed off the dust from the table. Surveying the other dusty pieces of furniture, she came to one conclusion—she had to dust the office.

An hour and a half later, tired and sore, she stumbled her way up the stairs.

The lights of Conner's car flashed in the driveway. Riley scooted into bed with the papers in hand before he pulled to a stop near the house.

Chapter 18

Riley fidgeted in her chair. They sat in the conference room at the lawyer's office—Shannon, Conner, and her—as they waited for the lawyers to show. They were on the second floor of the old brick-and-mortar building in downtown Hudson. She gazed out the window at the tiny flakes of snow that fell from the sky. She hoped they didn't stick to the ground, making the roads slippery.

What an unusual October. The events of the last week, her emotions and decisions, and the weather were totally bizarre. And now they were there—for the reading of the will.

She followed Shannon's eyes to the picture of Hudson, an old logging town built in the 1800s. Today the town had quaint shops, restaurants, and bars—not to mention that it was next to the St. Croix River. In high school, Riley would always hang out on the beach at the end of the dike. They'd swim or wade to the island next to it, depending on the river's height. A few times they'd stay for the weekend, camping in a tent overnight.

Conner whispered something to Shannon, bringing Riley back to the office. She wished he weren't there, but her sister was adamant that he be present. Or, she figured, he'd insisted on being there. Thinking about it, he did have a right, being part of the family. He also had business smarts, most of the time.

She was more concerned about the events after the reading than the actual reading. As far as managing the estate, Dad wanted her in control. She didn't know if Conner was aware of it or how he would react. Riley glanced at Shannon, who sat straight in her chair and stared at the same picture Riley had been studying seconds before.

The night Riley found the papers, she listened from her bedroom as Conner fumbled around in the kitchen. In the morning, he had left a mess—the bread uncovered, butter smeared on the counter, and pieces of lettuce on the floor. At least he placed the knife and plate in the sink. As far as she could tell, he hadn't gone downstairs.

She called Detective Torrence the next morning to tell him about the papers. He offered to come over to collect the folders, but she decided to take them to him. She didn't want Conner or Shannon to be suspicious. Again, she kept her findings a secret. Not that she wanted to, but Riley didn't want her sister to accidently leak information or have to tell him what she knew. As a faithful wife, she told him everything if asked.

The lawyer, Mr. John Endellright, a stocky man in his late fifties, made his entrance. She liked the new lawyer. She'd talked to him on the phone a few times, and he was very knowledgeable with trusts. They'd met him in person when he came to Dad's funeral to pay his respects.

In the conference room, they all shook hands and then he set his laptop computer on the table, opposite them, and opened the lid.

"Can we get this done?" Conner asked as they continued to wait for another partner of the firm to arrive. He tapped the top of the table with his fingers. His restlessness carried to Shannon. She fidgeted in her chair, which was so unlike her.

"Mr. Lavonne will be here shortly," Mr. Endellright stated.

Riley kept still. Her hands rested on her lap. She stared at the cup of coffee in front of her, noting the fancy gold lettering of the firm's name. The coffee was too hot to drink and she needed to let it cool down. She should have asked for cream and sugar too.

The lawyer offered some small talk as he typed on his computer. She assumed he entered his password—twice. He then tilted his head back to peer at the small screen through bifocals.

The noise outside the conference room made them turn their heads. Not one but all three partners who owned the firm entered through the frosted-glass door. If Riley remembered, based on the billboard along I-94, they were two brothers and one cousin. Gray suits, black ties, and polished black shoes. One overweight, one with a gut, and the other thin as a rail. The three offered their condolences to her and Shannon. They shook Conner's hand but acted a bit distant toward him. They sat on the same side of the table as Mr. Endellright. Once settled, the thin partner gave the nod for their lawyer to begin.

"I will give both of you copies of the legal will. What I plan to read today is one that has the same content but is short, simple, and in plain language. Both documents were signed by your father, Maxwell Walsh."

Silence filled the room. Riley realized he waited for their consent to begin. "Please, continue."

Most of the reading was information Dad had already discussed with her and Shannon about dividing the furniture and personal belongings. The one surprise was learning Dad rented two safety deposit boxes at the bank he'd been a member of for years. Based on the reading, the boxes stored both their grandma's jewelry and Mom's jewelry. Shannon controlled the safety deposit boxes, but she could not remove or disburse the contents of the safe until one year after his death.

"Who has the keys?" Conner asked.

"We do," Mr. Endellright stated.

"The jewelry belongs to us. Not you," Conner growled.

Instead of responding, the lawyer continued with the instructions as described in the short version of the will. Within one month of the reading, the lawyer and Shannon would inventory the jewelry, now stored in the safe, and verify that the contents matched the list attached to the will. One year from his death, Shannon would get the keys and could then divide the jewelry between the sisters if all affairs were in order.

Conner made a noise of disgust. He swung his leg over his other one and stared at the back wall.

Riley frowned at his behavior. Jewelry was jewelry. It was no big deal to keep the pieces locked in a safe for a while. They didn't have it before and wouldn't need it now.

She thought it was clever and fair. If she turned into a bitch or became irresponsible with Shannon's portion of the estate, then her sister could keep all the jewelry instead of sharing with her. Mom acquired quite a collection, but Riley thought they had sold it years ago, seeing Mom wear only a few pieces in the last year of her life.

"So," Conner said, returning to the conversation. "What you're saying is Shannon gets the jewelry and Riley gets the rest."

"That is not what he said," Riley snapped back, annoyed he hadn't been listening.

The lawyer cleared his throat, repeated what he read minutes before, and then moved on. "For the trust, all financial holdings that include investments and property are the responsibility of Riley Catherine Walsh. She will manage the trust and disburse funds as needed. Riley will also have full control over financial bank accounts, personal belongings, and any other items not carried forward within the trust. Again, the stipulation is that no major change would be made until one year from his death."

"Bullshit!" Conner's voice rose in anger. "He can't dictate that nothing changes for a year."

"Yes, he can," Mr. Endellright said and remained calm. "Everything is stated here and our firm will carry out the will. Mr. Walsh has been a client of ours for over thirty years. We understand his wishes clearly."

Conner glared at the man.

Dad never said anything to her or Shannon that they'd need to wait for a year before making any major decisions. In a way, it would prevent them from doing anything irrational. But then, it was going to be a major headache trying to manage the estate with her living in Arizona and Shannon living in Milwaukee.

"Don't worry, honey," Conner said to Shannon. "We can contest it."

Her sister stared at her husband with widened eyes. Her throat moved as she swallowed hard.

Riley sympathized with her sister. She had been put on the spot by her husband. The lawyers stared at them with some nervous apprehension.

"We have no issues," Riley said, speaking for Shannon as well. "Neither of us were aware of the jewelry or the stipulation of holding steady for one year. We can manage it."

"There's a pending sale on the estate." Conner leaned over Shannon to glare at Riley. His face turned beet red. The veins on his forehead were ready to burst.

The lawyers glanced at one another. The overweight partner said, "A sale?"

"We do not have a pending sale," Riley assured him.

Conner pronounced each word. "We have a sale."

Riley cocked her eyebrow. Her hot Irish blood kicked in, ready to boil.

Keep it in control.

She placed her arms on the table with her hands flat against the polished mahogany top. She looked to Conner and then to the lawyers. "We did not sign any agreement on a sale nor do we have any pending—"

"We talked about this." Conner cut her off.

"*You* talked about it." After one quick look at Shannon, who stayed silent, she turned back to the lawyers. The words fell out. "We're keeping the property. I'm going to move back here, live at the house, and manage the estate."

Shannon's head jerked and she stared at Riley. She came out of her withdrawn state as she took in her sister's words. "You'll move back?"

"Yes." Riley's heart raced. She wasn't sure where the decision came from, but it happened. Just like that.

"Don't you have a pathetic job you need to go back to?" Conner asked.

His snide remark drew her attention back to him. "First, my job isn't pathetic." She worked her ass off at that job. She was well-respected when it came to getting stuff done. "Second, this is more important. It will be easier managing the estate and Dad's finances if I'm here."

She didn't say but thought how it'd be easier to protect it all as well.

Conner rose from his chair in a huff and stormed out of the conference room.

Mr. Endellright cleared his throat. With a relieved smile he said, "I look forward to working with you. Your father would be pleased."

She took a sip of her coffee. Her hand shook.

Shannon waited until she placed the cup down before squeezing Riley's arm. "I am *so* excited. You're moving back!"

The lightness in the room faded when Conner came back with a cup of coffee in hand. His face wasn't so red. The break gave him a chance to calm down. He wasn't done though. He started in again, in more of a business-like manner. "How do we acquire our portion of the estate?"

"Conner." Shannon frowned and blushed at the same time. "They just explained."

"What?" he snapped at her. "We need to look out for our investment."

"Investment?" Riley rocked back in her chair, struck by his comment. "This isn't about the money."

"Yes, it is," Conner said without thinking much about it. "I want our money before you blow it away."

"She wouldn't do that." Shannon was aghast. For the first time, she showed anger. She straightened in her chair and balled her hands into fists.

The air in the room became thick as the lawyers on the other side of the table watched the dispute.

"Mr. Doyle," the largest partner spoke up. "The will states no changes will be made for a year. We'll also provide assistance to ensure the estate and trust are sound."

"I would like to see the will. Let my lawyers take a look at it," Conner leaned back in his chair. His expression changed. "Did he say what happens if Riley dies? Would it all go to Shannon and me?"

Riley's eyes widened and she sucked in her breath. "What the hell, Conner? You're leaving me for dead?"

Conner shot her a look. His eyes turned cold and dark, but his face relaxed as if realizing he'd better behave in front of the lawyers. "Of course not. If your dad was thorough in his will, he'd include provisions if you or

Shannon died. I'm merely asking if he did. I need to look out for Shannon and our kids. Your father has an estate that would benefit them."

And him, she thought but didn't say. Her attitude and respect for Conner went downhill. She would be the one needing to look out for Shannon and herself.

Ugh, Riley thought. Her stomach turned queasy. What kind of mess were they getting into?

"Do you have any questions or concerns, Riley?" Mr. Endellright asked her directly.

She shook her head.

The papers were ready for them to sign. The one form was for acknowledging that they participated in the reading with the other lawyers as witnesses. The other stack was for signing the accounts and trust over to Riley and then the safety deposit boxes to Shannon.

"We will be in contact again. We'll go through more of the details, help answer your questions as they arise. Your father left us a stipulation to ensure you get the assistance you need."

By the smile on their faces, the accompanying stipend must have been decent in size.

Conner pointed his finger to the table and then tapped on the surface. "Nothing gets discussed without Shannon and me being involved."

The lawyers gathered the papers. The lean one said, "That will be Ms. Walsh's decision."

Mr. Endellright drew his attention to Shannon. "Mrs. Doyle, do you have any questions or concerns at this time? Do you under—"

"I have lots of concerns," Conner said.

The lawyer ignored him. "Do you understand your father's wishes?"

"I have no questions," she responded. "Our father explained this, what would happen, when he updated his will after Mom died."

This set Conner off again. He stood, disbelief on his face. "You- you knew about this? Riley getting full control?"

"Ye-yes," Shannon stuttered. "This was Dad's wish."

"And you didn't fight it?" He pushed back from the table and growled in frustration. "You idiot. We could've taken care of this and made him change the will, before he killed himself."

The air heaved with tense pressure. No one spoke.

Riley clutched the arms of her chair, ready to attack Conner. She didn't know what he could or would do being this angry, but she'd give it right back. Seeing Shannon's shocked expression, she held back. Shannon sat frozen to her chair and stared at him as if wondering who she married. She didn't need Riley to aggravate him more.

The partners glanced at each other, unsure what to do. The lean one took the lead. He wiped the sweat from his balding forehead with a white handkerchief and then stood. "I believe this concludes the reading."

"I agree," Riley said and followed their lead. She tapped her sister's shoulder, wanting her to get up quickly. She turned to the lawyers. "Thank you for your time."

"Yes, th-thank you," Shannon stuttered.

Detective Torrence sat outside the conference room. A security guard leaned against the high-top desk, in conversation with the receptionist. The darker-skinned guard was built. He lifted to his full height when they piled out to the reception area. He kept his stance casual, as if he merely happened to be there, but his eyes watched Conner. Riley wondered if he'd been called to the front, through email, by one of the lawyers.

The detective stood. He stared at Riley for a second before turning to Conner and asking if they could have a moment to talk. She took this as a cue to get Shannon out of there. "Why don't you come home with me. Let Conner cool off."

"I can't," she said under her breath. "I must go with my husband." She kept glancing toward him. "He's stressed."

"This isn't good." A pit of dread grew in Riley's stomach.

"I'll be all right." She placed her hand on her shoulder. "It's you who I'm worried about. He still needs me."

Shannon left her to join Conner and the detective. She stood by her husband's side. Again, waiting like the perfect wife.

Riley shuddered, dreading the conversation at the house.

Mr. Endellright stood behind her. "Ms. Walsh, we'd like a private conversation with you, if you can spare a few minutes."

"Of course," she said and followed him down a hall while the detective continued his conversation with Conner and Shannon.

They ducked into his office, and he closed the door. The thin lawyer was already sitting at the smaller table in the room.

"Please sit." He offered her a chair.

"We're sorry we didn't ask Mrs. Doyle to join us at this

time. We had specific instructions to omit part of the reading if Mr. Doyle was present."

"Oh?" Riley sat, paying attention. One side of her brain was still on Shannon, hoping she was okay. The other side was curious about this secret gathering. What else was Dad up to?

"Your father was not on friendly terms with Mr. Doyle." The thin lawyer said.

"I gathered that."

"He, Maxwell, did not want you to worry or be without money during the one-year transition of the estate. The trust."

She nodded, thinking about the money hidden in the books.

Mr. Endellright pulled out papers from a folder and set them on the table next to her. He placed a pen next to the papers. "Your father has another account we'd like to sign over to you today. This account assures you have sufficient funds to take care of the estate, which includes an allowance for traveling. However, if you are moving back to the house, the funds can go to other uses at your discretion."

"I've known Max for a long time," the thin lawyer stated. "He'd be pleased you're keeping the house. He always wanted one of his girls to take it over and run the show."

Riley smiled. He used Dad's favorite saying: "to run the show." She scooted forward in her chair and examined the papers. Two pages explained the necessities of running the estate. While scanning through the information, she spotted another set of numbers with an agreement of transferring ownership. "What's this for?"

"A safety deposit box at the local bank. The documents for all your father's accounts, assets, and original leases are in the box."

Now she knew why she couldn't find anything. She grabbed the pen and signed the papers. The sooner she gathered all the information, the sooner she'd be able to piece together the accounts. Geo's lease was what interested her, and then if Dad had anything about Conner or Satchel Casing.

Riley slid the document and pen over to Mr. Endellright. He excused himself from the room with the document in hand and stated he'd be right back.

The thin lawyer stood and shook her hand. "We're looking forward to continuing our business with you, Ms. Walsh. Don't hesitate to ask if you have any questions."

"I'm sure we'll be in touch," she said with a slight laugh. "It's a little overwhelming for us these days."

"You'll do fine. Your father was well-organized." After a moment of reflection, he added, "He was both a client and a friend."

She believed him, which made her think …

"Mr. Lavonne," she said to catch his attention before he left the office. He turned, lifting his head to her. "Do you know anything about Geo Le Monte?"

He puckered his lips together to think and then asked, "Do you have something particular you are interested in?"

"Did my father trust him?"

The thin lawyer hesitated for a moment. Her breath caught as she waited for him to formulate his response. Finally, he said, "If you're concerned about him, the lease, and his staying in the second house on the property, you couldn't have a better renter or business partner."

Riley let go of her breath. "Thank you."

"And …" He paused. His face relaxed, turning more personable. "If you are wondering about him on a personal level, your father respected him highly. Only once did your father get angry with him, that I remember. I'm not sure if they settled their matter before his death. I don't recall seeing anything cross my files, but I'll check."

Mr. Endellright almost ran into the thin lawyer as he returned to the room. Before Riley could ask him about what he had meant by anything crossing his files, the man disappeared.

"Here's a copy of the document you signed," Mr. Endellright said and handed her a large white envelope with the firm's name in the upper left corner. "Inside, you'll also find the key to the safety deposit box."

She hesitated to take it from his hands, not wanting to leave the lawyer's office with an envelope. If Conner noticed, he would ask all kinds of questions and want to see them.

He sensed her concern. "Don't worry, your sister and her husband left the office. And remember, you are in charge of your father's estate and trust. We're here to help in any way, including protecting you."

Riley smiled. She took the envelope and shook his

hand before slipping out the door.

Once outside the old building, she scanned the street for Conner's vehicle. She wondered how many times she'd need to contact the lawyers to rely on them to referee matters between her and Conner. She shuddered. This could turn ugly.

Chapter 19

Downtown Hudson was quiet for a Wednesday. Mainly business people milled about, instead of the tourists or visitors who spent their day shopping or eating near the St. Croix River. With summer ending, the town was settling in for the winter months ahead.

Cold, snow-filled days.

Riley hugged the white envelope to her chest as she stood outside the door of the lawyer's office building.

I am moving back to Wisconsin.

Was she crazy? Was she doing the right thing? Nobody told her how drastically her life would change the minute she picked up the phone to be told Dad had died. Yesterday, she had every intention of heading back to Arizona. She waited to buy her airplane tickets, thinking she'd have time this afternoon. Every day she'd procrastinated about buying those tickets. Was this why?

The bank was on the south side of town, only a few blocks away. She had time to pull the contents out of the safe deposit box and look through them this afternoon.

The sooner she had a handle on Dad's finances the more comfortable she'd be.

Riley window-shopped as she passed the cute boutique stores selling their kitchenware, clothing, and touristy items. As she waited at the corner to cross the street, she glanced into the restaurant and bar with the large front windows. Geo sat at the bar. She recognized his green coat before seeing the locks of hair curl out from under the knit cap on his head. He was with Detective Torrence. And they were deep in conversation.

Her bottom lip trembled. She edged closer to the door. Riley longed to see him, missing Geo's eyes and how they smiled at her. She missed being with him.

Not yet.

As much as she wanted to apologize for her behavior, she still needed more information before confronting him. If her dad had additional information in his safe deposit box about the lease or Geo buying the property, she wanted to know before they talked.

The light turned green with the lighted walk sign. She hurried across the street before either one of them saw her gawking at them through the window. The bank was at the end of the block. She entered through the double doors and walked over to the woman at the desk to get her help with the safety deposit box. After some digging, the woman returned and apologized, but they couldn't help her today. Riley should have known it'd take a few days to get access to the account and box. Even though she had a copy of the papers giving her access, the bank had to wait for the original documents from the lawyer's office.

She left the bank frazzled. She didn't want to pass the restaurant again where Geo and Detective Torrence sat, so she crossed to the other side of the street, thinking she'd be safe. Right before she got to the point where she'd pass the restaurant, Geo and Detective Torrence came out of the wooden door. If they looked up, they would see her.

Riley panicked. She ducked into the nearest store, which sold home decor. She glanced about. She'd been in the place many times before with her sister.

A gray-haired woman sat behind the counter near the middle of the store. She leaned forward as the door jingled. Riley moved closer and the woman smiled, recognizing her.

"You're Maxwell's daughter. Shannon or Riley?" She raised a finger. "No, let me guess ... Riley."

The woman looked familiar but Riley couldn't place her. Had she been at the funeral? She seemed fragile. The skin on her arms and hands looked paper thin. She wore a thick hand-crocheted sweater, buttoned tight as if she was permanently chilled.

"I've known you since you were a little girl." The woman continued to admire her, making Riley feel bad that she didn't recognize her. "My, how you've grown."

Riley's head spun, trying to figure out who the person could be.

"I'm so sorry about your father. Such terrible news." The woman's face turned downward and her eyes unfocused, as if thinking about him.

"Thank you," Riley said, unsure what to say. She

glanced toward the door. Geo and Detective Torrence were standing in front of the building and continued their conversation outside. They didn't seem to be in any hurry to leave.

"Come in," the woman said and motioned with her hand. "I made a pot of tea. Would you like a cup?"

"Sure." Riley guessed she might be in there for a while. She followed the woman to the back of the store, passing by the section with unique kitchen items—handmade wooden bowls and spoons, different timers, towels, aprons, and potholders.

"I like your store."

"My sister owns it. I help on occasion. My hip doesn't allow me to work full-time." She glanced back at Riley. "The reason why I missed the funeral."

The woman shook her head with a sadness that even made the bun holding her hair droop. She walked with a slight limp, shuffling her way to the back of the store. She went through a door to a small room that held a desk filled with papers and wall-to-wall shelves topped with office junk. In the corner was a square table with a coffee maker and electric pot. She grabbed a cup off the shelf and then motioned for Riley to select a tea bag from the basket filled with different selections.

"We were friends with Helen and Max for a long time. Since right when they moved here. My husband, God rest his soul, used to hunt with your dad every fall. Deer and grouse."

Riley's memory of the woman and her husband came back in an instant. Jo Ann Anderson, that was her name. She remembered going over to their house, actually their barn, to help pack the venison after the hunt. Shannon's job was to weigh the freshly ground meat. She would pass it to Riley, whose job was to freezer-wrap the meat, tape, and mark what was inside. It was quite the production. Everyone had their station. Mrs. Anderson always fluttered about, making sure no one ran out of meat on the assembly line. She'd wear her white lace apron with the old and new bloodstains.

Jo Ann poured hot water from the electric pot into their cups. They walked back to the register in the middle of the store.

"Please, sit." She pointed to the stool behind the counter.

"Oh no." Riley couldn't take her stool. The woman needed it way more than she did. "You sit."

The front door dinged when the postman came into the store to hand Jo Ann the mail. After pleasantries between them, he left and they were alone again.

"This is our quiet time during the day," she said and seemed relieved to sit and be off her feet.

"Do you still live on your farm?" Riley was curious. "I remember spending time in your barn. I loved your picnics."

As a teenager, packing venison was the last thing she wanted to do, preferring to be with her friends instead. They worked their asses off trying to get all the meat packaged and divided out before the evening. But the summer picnics were different. They were able to ride their horses and get tractor rides around the fields.

"Yep. Still got the farm. My two sons are farming the

land. We now have cattle and sheep."

Riley sipped her tea. She asked, "Do you board horses?"

"Three of them. You should come visit and go riding sometime." They were silent for a moment as they drank their tea. Jo Ann made a noise, having been lost in thought again. She said, "Your father was very proud of you girls, especially you."

Riley coughed, nearly choking on the tea. "Why me?"

"You got a strong head on your shoulders. Like him. Shannon is a lot like your mother, but you have the business smarts."

Riley bobbed her head. She could agree. She was the math whiz and organizer. Shannon was the caretaker and planner.

"Are you taking care of his place?"

"I am."

"You live out in … New Mexico?" She paused. "No … no, Arizona. Right? How long are you staying?"

"I'm moving back here."

Jo Ann's face brightened. "That's great to hear. Max always wanted you to come home." She reflected again into her memory bank. She explained. "After your mom died, your dad and I had a long conversation over coffee and dessert. Did they tell you how, before they met, your mom planned to be a model in New York?" Mrs. Anderson sipped her tea. "Your dad said she had everything lined up to go—a contract with a modeling agency, an apartment, and tickets to fly out there."

"Mom, a model?" Riley was floored. Mom had striking features with her high cheekbones, perfect skin, and thin body. She never said anything to them about it.

"According to your dad, she caved and stayed with him. She got smart fast and figured out she'd never find anyone like him again." The woman chuckled. "Of course, this was your dad's story. He might have stretched it a bit. Boy, he sure loved her. You girls are the reason why they stayed. They wanted a good home for the two of you to grow up in. A place you could always come back to."

"And here I am," Riley said.

They continued their conversation while finishing their tea. She liked Jo Ann and hearing stories about her parents. What she said about Dad wanting to raise his girls in a decent town was true. Riley felt better about her choice to stay. This was a wonderful place to live, with great people. She felt an instant connection to Jo Ann.

Two women shoppers came into the store. Jo Ann stood, her break over. Riley said her goodbye and promised the woman that she'd visit the farm and take Shannon with her. And thinking of Shannon, Riley needed to return home and see how her sister was doing.

When she pulled into the driveway, Conner was loading a suitcase into the car. Good. He was leaving. She got out of her car.

"Say goodbye to your sister," Conner said with a sneer.

"Why?" Riley's heart skipped a beat. She frowned. "What are you talking about?"

"She's coming with me."

"What? She needs to stay here." They had work to do. They had the charity ball. What the hell was he talking about?

Instead of staying with him, she rushed into the house. Shannon was walking down the stairs from the bedrooms with her carry-on bag.

"Are you leaving?"

"I am," Shannon said with a solemn expression. "We're heading back."

"Shannon!" She couldn't believe it. How could she do this to her?

"I feel bad, for your sake, but I have to go." Shannon's forehead creased with wrinkles. "I need to make things all right on my end, with my marriage."

"Why? You don't have to go."

"Yes, I do." Shannon set her suitcase down on the floor when she reached the main floor and stood next to her. "Three children need me to care for them."

She flipped Riley's hair away from her face. Riley couldn't argue. She was selfish to think her sister could stay, but she thought she had until Sunday.

"What about the costumes and the charity ball?"

"You can go without me," she said with a sad smile. "I finished your costume. It's on your bed."

She didn't want to go alone. Riley growled in frustration. She understood Shannon's reason, but it still concerned her. "Are you sure?"

"I'll be okay," she promised. They heard the car door slam. Shannon offered a regretful smile. "He's waiting."

Riley's lips tightened. "When are you coming back?"

Shannon hugged her, squeezing tight. "I will find a way to see you soon. We can always say something about signing papers with the lawyer. That'll get him to come."

"I want you to come, not him."

Conner honked the horn.

She didn't have much time. Riley pointed a finger at her. "I expect a call from you every day."

"I will."

"If not, I'm calling the police."

"Don't worry, I'll be fine." Shannon gave her a look to say she was being ridiculous.

Riley's heart sank when the car sped off with her sister inside.

Chapter 20

After Shannon and Conner left for Milwaukee, Riley sent her resignation to her boss and to HR at Sikerte Investment Firm by email. She explained her reason for quitting, how it had been a tough decision, and how she would miss working there. After hitting send, she went to work on Dad's bedroom. She finished going through the closet, picking up where her sister left off before the funeral. Dad's aftershave, resembling a smell similar to whiskey, coated everything, including his clothes. She went through the nightstand where she found his wallet. Funny how he hadn't been carrying it when he died. Inside were four crisp one hundred-dollar bills, two twenties, and three ones. She put the wallet in her back pocket to take down to the office later on. She'd have to call his credit card companies, telling them to cancel the accounts since he passed away.

With the room cleaned of old stuff, it looked more like a guest room. The windows, with the curtains opened, let in a lot of sunshine. The connected bathroom featured a clawfoot tub centered in an alcove surrounded by windows. They always loved taking baths in Mom's tub when she let them, but she agreed only on special occasions. Now Riley could take one any time. No more rules, she thought with a smile.

She flipped the hot water on and plugged the drain. The different potions lined up on the shelf drew her eye, particularly the eucalyptus bath oil and bubble bath soap. She wanted bubbles.

Her cell phone pinged as she stepped into the bathtub. She reached over, grabbed her pants from the floor, and slipped the phone out of the back pocket.

Shannon. They were home with the kids. Everything was fine and she'd call her in the morning.

She responded and then put her phone down on the shelf under the window.

The water was a little too hot but she didn't care. Riley sank in, letting the water and bubbles surround her.

How long had it been since she'd taken a bath? Her apartment's small, shallow tub was hardly worth getting into compared to the deep, oversized tub Mom and Dad used. While the bath water steamed and the eucalyptus fragrance blossomed around her, she closed her eyes to enjoy the peacefulness and openness of the room.

Riley drifted off, thinking about the days' events since she'd arrived home. The ups and downs of her emotions had her on a roller coaster. She still had moments when her heart sank with grief, and then she'd laugh when thinking about something silly Dad would do to cheer her up. She'd have more time to think and reflect without a job.

She needed to make one more call. Gary. Reaching

across the tub to the shelf, she picked up her phone. He answered on the third ring.

"Riley. How's it going?"

"Good, I guess."

"Funeral now done? How about the will? Did you attend the reading?"

"Yes, everything is done." She watched the bubbles swirl around her breasts.

"I'm looking forward to your coming back. Did you buy your tickets? I've scheduled our first meeting."

"Gary—"

He cut her off. "By the way, they gave the position to Rita. She starts next Monday. The guys here in the office weren't happy that you didn't take the job."

"I'm—"

"Tell me your flight info. Better yet, text it to me. I'll pick you up."

"Gary." Riley raised her voice to grab his attention.

"Plan on working some hours, girl. Your desk is stacked with papers. You'll need a happy hour. We can call Terri, Vern, and Mike for a night out. How about next Friday?"

She laughed at Gary's enthusiasm, thinking she was coming back. Poor guy.

"What?" He finally heard her—the laugh must have caught him off guard.

"I hate to say this, but I'm not coming back, Gary."

The other end of the phone turned silent.

"Are you still there?"

"You must come back," he said. "You don't have any more

vacation time."

"No, I gave my notice."

The phone went silent again.

"Hello?" She glanced at the screen to make sure he hadn't hung up on her.

A long sigh came from the other end. "Oh, Riley. You can't quit."

"I can and I am."

"What am I going to do without you?" He whimpered like a puppy. "This office needs you here."

"No, they don't."

"Yes, they do."

"I expect Rita will take care of everything."

"She's not you," he said between his teeth. "You kept the office together. Everyone's eager for your return."

"Not without the pay."

"I'll get you more money."

Bless his heart for trying. "You don't have control over that. Besides, the money isn't important anymore."

The words sounded odd coming from her mouth. Getting a decent-sized raise had always been a top goal for her. She wanted a house in Arizona. And now she had it, only in different circumstances. And a different state.

She talked with him for another ten minutes, then finished with "I'll call you later. I have to go now."

"You always need to go," he complained.

"I'm taking a bath. I want to relax a bit more before the water turns cold."

"Bath, smash." He blew her off until her end of the

conversation turned silent. "Fine. You have better things to do than console me."

"I'll let you know how it goes."

"The bath?"

"No, silly. How they respond to my resignation."

"Fine."

Riley let him talk for another few minutes before hanging up. In the quiet, she waved her fingers through the water. The bubbles popped and formed into different shapes. Like the bath soothed her, she hoped her life here would be simpler, less stressful. Her thoughts wandered to her moving. She'd have to fly back to Arizona by the end of the month. She rented the apartment on a month-to-month lease with a 60-day notice to vacate. Within that time period, she'd have to figure out how to pack and move her belongings here. Gary could help her drive back with all her stuff. He'd like Wisconsin. She laughed, thinking of him visiting in below-zero weather. He'd love her for that.

Funny, if she had been offered the promotion six months ago, she would never have considered moving back to Wisconsin. Was she meant to be here? She thought of Mrs. Anderson's story about Mom dropping her modeling career for Dad. If Riley had fallen for Geo earlier, would she have agreed to move back? Would he move to Phoenix?

Riley reminded herself that it was because of her situation and the estate that she stayed. Not because of Geo.

She closed her eyes and remembered the feel of his hand on her back. Her reaction to his touch was more than a casual gesture. The desire built again when she caressed her breasts, imagining him in bed with her, naked. She bet he'd be gentle, kind, and want to please her more than himself. Definite happy thoughts.

Chapter 21

The next morning, Riley was sitting at the kitchen island drinking her coffee when Shannon called, as promised. Her sister couldn't talk long but wanted her to know Conner was leaving again on a business trip to Atlanta. He acted anxious about it.

Good. Riley liked the fact that she didn't have to worry about his being around her sister or the kids. But something in her sister's voice sounded different, sad. "Are you okay, Shannon?"

"Why?"

Something was wrong. Her sister never hesitated with a response. "You sound different. Is he with you now?"

"Not with me, right here. He's out in the garage."

Shannon's voice lowered. "I don't know. I think ... I'm not sure if I want to be with him anymore. He's changed, Riley. Every time I try talking to him, he's distant—not himself."

"You did say he's anxious about this deal in Atlanta."

"I think it's something more than that. He won't even ... be with me. You know ... touch me."

277

Riley made a face.

"And the sad thing is that I'm okay with it."

"What are you going to do?" She put down her cup for the serious conversation.

"He'll be away for three days. Maybe four." She paused and whispered, "He's coming back inside. Don't worry, I'll be fine."

"Call me later."

"I will." She ended the call.

Riley's heart turned heavy for her sister. She couldn't imagine having a loving, caring husband one day and a total jerk the next. What set Conner off? Did he stop caring for Shannon when Dad wouldn't give him what he wanted? He had to have known that Dad would never give him control over his finances. Or was there more to it? A deal gone bad?

She checked her messages on her phone. Her boss had responded. She raised her phone closer to her face and clicked to open.

The best of luck to you.

That was it?

One lousy sentence acknowledging her resignation.

Bastards.

In one way, she felt better about her decision.

Riley needed fresh air. The weather outside was sunny and in the mid-forties. She slipped on her jacket, hat, and boots to go for a walk. The cemetery came first.

A mound of black dirt covered her parents' grave. The flowers from the funeral, now shriveled and dried, were still scattered on the ground. She picked up the debris and piled them near the bench for the caretaker to dispose of.

The plot looked better now without the dead flowers.

A truck door slammed, causing her to look toward the direction of the hunting shack. The hill and trees blocked her view, but she heard the engine rev and the fan belt squeal. She waited for the red roof to appear over the hill-line.

The truck slowed when it passed the cemetery. The driver's side window reflected the trees, like a mirror. Geo must be driving. No one else would take his truck. She hoped he would roll down the window. She wasn't sure if he even saw her.

Riley's head lowered as he continued on and turned the corner, out of sight.

This could be a long, long winter.

The breeze picked up. The air turned colder. She sensed someone behind her and spun around. No one was there. Maggie? Geo's grandfather? She stood still and continued to look around the trees and headstones for a shadow or a little girl to appear.

The hair on Riley's arms prickled. She wasn't alone.

"Maggie?" She called out to the open air.

The wind swirled the leaves that had fallen on the ground, making them dance across the graves.

"Watch out."

Riley's feet did a little dance. The voice came quick, almost like a squeak. Still, the cemetery was devoid of any living person. As she turned to leave, she spotted Maggie next to her own grave. Her eyes were dark, her mouth turned in as if she was worried.

"Why?" Riley asked, but Maggie was gone.

She circled around and headed toward Maggie's grave. One rose rested on top of the girl's headstone. Riley wondered if Delana left it for her.

The feeling of a presence was gone. Only the leaves rustled. But the words continued to repeat in her head. What did she need to watch out for?

Riley gave up on her walk and headed back to the house. She locked the back door, which she rarely did. She checked the front door and locked that one too. Her nerves got the better of her; she was being ridiculous. She'd always felt safe in the house … until now.

Riley stayed in the kitchen. The hub where family gathered. She wasn't keen on the idea of being alone for the next week or month. Geo had invited her to his place, but she couldn't go over there. They weren't on the best of terms right now. Instead, she should keep busy. Tackle the kitchen. With a new purpose, she went through the cupboards and drawers to get rid of unnecessary items. Even though she told herself it was silly, she kept a knife on the counter to protect herself if needed.

The night was worse. Every noise in the house, every crack and snap woke her from an unsettled sleep. Being paranoid drove her nuts. At four in the morning, she finally gave up and left her warm bed to clean around the house. She heard a few noises and went to explore. Nothing.

Having enough, Riley stood in the hall, near the den. She said, "Okay, Maggie, or whoever is in this house, you need to be quiet." She placed her hands on her hips. "If someone is in this house and shouldn't be, I can't be guessing if it's you or a bad guy. Understand?"

The light in the hall near the front door flickered. She hadn't turned it on.

Riley shivered. She communicated with a ghost. Is this what her life would be from here on out? She shook her head to dismiss the idea. She went about doing her chores again until Shannon called for their morning checkup.

"Tonight's the charity ball," her sister sang. "Are you excited?"

"Not really," she answered in truth. She didn't want to go to the ball without Shannon. But the guilt, if she didn't attend, would weigh heavily on her. This was for Dad.

"You're doing this for Dad." Shannon must have channeled her thought. "You need to go. And look your best. Besides, Geo is going to be there."

"How do you know? Did he tell you?"

"When he found out you were going, he changed his mind. He's going. Wear a push-up bra with your costume. Let him drool for you."

"Shannon," Riley said and blushed.

"I'm giving you advice. You two make a perfect couple."

"But he's not talking to me."

"Are you sure?" Shannon's voice turned into their mom's. "Or is it that you're not talking to him?"

When she didn't say anything, Shannon continued, "Just what I thought. Make amends with him."

"What if he doesn't want to?"

"He will," she said. "I've caught the way he looks at you.

And *you* him."

"Fine. I'll go to the ball."

"Don't forget the push-up bra."

"Yes, dear."

When she hung up from their call, Riley loaded the car with the boxes and bags of discarded kitchen items for the thrift store. Since she was headed to town, she might as well shop for a white push-up bra. The ones she packed in her suitcase were black or plaid. They'd show through the shimmery fabric.

As she drove into River Falls, she noticed a black car following her on the country roads. The smaller vehicle had tinted windows and rode low to the ground like a sports car. She couldn't tell the make. The person could be a college student, taking a drive to find different routes to avoid the police if they'd been out partying. She passed it off.

Her first stop was at the thrift store. When she came out after dropping off the boxes, she noticed the black car idling in a parking spot on the side street. With the windows so heavily tinted, she couldn't tell if anyone sat inside. She drove to her next stop, the grocery store, to grab a few items. Coming out, she spotted the black car again, this time in the back corner of the lot. She drove to the boutique store and parked on the street. Lucky for her, they sold bras. She found one—not her style with all the lace, but it would work. When she left the store, the black car was parked a block down.

Riley stared at the car. A man moved inside. From the

angle of the car, she saw the outline of his head follow her as she walked to her car. Why was he following her? She stepped out on the street to walk over to him. As if knowing her intent, the car drove off, and she squinted to see the license. The plate came from another state. A splatter of mud prevented her from seeing which one. Even the numbers were covered.

Creepiness clung to her like an ominous cloud hanging low in the sky. She wondered if that car had any connection to Maggie's warning. Riley's nerves jumped. She didn't want to drive home, afraid he might follow. She stood in front of her favorite bar, a small brick building where locals liked to hang out. On a whim, she darted to the door and went inside.

Two guys sat at the bar. An older woman sat at one of the tables with a pile of pull-tabs in front of her. Riley sat on the stool at the end of the bar and ordered a breakfast shot. The bartender poured Jamison Irish Whiskey and butterscotch schnapps into one glass. He grabbed another glass and poured an orange juice chaser. He slid the two toward her. She wasted no time downing both.

Enough to calm my nerves.

She ordered another.

The back door to the bar slammed shut, making her look. Detective Torrence swaggered into the bar. He didn't see her at first, since she sat near the front. The bartender held his hand out, leaning over the bar to give him a handshake. They talked for a few minutes before he scanned the rest of the place. The detective spotted Riley and walked over to join her.

"Hello, Ms. Walsh." He purposely glanced down at the empty glasses.

"Breakfast," she explained. "Tastes just like pancakes and sausage."

"Rough morning?" He leaned his elbow against the bar. He wore a tight black polo shirt underneath his unbuttoned gray sports coat. Shannon would like the look.

"Yes, a little," she said, remembering his question. The bartender placed the second breakfast shot in front of her.

"Then I don't blame you." He smiled with understanding.

"How's it going with the investigation?"

"We're getting close."

Riley sat straighter in her chair. "What? You know who killed him?"

He winced at her raised voice and glanced behind him.

"Sorry. I didn't mean to be so loud." She lowered her voice. "This is good news. Right?"

"I'll be happy when it's over." His response was lame. He didn't act excited for someone who solved a case.

She assumed he wouldn't be able to tell her the culprit without having made the arrest first.

"How's your sister?" He glanced about as if hoping to find her.

"Shannon's back in Milwaukee with Conner and the kids. The kids, I mean. I guess Conner is away on another business trip."

Detective Torrence frowned. "When did he leave?"

"Yesterday afternoon?" She tried remembering their conversation. "I think that's what she said."

He tapped his finger on the bar as if calculating

something out in his head. He shifted to a standing position. The detective pointed to the drink. "Be careful. Those can knock you out."

Riley chuckled. How true.

He stopped before turning away. "Are you going to the ball tonight?"

"I am."

"Geo will be there." He leaned in and said in a softer voice, "He misses you."

A lump formed in her throat. She missed him too.

The detective stepped back to leave. "He's one of the good guys, you know."

"Thanks for the warning." She downed the whiskey and schnapps, followed by the juice.

Chapter 22

Riley forgot to tell Detective Torrence about the black car. She paid for her drinks, grabbed her purse and bag to catch him, but he had already disappeared. The alley was empty. Instead of going back into the bar, she walked around the building to the street. She searched the area for the black car and didn't find it. Maybe it was a coincidence or her being too paranoid. She had to stop it. Be herself.

Once home, she took a nap in the den before getting ready for the charity ball. Shannon did a beautiful job with her costume. Once Riley put it on, the shimmery dress flowed across her body, making her look more like a goddess than an angel. The low-cut bodice showed a portion of her rounded breasts. She thanked Shannon for telling her to buy the white push-up bra. Riley didn't have big breasts, so the bra took over where needed.

The wings were attached to a matching bolero-style jacket. She opened and fluffed the wings before trying it on. The white feathers were beautifully aligned and not too small or big for her size. Riley couldn't figure out how

Shannon got the wings to stay firm and pointing upward, not drooping from their weight. Impressive.

The last piece of the outfit was the halo. Riley placed the fluffy white crown on her head. She kept her hair down, letting the curly locks flow across her shoulders and contrast with the dress. With her ensemble in place, she stood in front of the full-length mirror and took a few selfies with her phone. She sent the pictures of her costume—front and backside—to Shannon.

She responded back.

Beautiful. He'll be eating from your hand.

Riley rolled her eyes at her sister's text.

Not wanting to come home to darkness, she turned on the desk lamp in the den and the one above the stove in the kitchen. She locked the house and headed to her car. The wings, she discovered, caused an issue when sitting in the driver's seat. She took the jacket off, opened the back door, and then laid the wings on the seat so she wouldn't have to fold them in.

The parking lot was already full when she arrived at the red barn. She found a spot beyond the lot and in the grass field. Once out of the car, she donned her jacket. She searched for Geo's truck, hoping to see him. No truck yet. A few other couples headed toward the barn. Like her, the women walked with care in their high-heeled shoes. Unlike her, they hung on to their male's arm to keep their balance. Riley lifted her dress, not wanting grass stains on the fabric or to trip on the edges. She kept her eyes to the ground. Her wings flapped behind her.

When she neared the entrance of the barn, Riley let go of

her dress so the skirt flowed evenly again. She glanced up toward the sky—the first time she dared while walking. The stars sparkled like her dress. A beautiful night for a ball, even if the air was chilly without a proper jacket.

The music filtered outside through a set of speakers. If she remembered from what was printed on the brochure, the first band was an eight-piece orchestra. A waltz filled the night to greet the guests. Riley found herself swaying to the music as she stepped onto the black runner lined with potted bushes covered in tiny black lights.

A young man dressed as a zombie butler held a clipboard. He walked up to her and bowed. "Welcome to the Ball."

She curtsied.

"Your name please."

"Riley Walsh."

He checked the list. "Riley and Shannon Doyle?"

"Shannon won't be attending."

The butler bowed and held out his arm for her to take. He played the part, walking stiff-legged and making it awkward to walk beside him. He stared at her on occasion and moaned as he walked her to her table, making Riley giggle. He held out a chair for her and said in a dull tone, "Enjoy your evening."

"Thank you."

He pushed her chair back in when she sat. With another groan, he backed away to greet the next guest.

Riley adjusted her skirt while she admired the decorations in front of her. She sat at a table with an orange tablecloth. The dinner places were set except for the plates. In the center of the table sat a black lantern, black-painted branches with orange glitter, and three black candles protected by a glass cylinder. Other tables were decorated in a similar style but with a white and black or a green and black color scheme. Above her, yards of white tulle and lights draped across the rafters and met in the middle, where a large crystal chandelier commanded center of attention.

Shannon would have loved the ambience, the glitter, the costumes, and the orchestra playing on the stage. Riley wished she were there to experience it. She took out her phone and snapped pictures, then sent them off to her sister.

Guests continued to arrive, and the tables filled fast. A zombie waitress came by and removed the place setting next to her, including a small stick with Shannon's name painted on it. Riley noticed her own. She looked to see who was supposed to be sitting next to her. Geo. She smiled. Perfect. She could devote her attention to him and repair their friendship.

An older couple, dressed as Fred and Wilma Flintstone, and another single woman, dressed as a flower pot with her head as the flower, joined her at the table. Once settled on the opposite side, they introduced themselves. The older couple knew her father. The man was his dentist.

"Did they solve your father's murder?" he asked.

The flower pot woman made a noise of disgust as if not wanting them to talk about it in front of her. The subject was dropped.

When the next couple arrived, Zorro and a female cat, the conversation changed. The couples knew each other and talked amongst themselves. Riley felt awkward. She had no intention of being friendly with the flower pot woman, and she doubted if the woman would talk to her anyway.

Where is Geo?

As they served the salad, a ballerina sat on the other side of Geo's empty chair. The woman was about Riley's age. Her hair was pulled back in a bun and she wore dark, dramatic makeup. She looked like a model. A pang of jealousy hit Riley in the chest. Was the ballerina Geo's date? After introducing herself, Ms. Ballerina had no issues with talking. She was recently divorced, a mother of two, and the head of a successful textile company located in the industrial park. If Shannon had been there, the two would be chatting like old friends. Riley liked her, despite being unsure if she was there for Geo. She was about to ask if she knew him when the woman beat her to it.

"I see Geo's not here yet. I hear he's coming."

Riley's heart dropped as Ms. Ballerina searched the room for him.

"You know him?"

She smiled like a cat. "Every single woman in here knows who he is."

"Of course." Riley swallowed hard.

After the salad, the soup was served. Still no Geo. She kept her eyes on the door, hoping he'd arrive.

Ms. Ballerina engaged in conversation with Fred Flintstone. His wife kept an eye on them.

The main course arrived—chicken and rice pilaf.

Riley lost her appetite. Her stomach tied in knots,

making it hard to eat. If he found out earlier or saw that they were sitting next to each other, Geo could have chosen not to come. Or taken a seat elsewhere. She searched the room. Most people dressed in very ornate costumes and masks, making it hard to identify anyone. However, she would find Geo in the crowd if she saw his blue eyes. She searched harder.

A large man dressed in black and wearing a vampire cape with a pointed collar stared at her from across the room. His dark eyes, visible through the openings in his mask, targeted her. She turned her eyes away and focused on her plate. She picked at her food.

On occasion, she glanced over at the vampire. He continued to watch her and didn't care that she knew.

The black car.

He carried the same evil persona that she felt with the car.

A man wearing a surgeon's gown and mask walked between the tables and broke their eye contact. Riley needed a distraction. She turned to the ballerina and asked about her kids. Moms liked talking about their children—good or bad.

On occasion, Riley glanced over toward the wall where the vampire stood. He stayed in position with his eyes on her. A detective or police officer? No, she didn't believe he was there to protect.

Where in the hell is Geo?

As the two couples finished their main course, they rose from the table to mingle with the other guests. Riley spotted Detective Torrence. He was on his phone. A scowl crossed his entire face. He darted out, leaving the barn in a rush. Two more men followed behind him.

The other guests didn't notice as they carried on with their conversations. The vampire hadn't moved. He kept staring at her.

Riley wanted to sink down in her chair but the wings on her back prevented her from moving too much. Ms. Ballerina continued to talk.

The Master of Ceremonies for the ball, the mayor, hopped on to the stage with microphone in hand. He was a stocky, short man with a wide grin.

"Attention. Attention everyone."

The room quieted. Forks clinked as the guests placed them on their plates. Ice rattled as water poured into glasses.

"We'd like to start our program." The mayor held up his hand and waved it at the crowd. "Don't worry. Don't worry. We won't bore you with a lot of talk. But we would like to take this time, before the dancing begins, to talk about the charity we're sponsoring tonight."

Riley couldn't sit any longer. She got up from her chair, taking her clutch with her. Wanting to avoid the vampire, she took the long way around the edge of the barn toward the bathroom. She also scanned the tables for Geo. No luck. She checked the bar in the other room. Quite a few men hung out, but still no Geo.

She slipped into the bathroom. The wings were difficult to handle in the stall, but she managed to sit on the toilet without crushing them into the tank.

When she came back out, the vampire's form blocked her exit. He stood at the end of the hall so she couldn't pass him. Two women came out of the bathroom. Riley followed behind them, hoping to use them as a shield to protect herself.

The vampire grabbed her arm as she passed him, and she jerked back. His gloved fingers pinched her, and she flinched in pain.

"Let go of me." Riley tried to free herself.

He pulled her over to a dark corner of the bar. His piercing eyes grew hard and cold. His lips tightened into a white line. The rest of his face was hidden by the mask.

"We have a deal." His voice was low and hoarse.

"What the hell are you talking about?" Her heart pounded as she struggled to free her arm from his grip.

"The house. The estate belongs to us. Sign the papers."

Riley's heart went to her throat. She turned her fear into anger. "You can't tell me what to do."

"No," he said. "But I can do things you'll regret."

He blocked her in the corner. If anyone glanced their way, they'd think the two of them were in a private conversation— a lover's quarrel. She tried moving around him to call for help. His cape blocked her view. The vampire's hand grabbed her throat. Riley smelled whiskey on his breath and bad aftershave lotion. She choked.

"The house. The estate. You will sell to Satchel."

Her eyes widened at the mention of the name, part of Conner's company.

"Max Walsh owes us."

"No, he doesn't."

The man half-growled, half-laughed. He pressed his fingers

harder against her throat and she gasped for breath.

Riley froze. He couldn't kill her there in front of everyone. He'd have too many witnesses.

She started to shake and he noticed. A low-pitched laugh came from his throat. "Now you're getting it."

Her headed pounded from the pressure of his fingers on her neck. She stared at his masked face. For one second, she wondered if he had killed her dad. He looked like he'd have no issue killing her.

"You got three days to sign the papers."

"How can—"

"You'll have them soon. Instructions will follow."

"But—"

"If you don't, one by one, you'll drop." He pushed her toward the wall, crushing her wings into her back. "Shannon. Delana. You get the picture."

Oh God.

She wanted to faint. Stars swirled above her.

"You'll be the first."

Riley's knees buckled when the vampire released her. She didn't see where he went as it took all her strength to stay upright. She grabbed the edge of the high table next to her and managed to sit on the stool. She didn't know how long she stayed there as she caught her breath and recovered. Her legs continued to shake.

A zombie waitress passed by. The woman stopped when she noticed Riley in the corner. "Are you feeling okay, sweetie?"

She nodded but couldn't talk yet.

"Let me grab you some water ... and a cold rag. You look faint."

The waitress didn't take long. She gave her the water first, made Riley drink, and then handed her the rag.

"Thank you," Riley said. Both helped.

"You want me to call for a ride?"

She shook her head. "I'll be fine."

The zombie waitress disappeared. Riley slid off the stool and set the rag on the table. She needed to be outside. Leave. For her, the party was over.

The night air was a blessing. The briskness made her catch her breath and cough, but it brought her back to life. The shock of being cornered by the vampire wore off as she darted to her car. Her heels pinched her feet and were hard to walk in, but she wasn't going to stop.

Get to the car.

She glanced about in search of the vampire. Two men dressed as cows lingered outside, smoking cigars. She'd cry for help if needed.

Luckily, a car on the road slowed down to turn into the parking lot. It was enough light to see around her car before Riley dashed to the door.

Once inside, she locked the doors and placed her head against the steering wheel.

"Pull yourself together. Pull yourself together," she said and grabbed her car keys and cell phone from her clutch. She tried calling Shannon. No answer. She hadn't responded to the picture she sent earlier.

"Fuck," she swore under her breath.

Riley started her car. She had a clean sweep from the parking spot to the road—no fence or ditch. She pulled straight through and turned on to the road, taking a left. The smaller rocks from the edge of the road sprayed out from under her tires as she sped off.

Watch for deer.

She slowed down, knowing the damage caused by a deer crossing the road. Her wings dug into her back. She flipped her arm around and tried flattening one of them. Riley didn't notice the black car waiting on the side street until seeing the driver flick the remains of a cigarette out the window when she passed.

He turned on to the street and followed behind her.

Riley grabbed the steering wheel with both hands, forgetting about her wings.

She guessed it was the vampire following her. She refused to let him intimidate her like he did at the barn. Being in the car, she felt protected. If she was going to die, she'd go down fighting.

To make sure she wasn't being paranoid, Riley turned right on the next street to see if he followed. He did. She sped up and turned left at the first street. From the driver's side, she glanced out the side mirror and saw the pointy ends of his cape, confirming it was the vampire. Asshole.

On a straight stretch, Riley bit her lip to think. She could drive the backroads blindfolded. As a teen, she liked to race around the curved roads as if driving on a race course. Only once had she lost control and ended in a ditch. Lucky for her, a friend pulled her out. She calculated a plan.

"Let's see if you can keep up," she said while glancing into the rearview mirror.

Riley put on her serious driving face. The vampire didn't know what he was getting himself into.

She turned right on a long, winding road that would take them into a valley. She didn't slow down as she made the turns, left and then right. She let up on the gas pedal before hitting the dip in the road. Her car bounced. She kept a tight grip on the steering wheel, despite the wings jabbing into her back.

Behind her, the black car's front bumper hit the dip without first slowing down. Sparks flew up. He fell behind, which told her that he wasn't familiar with the roads. It didn't take long before he caught up to her again. She accelerated to give the car more gas as she climbed the next hill. She lifted her foot off the pedal as she crested the top. Down she went. The decline was steep—not one to take at 55 miles per hour.

The black car gained speed, almost kissing her bumper. At the bottom of the hill, the road turned sharply to the left before starting up the next hill and out of the valley. She waited until she passed the "slippery when wet" sign near the bottom before applying the brakes. Thank God it wasn't icy or snowing. She slowed the car enough to make the turn. Her back tires fishtailed. She steered to correct, gaining control again.

A loud thunderous crash of tires squealing and metal hitting came from behind. Riley looked out the rearview mirror. The car's headlights glowed in the trees at an odd angle. She applied the brakes and stopped her car. The vampire had flipped his car sideways and wedged himself between two trees. He wasn't going anywhere.

The last thing she wanted to do was help him. Instead, she called Detective Torrence's number and received his voice mail. She left a brief description of what happened, and where he could find the vampire's car. She headed back to the house.

Guilt riddled Riley for not calling 911. She could be in trouble for leaving the scene of the crime. But as she'd explained to Detective Torrence in her message, the guy had threatened to kill her.

She'd have to deal with it later. Riley focused on deer and the vampire for the rest of the drive home. Like it happened in the movies, he could easily appear out of nowhere.

The glow of red, flashing lights lit the sky as she reached the road she lived on. Riley squinted to see better. Smoke billowed upward, beyond the trees. She calculated where both came from. Not the house. Behind it. Geo's?

Riley's heart pounded as she drove closer and smelled the fire. It had to be the field behind the house. As she drove closer, the glow of the fire lit the night.

"Oh shit."

The grape vines. The vineyard.

She turned onto the road in front of the cemetery, wanting to turn into Geo's driveway. It was blocked by all the firetrucks and police cars. She spun the car around and drove to her house and parked in the driveway. Riley ran to the cemetery. One heel sank into a soft spot in the ground, and she twisted her ankle.

"Fuck!" She cried out and stopped. She took both shoes off, leaving them in the grass, and hobbled toward the path to the shack.

The crackling of fire, the yelling of fireman, and the spraying of water from the hoses became a symphony of horror. Riley ignored the throbbing pain in her ankle as she reached the driveway.

There couldn't be a fire. Not now. She let out a sob. Geo's hard work—gone.

The smoke, heavy in the air, burned her eyes. She searched for Geo.

"Ma'am." A firefighter stuck his arm out to block her. "You can't go past the vehicles."

"I own this place!" Riley yelled at him.

"Chief," he hollered and waved his hand to grab his boss's attention and pointed to her.

Detective Torrence was near the shack talking to a police officer. Riley left the firefighter and struggled to climb the hill. The detective saw her and came over to help.

"I got your voice mail. The police are heading there now. Are you hurt?" He looked down at her leg.

"I'm okay." She didn't care about herself. "Where's Geo?"

"Over next to the firefighters." He pointed toward the vineyard.

Riley left him while he continued to direct people. She found Geo standing by a tree and out of the way. The firefighters sprayed down the blackened strip of land and beyond where it continued to burn.

"Geo," she called out. Like him, there was nothing she could do but watch in horror.

He turned. He stepped toward her. It was all she needed. Riley flew into his arms, not sure who needed the hug more—her or him.

"Geo. Geo. What happened?" she asked between sobs and catching her breath.

"Someone set it on fire."

He was so calm—too calm. He had to be in shock.

"Who would do such a cruel thing?" She stared at the ruins. "Your grapes."

She brushed away her tears. He continued to hold her, placing his hand around her backside. They watched the flames and the water from the hoses collide. Smoke billowed upward. The wind changed directions and the water sprayed them. Geo stepped in front of her to shield her from getting wet. They backed away.

Detective Torrence met them by the driveway. He carried a blanket in his hands and wrapped it around her. Both men helped her to the ambulance near the shack. The EMT examined her ankle. They thought it was a bad sprain but wanted her to go to the hospital to make sure nothing was broken.

No way was Riley leaving now. She promised to go to the doctor tomorrow.

Geo unlatched the tailgate on his truck and lifted her so she could sit with her bad leg up. Even with the blanket, she shivered from the cold.

"I don't understand," she cried. "Who would set your

vineyard on fire? Why?"

"Revenge. Distraction. Threat." He leaned against the edge of his truck, next to her. The lights from the firetruck glowed against his face. "To encourage you to sell?"

Geo's gaze swept the ground, filled with a sadness that made her heart ache and melt at the same time. His new life, one he was so proud of, now in ash. Gone.

"I'm so sorry."

"You're not at fault."

"It is. I should never have doubted you. I should never have shut the door in your face."

He did a double take and then realized she was talking about them, not the fire.

"Please don't be mad at me," she said and brought the blanket up close to her neck. "I just—when I found the papers—everything—"

"I'm not mad at you." Geo moved closer and took her by the shoulders. "Believe me, I'm not mad at you."

She saw an emptiness in his eyes that worried her. She lowered her leg to be even with him. "I found the papers. How Dad wanted you to buy the shack and the land."

"I couldn't accept his price. Your dad was too generous." He placed his hands on the tailgate, one on each side of her.

"I didn't understand at first, but then it dawned on me that you were the one who refused to sign the papers. Is that why the two of you had been arguing?"

"I couldn't take advantage of your father."

"I'm so sorry." Riley covered her face with the blanket, angry at herself for not giving him a chance.

Geo hugged her, bringing her into his warmth. She wiped her cheek with the blanket.

Pulling herself together, she lowered the blanket and asked, "Can you rebuild? Grow more grapes?"

He hesitated. "I'm not sure if all the work is worth it. If you're planning—"

"I'm not selling. I'm not doing anything," she said as she scanned the property. "I'm staying."

Geo froze. He stared at her. "Why?"

"This is my home." She then pointed toward the shack with her head. "And that's your home."

He continued to think about what she said, as if not comprehending. Riley waited, letting him process it. The color returned to his face. His expression brightened. "You're staying?"

"Yes." She laughed. "Because of you."

Until she went to the charity ball, Riley didn't realize how much she truly missed and wanted him. The empty chair beside her hit hard, like a wakeup call. She didn't want to lose him. "I've fallen for you, Geo Le Monte."

He cracked a tired smile as he stepped back. "Really?"

Why was he making this so difficult?

"Is that the response I get?"

Geo stepped back while taking in her costume. His smile turned genuine. "You have no idea how you just made my day. You truly are my angel."

Riley buried her face against his neck when he wrapped his arms around her. She loved his scent. Even with the smoke permeating his clothes, she could smell him.

His mouth was close to her ear and he kissed the top of it. "I've fallen for you as well, Riley Walsh."

She would have been content to sit on the truck's tailgate all night with him holding her, but their time together was short-lived. Detective Torrence returned.

"Riley, I need to talk to you about the vampire."

Geo jerked back. "What?"

He looked to her and then to the detective for an explanation.

Chapter 23

Riley sat on the couch in the hunting shack with the blanket still wrapped over her shoulders. She couldn't warm up. The living room held plenty of heat, but the shock from the night's events continued to chill her bones. She couldn't stop shaking.

Detective Torrence sat on a kitchen chair that Geo brought out to the living room. He wanted a statement from Riley, from the time she arrived at the charity ball until she left the vampire's car crumpled within the trees. They had dispatched a police car out to the scene and found the car as she stated. The man was now in the hospital in critical condition. They were trying to determine if they could charge him.

"He threatened me," Riley said with a scowl. "He had his hand on my neck. He choked me. I couldn't breathe."

"It's not enough to keep him in jail. He has no record."

"Let me take a look at your neck." Geo wanted her to turn her head. He lifted her chin. His fingers traced over her throat. He glanced at the detective. "She has marks."

"Not enough."

Riley put her head down as she remembered his threats. "He mentioned Satchel. He said my dad owed them. The house belonged to them."

Geo's head rose. He stared at Detective Torrence. "That should be enough."

The detective nodded.

"What?" She glared at one and then the other as they silently talked to each another. Her voice hardened, wanting an answer. *"What?"*

"There's something else I need to tell you." The detective shifted on the hard kitchen chair. "The Milwaukee police searched your sister's residence earlier this evening."

Riley gasped. "Where's Shannon?"

She sat up, in a panic, as she remembered the vampire's threats. She was about to stand, to pace, but pain shot through her leg as she put weight on her foot.

"Your sister's fine." Geo made her sit back down. "We made sure she was escorted out of the house before the search. She's staying at a hotel with the kids."

Riley caught what he said. "What's with this 'we'?"

"Geo has been helping us. The papers you gave us, and other evidence we collected, including Delana's drawing, helped build a case against Conner Doyle. He's been arrested for first-degree murder."

"Conner?" The suspicion had been there. But to hear him actually say Shannon's husband was arrested for Dad's murder unnerved her. She wanted to throw up. Her stomach churned. The horror of having someone turn so violent and kill her dad.

"Oh my god," she said, not knowing if she could take it. Her hand trembled as she brought it up to her mouth. "Conner killed my dad?"

"He's been arrested," Detective Torrence stated.

Riley shook her head. "Picture? What did you say about Delana's picture? Being evidence?"

"That day I came to visit," the detective said. "She drew a picture—a piece of jewelry."

She thought back and nodded. The detective had taken it with him.

"We found a cufflink, similar to the picture, at the scene of the crime. The matching cufflink was found at the Doyle house during the search. We arrested him today, here in River Falls."

"Here?" Riley's head jerked. Her mind raced with too many questions. Shannon had said he was going on a business trip to Atlanta.

"He had the papers for you to sign."

She didn't care. "I have to call Shannon."

"I need a statement."

Riley searched for her phone, ignoring him. She'd left her clutch in the car. She stared at Geo, unsure what to do.

"Give your statement. I'll grab your phone."

The interview took forever. Riley closed her eyes, trying to remember the details, not wanting to leave anything out. Geo came back halfway through. He kept his distance, as if not wanting to distract her from giving the detective the information he needed.

When Detective Torrence was satisfied, stating that

they were done, she held her hand out, ready for her phone. Geo placed it in her hand. The men left, giving her privacy.

"Oh God, Riley." Shannon's voice was a strained whisper. "I finally got the kids to sleep. They sense something's going on." Her voice shook, her control ready to burst. "How am I supposed to tell them?"

"I don't know. I don't know." She matched her sister's pain. "I'm going to drive down tonight. Help you."

"No," she said. "You need to stay there."

Riley would have her hands full. Her sister was right.

"How's Geo? I can't believe what happened—the fire."

"We'll get through it."

"We?" For the first time in the phone conversation, Shannon's voice lifted.

Chapter 24

Geo helped Riley prepare the Thanksgiving turkey. Neither one of them had made a turkey before.

"Is that it?" He stared at the raw bird in the roaster pan. He held up his hands, coated with butter and seasoning, trying not to get anything else dirty.

Riley stood beside him at the kitchen island. She struggled to read the handwriting on the index card where the print had faded. A week ago, she dug through the old shoe box filled with Mom's favorite recipes to find the instructions for prepping the bird and making the stuffing.

"Let's hope," she said. She recollected their steps. They had rinsed the bird thoroughly after removing the brine and then polished the skin and cavity with butter and seasonings. "Yep, I think we're good. We just need to put the cover on and place the roaster pan in the oven."

The turkey was too large for the lid to fit. Geo washed his hands and then, using tin foil, created a makeshift cover for the roaster. Once he was finished, Riley opened the oven door so he could place the heavy bird in the oven.

"Anything else we need to do? Peel the sweet potatoes?" he asked, washing his hands for the second time.

"Not yet. Ready for the cemetery?"

"Shouldn't we wait for Shannon?" he asked. She was on her way from Milwaukee and would be staying for the long weekend.

Riley pondered for a minute. She would like to wait for her sister, but this was the perfect opportunity—between chores and all the bustle of the day—being Thanksgiving. "If we have a chance, how 'bout we do another round after dinner. Or we could take wine."

He nodded, liking the idea.

They put on their coats and boots and then headed outside with four shot glasses and a pint of whiskey.

Most of the leaves had waved goodbye to the trees, making the cemetery bare. The pines and cedar bushes still stood tall, but they seemed lonely without the color of summer or fall. From the snowstorm that hit their area the day before, patches of white puddled the ground. The statue of the angel had snow on its hands. Riley stood on her tiptoes to brush them off. The angel smiled down at her. Riley smiled back.

"Brrr," Geo said and shook as a shiver ran through him.

The air was brisk and his breath came out like steam from a locomotive as they stood at the family plot. Instead of sitting, Geo set the bottle of Irish whiskey on the bench. He pulled out two shot glasses, one from each pocket and handed them to Riley. She held while he poured. He kept the open bottle in one hand while she handed him one of the poured shots.

Geo lifted his glass. "Here's to your dad."

"May he rest in peace."

The sun appeared from behind a cloud as they drank their shots. Riley glanced over at Geo. He laughed. "I think he's trying to tell you something."

She smiled while casting one eye to the sky. She agreed. "He is at peace."

"He knows his daughters are safe."

With Shannon's husband arrested for Dad's death, they had closure in knowing who did it. Geo was confident Conner would be found guilty based on the evidence. He hadn't been sentenced yet, and they didn't know how he'd plead. The court date was next week. The police investigated Mr. Hathaway's death as well. The vampire was charged with his murder.

Geo stepped closer and put his arm around Riley and held tight. He said, "You will be safe."

Riley put her head on his shoulder. He would protect her, but what about Shannon? She'd be taking the brunt of it. She would carry the burden of her husband's action for the rest of her life. "I'm concerned for Shannon and what else is to come."

"She's got you. And me."

"But she lives so far away. I want to help her and the kids."

Geo rubbed her back. The bottle of whiskey hit against her back. Riley remembered they weren't done. She turned and held out her shot glass, ready for another pour.

With glasses filled, they walked the few steps to his grandfather's grave.

"And here's to your grandfather," she said and raised her glass.

"I'll be forever grateful. He invited me here, to move in with him, and it gave me another chance at life."

How true. If Geo had continued his career as a detective, would he even be around? After being shot twice, she was glad he had the sense to quit. She smiled, thinking back to when they first met in this same spot. Back then, he carried an edginess to him, as if holding a secret. With the suspects in jail, she now realized it was because he knew about Conner. Satchel Company was a front to a more dangerous business, and Conner was a partner who owed them a lot of money.

She wondered if this was Geo's last case. No matter, seeing him calmer was still quite amazing, especially after losing his vineyard to fire.

He raised his glass. They downed the whiskey in honor of his grandfather. The liquid burned her throat and she coughed. She would never get used to the hard stuff, preferring wine, but it was Dad's and Geo's grandfather's favorite.

A thought struck her and she laughed. "Do you think the two of them, your grandfather and my dad, plotted for us to get together?"

Geo chuckled. "I wouldn't doubt it. My grandfather always said I needed to settle down with a Midwest girl. I guess he made sure of it."

Riley's heart warmed. She remembered her tea at the store with Mrs. Anderson and what the woman had said. How Riley's mom chose to stay with Dad instead of becoming a model. This was the place to raise their kids. They were so right.

She glanced toward Geo. She pictured the two of them in a few years with little kids running around.

All was peaceful as they stood for a moment in silence.

"Other two glasses?" Geo held out the Jamison bottle.

"Oh yes," she said and pulled the other two shot glasses out of her coat pocket.

Again, she held the two new shot glasses up for Geo to pour whiskey into them. He took one and set the glass down on his grandfather's headstone. Riley let him do the honors of giving her dad one as well.

"Enjoy," he said and stepped back.

The crackle of tires against dirt made them both look toward the driveway.

Shannon was home.

Geo placed the cap back on the bottle. They went into the house through the back door to dispose of the whiskey and used shot glasses. Riley met the kids as they opened the front door.

"Hi, Auntie!" they chimed and gave her a hug after dropping their backpacks filled with toys. They giggled as they ran outside again.

Shannon opened the back of the SUV. She handed Flynn a box. She handed Delana a box. Elise grabbed a small bag to carry in.

"What the hell did you bring?" Riley asked her sister as she reached the back of the SUV. She glanced behind her, at the kids who were still giggling as if keeping a secret.

"Here," she said and handed her a box. "These are

Flynn's toys."

Riley struggled with the box, not realizing how heavy it was going to be. "All this for a long weekend?"

"Here, let me take it," Geo said and took the box. He shared a look with Shannon. Both of them carried wide grins on their faces.

"What are you two up to?" Riley grew suspicious.

"Stop standing around," Geo said as he turned to carry the box into the house. "Help your sister move in."

"*What?*"

"You heard him," Shannon said and shoved a box into her arms. "Help us move in."

It took a moment before it dawned on Riley what the two were saying. "You're moving here?"

Shannon smiled. "Yep. Whether you like it or not."

Geo came back out for another box.

"You knew about this?" Riley would have given him arm wings or hit him if she hadn't been holding a box.

"Maybe a little," he said.

Her sister laughed. "Oh, you should see your expression."

"But how—why—" Riley still couldn't believe it.

"I sold the house and all of our furniture. We're staying."

Riley hollered with joy.

Now she wouldn't need to worry about her sister or the kids. Everyone was home.

Epilogue

"I still can't believe it," Riley said as she opened a bottle of Geo's wine. "Shannon and the kids are moving in. Here."

Thanksgiving dinner turned out to be a success, and the turkey was close to how Mom made it. After dinner, they went outside to burn off all the food they'd eaten. Delana was excited to see Maggie again, but she sensed her friend wouldn't be around much longer and voiced her concern once they came inside.

"Why is that?" Riley asked.

"She did what she needed to do," Delana said. "She stayed to help, wanting to make sure I was okay."

"Because of what happened with grandpa?"

She nodded. "She knew my daddy was the bad guy."

Riley's mouth fell open. "Did you know?"

Delana lowered her head. "No. I think Maggie tried to tell me, but I didn't get it."

"It's a hard concept to understand." She hugged her niece. Her heart broke for her. "I'm glad she was here for you and for Grandpa."

"I'll miss him," Delana said like an adult. "But it'll be okay. Maggie told me that Grandpa would make sure of it."

Riley didn't doubt it.

"Your grandpa will always watch over you," Geo said and kissed Delana on the forehead.

Riley's heart warmed, seeing how attached they were getting. She couldn't be happier. Shannon took Mom and Dad's old room. Flynn grabbed one of the bedrooms upstairs while the girls took the other. Riley was glad she'd stayed in the guest room on the main floor, deciding not to take another room. "My sister and the kids belong here. This house is perfect for them. Doesn't it feel right?"

"Speaking of that …" Geo pulled her into his arms. "Remember when Delana asked at the table why she couldn't have her own room? Why she had to share with Elise?"

"Yes …" She waited, wondering where he was going with it.

"Well, you could give up your room. Let Elise have it so she's closer to her mom."

"Makes sense," Riley said and grinned. "But where would I sleep? Shannon's taking Mom and Dad's room."

"I have a spare bedroom."

"Ummmm …" She wasn't so sure if she liked that idea. She waited for him to offer her a better one.

Geo's eyes sparkled when he obliged. "How about half a bed? My bed is too big just for me."

"Well, now you're talking." Riley met his lips when he came in for a kiss.

"Hey, you two," Shannon said as she came into the kitchen. "Behave yourselves."

"We are," Riley said and laughed. "I think we found an arrangement that will work for all of us."

Author's Note

I hope you enjoyed reading *Peaceful Plots*. I had fun writing for the Common Elements Romance Project. I started this story a year ago, creating the characters and story outline based on a lightning storm, lost keys, a haunted house (or rumored to be), a stack of books, and a person named Max. Over fifty authors are participating in this project. Our stories are all different (including genre) and not tied together (except for the five elements). To learn more about the Common Elements Romance Project and participating authors, please find us at: www.commonelementsromanceproject.wordpress.com.

To read more about my books or current events, please join me at:

www.bethmjames.com
www.facebook.com/BethMJamesAuthor

And to note…I'd love a review on Amazon or another site to know how I'm doing. Thank you!

Author's Biography

Beth M James, a multi-genre romance writer, lives in the St. Croix Valley bordering Wisconsin and Minnesota. She writes character-driven stories filled with adventure, humor, and lessons learned. When she's not writing, she loves spending time with her family, traveling in her RV, going up to the glamper (tiny home), and discovering new wineries and breweries.